SUSAN WITTIG ALBERT

SOMEONE ALWAYS NEARBY

A NOVEL OF
GEORGIA O'KEEFFE
AND MARIA CHABOT

Persevero
Press
PP

Publisher's Cataloging-in-Publication data

Names: Albert, Susan Wittig, author.
Title: Someone always nearby / by Susan Wittig Albert.
Description: Bertram, TX: Persevero Press, 2023.
Identifiers: ISBN: 978-1-952558-20-7 (hardcover) |
978-1-952558-21-4 (paperback) | 978-1-952558-22-1 (ebook)
Subjects: LCSH O'Keeffe, Georgia, 1887-1986--Fiction. | O'Keeffe, Georgia,
1887-1986--Friends and associates--Fiction. | Chabot, Maria, 1913-2001--Fiction.
| Painters--United States--Fiction. | O'Keeffe, Georgia, 1887-1986--Homes and
haunts--New Mexico--Abiquiú--Fiction. | Ghost Ranch (Abiquiu, N.M.)--Fiction. |
BISAC FICTION / Biographical | FICTION / Historical / 20th Century / General
Classification: LCC PS3551.L2637 S66 2023 | DDC 813.6--dc23

Contents

A Note to Readers about This Book

We think we tell stories, but stories often tell us, tell us to love or to hate, to see or to be blind. Often, too often, stories saddle us, ride us, whip us onward, tell us what to do, and we do it without questioning. The task of learning to be free requires learning to hear them, to question them, to pause and hear silence, to name them, and then to become the storyteller.

—Rebecca Solnit, *The Faraway Nearby*

During the most active years of their extraordinary friendship, Georgia O'Keeffe and Maria Chabot exchanged more than seven hundred letters, telling each other the stories of their lives across a decade of war, peace, and cataclysmic personal change. In those years, O'Keeffe continued to prove herself as a prominent American artist, established a home at Ghost Ranch in New Mexico, lost her agent-husband of twenty years, and left New York to live permanently in the West. Chabot, a footloose, high-energy young woman, hoped to become a published novelist but instead became O'Keeffe's "hired man," the architect-builder of her celebrated house in the village of Abiquiu (pronounced **a**·buh·kyoo) and the ranch manager of Los Luceros, a culturally and historically significant Rio Grande estate. Their stories, told in the letters collected in *Maria Chabot, Georgia O'Keeffe Correspondence, 1941–1949* (University of New Mexico Press, 2003), document these enormous personal changes and the shifting dynamics of the volatile relationship that framed and to a great extent created them.

Someone Always Nearby bridges the space and time that separated the two women as they dealt with urgent obligations of work and family, apart from each other and away from the vast mesas and silent mountains of the Northern New Mexico desert that both longed to call home. Theirs was an often-tumultuous relationship across a rollercoaster decade of world war and start-and-stop recovery, through which Maria and Georgia supported, sustained, depended on, rejected, and reconciled with each other. It began with the creation of Georgia's home at Ghost Ranch and continued with Maria's rebuilding of the ruined, centuries-old adobe hacienda that the artist purchased in the then-remote village of Abiquiu—a remarkable feat that made visible the dreams and desires of the woman who built it for the woman who would live in it the rest of her life.

Someone Always Nearby is as true as I can make it to documented events, people, and places. Its scenes and storylines are crafted from events I have found in letters, biographies, historical works, and unpublished archival material. Its dialogue is imagined, but not exclusively; I have included quotations from the women's letters and other writings. Its landscapes are real, evoked by my experience as a two-decade part-time resident of New Mexico and by my research into the past and present of this historically rich region. Because this is a novel about real people, their lives and times, I have relied on the extensive work of biographers of Georgia O'Keeffe and Alfred Stieglitz, as well as on the couple's published letters, interviews, exhibit catalogs, and other works by and about them. Maria's life has not yet attracted a biographer, but I have had access to the collection of her papers held at the Georgia O'Keeffe Museum and Library, including Chabot's extensive correspondence, the manuscript of her unpublished book "Life With O'Keeffe," and many other documents. And because this is a historical novel, set chiefly in the first half of the twentieth century in a place deeply rooted in the New Mexican past, I have consulted the work of historians of the Piedra Lumbre region. I have documented these sources at the end of the book and more extensively in a separate *Reader's Guide*.

But none of this reliance on factual material alters the fundamentally *fictional* nature of this book. Please remember: however real-seeming the narrative may be, *Someone Always Nearby* is first, last, and entirely a work of the imagination and the characters in it live an imaginary life. I agree with memoirist and novelist Rebecca Solnit: learning to be free of our stories means that we must first hear them, then question them, and then become the storyteller.

Susan Wittig Albert
Bertram, Texas, 2023

For Maria Chabot, who made the Abiquiu House a place to live and has dreamed other dreams with me here near the cliffs and the red hills.

—O'Keeffe's inscription in Chabot's copy of *Georgia O'Keeffe*, 1976

PART ONE

Always Nearby
1941

Chapter One

_____

Someone Always Nearby
Maria

I haven't written what I plan to do because I havent known—Also
I've felt a bit uncertain about your really liking me as something
always nearby.

—Georgia O'Keeffe to Maria Chabot
New York, May 12, 1941

On the contrary I think I shall really like you as something nearby
. . . I am very happy that you want me and I think we can live a quiet
life and each get our own work accomplished.

—Maria Chabot to Georgia O'Keeffe
San Antonio, May 15, 1941

San Antonio, Texas

An open suitcase on the lace-canopied four-poster bed. In the suitcase,
two pairs of Levi's and a pair of khaki shorts, socks, pajamas, underth-
ings. Beside it, folded cotton blouses, long-sleeved and short-sleeved.
A button-up sweater and a couple of sweatshirts. Hiking boots, huaraches, a canvas outback hat.

"Mary Lea," my mother said plaintively, "I don't think you've
thought this through. You haven't considered the consequences. You
won't be back until November. Why, you'll miss your cousin's wedding!"

I gave her a reassuring smile. "Oh, but I have, dear Mudds. I've thought all about it, carefully."

I might have added, *And I want it more than I've wanted anything for a very long time.* But I didn't. She had enough on her mind these days, trying to keep the Chabots afloat. No need to let her know how almost frighteningly eager I was for this chance at a new adventure, how intrigued I was by this artist, this woman. And how glad to miss my cousin's wedding and all the celebratory folderol—as if women had nothing better to do with their lives than find a husband and settle down to keeping house and making babies.

Still trying, my mother invoked the final authority. "Your father believes you should go back to your old job at Joske's. Mr. Christie told him they'd *love* to have you do advertising copy for them again. They think you're a marvelous writer." She pursed her lips and folded her arms across her ruffled bosom. "And neither he nor I can understand why in heaven's name you want to work for this woman. You know who she is."

"Of course I know who she is, dear." It didn't take much to tweak my guilt strings. I heard the reminder (unspoken, of course) that the family could use a regular paycheck from Joske's. I folded the sweater and two sweatshirts on top of the Levi's and said the only thing that might mean something to my mother, who judges art by the fame of the artist.

"O'Keeffe is simply the best-known female painter in North America. She shows her paintings in New York every year. The newspapers say wonderful things about her giant flowers and—"

"She isn't as famous as Mary Cassatt," my mother said petulantly. "And Miss Cassatt paints perfectly charming little pictures of women and children, not those massive, voluptuous things that are meant to look like—" She shuddered. "I won't say it. But you know what I'm talking about."

I knew. I had read the Freudian critics (all men, of course) who want everybody to see O'Keeffe's flowers as erotic, especially given the photos Mr. Stieglitz had—

She wasn't finished. "You also know very well that she posed for *hundreds* of nude photographs, which her husband hung in his gallery and invited every Tom, Dick, and Harry in New York to feast his lascivious eyes on them. How any decent man could defile his wife in that way is simply beyond my comprehension." She gestured toward my suitcase. "And just look at the clothes you're packing. Nothing at all . . . civilized! You could at least take one or two of your pretty dresses."

I tucked my huaraches into the corners of my suitcase. I had spent several days at O'Keeffe's isolated ranch house the previous November. I knew how beautifully wild it was in the Piedra Lumbre, that magical desert basin so far from civilization that it might as well be on another continent. And the women I knew in New Mexico were *different* from the women my mother knew in San Antonio. They wore whatever they felt like wearing. Jeans, riding pants, bib overalls—things that were comfortable to work in. A pretty dress would be as out of place as a . . . as a tutu on a cactus. I smiled at the simile, but it fit. That's how I felt about the ruffled, lacy feminine dresses my mother wanted me to wear.

And there was a reason for that. I glanced at myself in the tall chevalier mirror in the corner of the room. There's no getting around it. I was five-feet-eleven in my stockings. My shoulders were broad, my hips wide. I was strong. I was . . . substantial. My thick, straight, dark hair didn't take happily to permanent waves and I wasn't crazy about lipstick and eyeshadow, which made it difficult to play the well-dressed daughter of my fashionably dressed and expertly coifed mother. But while I made up my own mind on such matters, of course I loved her. She didn't approve of the way I dressed but she always indulged what she thought of as my whims—maybe a little too often for my own good. So I tried to look for compromises.

"How's this?" I went to the closet and took out a denim skirt. "I'll wear my plaid skirt and flats on the bus and take this for trips to town." I added a narrow belt. "Levi's and cotton blouses and sweatshirts will be fine for the ranch."

Which is exactly the way I like it. I had decided I'd rather be a boy when I was twelve and began reading Willa Cather. Inspired by a sentence in one of her short stories—"There are some girls who would make the best boys in the world if they were not girls"—I cut my hair like a boy's and began calling myself Maria, which in Spanish (spoken often in San Antonio) is often a boy's second name.

And I began dressing like a boy, as Miss Cather did when she was a girl. My mother attempted valiantly to conceal her horror: "Mary Lea is just the tiniest bit rebellious." My father didn't notice. He's always treated me like a boy, anyway—his third son, born as a replacement for my much-older and alcoholic half-brother Fred (a huge disappointment to him) and my half-brother Charles, who disappointingly drowned, with his mother, six years before I was born.

Of course, wearing boys' clothes at school provoked questioning glances from adults and a barrage of taunts, some quite cruel, from the kids. Of course I envied boys. I would have been one, given the choice. They were clearly more independent and could do what they wanted, while the girls and women I knew mostly did what somebody told them to. But frankly, I liked the attention I got when I wore boys' clothes. I took pleasure in being singled out—being noticed because I was different from the other girls. In San Antonio in the 1920s, a girl dressing like a boy was *certainly* different.

So while the kids laughed at me, I was laughing at them for giving me what I wanted. I kept a photo of Miss Cather by my bed and copied her straightforward writing style and her brusque, muscular, get-things-done manner. With that close-cropped dark hair and my emphatic dark eyebrows, I even thought I looked like Cather, a little, anyway. Now, if I could only *write* like Cather . . .

My mother's *sniff* ceded the practical necessity of ranch clothing and she shifted position. "If you feel you absolutely *have* to go to Santa Fe for the summer, wouldn't it be better to work for that lovely Mrs. Dietrich again? You liked doing those Indian surveys, and you were certainly well enough paid for *that*. Or if it's an artist you want to work for, you could go back to her sister, to Miss Stewart. She paid you well. too." She sighed. "If you see them, please remember me to them. They are both *ladies*."

This was delicate. My mother only knew that I'd worked for Margretta Dietrich as an advocate for New Mexico Indian artists, and that I had helped her sister, Dorothy Stewart, with her murals, prints, and paintings. She also knew (of course) that the sisters gave me board and room in Dorothy's and Margretta's Canyon Road adobe and that Dorothy and I had traveled together, to Europe and Mexico.

What she didn't know was that we—Dorothy and I—had been intimate since we met at cousin Emily Edward's house in Mexico City eight years before, when I was twenty. Our passion had waned—that always happens, doesn't it?—and we had arrived at the mutual decision that it was time for a change. She had discovered someone else—Agnes Sims, whom I *detested*. On principle, of course, and out of sheer jealousy, because I had to admit that Agi was a reasonably likeable person, quite nice-looking and a very good artist. I didn't want to give up my place in Dorothy's life, you see, especially since I hadn't found someone to take her place in mine.

Still, I'd agreed that we needed a change. She was mother and sister and friend as well as lover. Because I depended so entirely on her definitions of me, I had become uncertain about who I was and what I wanted for myself. And while I loved her, I had to admit to being attracted to men, especially intelligent men who knew what they wanted and how to get it.

Rudi Staffle, for instance, whom I knew from high school. Rudi planned to be a famous ceramicist and I was sure he would. He was studying art in New York just now, with Hans Hofman. We went to Mexico together one year and saw each other when we were both in San Antonio.

And Dana Bailey, whom I met in England the summer I was studying Native arts management at Oxford. He had finished a degree in astrophysics and then sailed off to the South Pole with Byrd's Third Antarctic Expedition. (No women allowed, of course, not even to do the laundry and cooking.)

And Tony Long, whom I met in Santa Fe, who probably wouldn't ever be famous like Rudi or Dana or his father (a well-known poet) but loved the mountains and desert as much as I did.

So my uncertainty had intensified. Was I *this*—what I was with Dorothy—or *that*, what I was with Rudi, or Dana, or Tony? Or perhaps, in a different way, with O'Keeffe.

How would I know?

When would I know?

Would I *ever* know?

None of these questions were new in the litany of urgent inquiries

I continually posed to myself in those days. I was then and still am a restless and unsettled person, continually asking who I am. Who I am *at the moment*, because at the next moment, I'm likely to be somebody else.

In the meantime, Dorothy (who always knew exactly who she was) was still my deepest, truest friend, the kind of friend who would always hold my heart in her hand and be gentle with it. We continued to end our regular letters with *te adoro*, but she kept herself apart these days, giving to Agnes what had been mine. I knew I'd get used to the hurt but I wasn't quite there yet. And of course my mother knew nothing of this.

I cleared my throat. "I'm sure I'll see Margretta and Dorothy. I'll give them your best." In fact, Dorothy was expecting me to stay for a day or two on my way to O'Keeffe's ranch. She and Agnes had just gotten back from another trip to Mexico and they'd have photos of the wonderful folk art they had seen. Dorothy had asked me to go with them, but I'd begged off with the excuse (quite valid, really) that I had to deal with the apartment renovations I was overseeing at the old Chabot house. The truth: I was still raw around Agnes.

I added the blue skirt to the suitcase and closed it. There wasn't room for my hiking boots and my Aussie bush hat. I could wear the hat but I'd have to put the boots in the canvas carry-all I'd take on the bus—along with Mum's sandwiches, cookies, a thermos of coffee, my camera, and my Zenith portable radio, which was about the size of Webster's unabridged and heavy as all get-out. The train was faster and more comfortable, but Trailways was cheaper. As always, pennies counted.

"Or you could work for that very nice Miss Wheelwright, at Los Luceros." My mother wasn't giving up. "You helped her write that book about the Navajos. I'm sure she'd be delighted to hire you again." Staking the annual Chabot family claim to my winters, she added, "Just for the summer."

It was the arrangement we had worked out, the price I paid for an annual six or seven months of freedom from family responsibilities. At twenty-eight, I might consider myself my own woman, but my parents shared the Victorian belief that as long as a daughter was un-married, they had an indisputable right to her time and attention. My half-brother Fred, older by some two decades, enjoyed a man's freedom from family obligation. My half-sister Edith (the two are Dad's chil-dren by his first and second marriages) purchased hers by marrying at twenty-one and moving to another state. Marriage wasn't a price I was willing to pay. It wasn't a guarantee of independence, either, as far as I could tell.

I went to the desk under the window and put my portable Rem-ington into its case, along with an extra typewriter ribbon, the man-uscript of my novel about Mexico with a stack of typing paper, and the notebook where I kept the pieces I was currently working on. My well-worn copy of Cather's *Death Comes for the Archbishop* was on the desk, along with Bancroft's *History of Arizona and New Mexico*. I was taking both to reread on the bus.

My mother was going on, plaintively now, because my writing was a well-gnawed bone of family contention. "I realize that your em-ployment is your own affair, dear. But if you insist on working for this O'Keeffe woman, I do hope she'll pay you something. You know your father has had several more . . . reverses. He can't afford to give you an allowance this summer." Her voice took on a familiar edge. "Of course, I always hope you'll make at least a little from your writing. Otherwise, what's the point?"

What's the point? I loved my mother, but for her all effort of any kind is measured by how much it earns. Judged by that, she considers my writing to be pretty pointless. I had already produced a series of articles on Indian arts and crafts for *New Mexico Magazine*, but that was several years ago. The short story I submitted in January had been returned with a rejection (encouraging, but still a rejection) from *Ladies' Home Journal*. And I had temporarily shelved my feature article about O'Keeffe, "Profile of the Artist at Home," which I had been hoping to sell to *The Atlantic*. She didn't like the idea of somebody writing about her unless she could rewrite it herself, she said when I sent her a draft. She had her own definite ideas about the way people should see her.

I didn't know much about how art criticism was written, but this struck me as a little strange. Did people like Henry McBride, the critic who wrote for the *New York Sun*, clear his reviews with O'Keeffe? Of course, I understood why a celebrity might want to control what was written about her and her art, but I didn't think an *Atlantic* editor would accept what might be called a puff piece. There was time to sort this all out, though. I had all summer.

So I set the piece aside, thinking it could wait until I knew her better. O'Keeffe was more fascinating than anyone I had ever known. As an artist, she had succeeded where no other woman could. I was deeply curious about the sources of her creativity, her energy, the way she saw the world, the way she had made it her own entirely through the force of her disciplined will.

But the inner strength that produced her art was oddly mixed with an appealing waif-like helplessness when it came to the business of everyday life. I would learn later that she and her sisters, like many girls of their era, had grown up with hired help and had been given lessons in art and music in part to help them acquire husbands who would provide for them. And that someone who knew her in her early thirties would remark that she was "just like a child." She could never do any work and "would have to be done for" her whole life.

What I saw when we first met was that even the simple, practical things—planning a trip, buying a tire, starting the generator at the ranch house—seemed a challenge for her. I could also see that her life in New Mexico would be made much more difficult by the fact that she still couldn't speak Spanish, although she had spent a decade of summers in a world where it was the chief, often the sole, language. It seemed clear (to me, at least) that she needed someone to take care of her, and I offered myself. "Lock, stock, and barrel, no strings, at no price," I wrote. I would do everything I could to make her life simple and productive. To give her the time and the freedom to paint, because that was her great gift to the world. Her art had impressed so many people for so many years. She deserved whatever I could offer.

But there was a string, of course. I wanted to know her, to learn from her, to learn *about* her, because I wanted to *be* her. I wanted to write in the way O'Keeffe painted, with discipline and persistence and a perceptive eye. I couldn't know, then, what the time with her would teach me or what kind of price I might pay for the experience. I only knew that I wanted to know her and thought—silly thought!—that by the end of summer, I would.

For me, the best way to know something has always been to write about it, and since I write to learn, I write whenever I can find a spare moment. There hadn't been many moments for writing while I was home this winter, though. I had spent the last several months overseeing the conversion of my grandparents' once-magnificent mansion into nine rather pricy apartments. The Chabot House, a San Antonio landmark a block down Madison from the house where my parents lived, was built by my grandfather, who had left England to serve as a British consul in Mexico. Unsettled by the rise of anarchism there in the 1870s, he and Gram had brought their family to San Antonio. Here, he built a flourishing wool-and-cotton business and an elegant house with lush gardens and a stone carriage house, and Gram enjoyed music, the arts, and a glittering life in the city's most dazzling social circles.

The grandparents were both dead now, the family business had disappeared into the dismal swamp of the Depression, and while some of our cousins owned oil land in West Texas, our branch of the Chabot family had slipped into a dim and shabby respectability. The Chabot House wouldn't have brought much in a property sale, but I had finally persuaded my father that it would pay to convert the old mansion to apartments. I'd had to oversee the work and do some of the painting myself. But the job was done and the apartment rentals would be my parents' most reliable source of income. We couldn't breathe easily yet, however. The Depression still cast a shadow. And Hitler's ugly war in Europe, now in its second year, was making recovery uncertain.

The waning of the family fortunes meant that I was left to fend for myself, a fate that did not daunt me. I had dreamed of being a writer since I could hold a pencil, and everybody knows that writers have to learn to live on practically nothing. I've learned better since, but I was sure then that succeeding as a writer—getting published, earning enough to buy groceries—was only a matter of time. Time and focus, which had never been my strong suit. I got bored easily and tended to flit from one project to another, following my passion of the moment. Focus and self-discipline were things I hoped to learn from O'Keeffe that summer.

So that was my plan. I would arrange meals, handle the shopping, manage the household help, and organize the logistics for O'Keeffe's painting trips in the desert, freeing her from all those domestic chores. In return, I would earn bed and board, as much pin money as I could save out of a fifty-dollar-a-month household expense budget, and time to work on my writing. With O'Keeffe as my model (and my mentor as well, I hoped), perhaps I could learn to manage my impulses and stop jumping into new projects just because they interested me.

As I would discover, however, O'Keeffe thought that a plan was a thing to be constantly changed. In the two dozen letters we had exchanged that spring, Georgia (I was invited to call her that, although I often preferred O'Keeffe) had kept remaking her plan to leave New York. First it was the art business. Then her elderly husband (she usually called him Stieglitz, sometimes Alfred) was ailing. Then her live-in help quit and she had trouble finding someone dependable to look after Stieglitz while she was gone. Twenty-two years his wife's senior, he was a famous photographer and gallery owner who featured her canvases in a one-woman show every February and March, keeping her art before the public. I had visited his gallery on a trip to New York five or six years before. I remembered him as a white-haired, white-mustached old man who had something to say about everything, endlessly—but most of it quite interesting.

Georgia had also written that she was a little uncertain about our compatibility, wondering whether I would actually like her "always nearby." I had read her letter carefully, studying the oddly embellished handwriting. Its stylized, formal elegance was distinctly at odds with its frequently interrupted, often unfinished, always breathless sentences, like a little girl who is trying to recite a poem while she runs up the stairs. That disconnect, and what it might say about O'Keeffe, deeply intrigued me. But I had replied that I thought we would get on together very well, especially since we both wanted quiet lives with few interruptions and time to work on our projects. All I asked was permission to bring my portable radio so I could stay in touch with what was going on in Europe these days.

Europe. Dorothy and I had traveled there just a couple of years before and I felt a hard knot in my stomach every time I thought about what was happening now. In the countries where we had bicycled blithely—Holland, Belgium, France—Hitler's Nazi storm troops now held the streets and countryside. Denmark and Norway had fallen, Yugoslavia too, and there were rumors that Russia would be next. Which surely didn't make a lot of sense. Weren't Germany and Russia supposed to be allies?

And worst of all, the Luftwaffe was bombing England, especially London, Liverpool, and Birmingham—but not yet Oxford, where I had studied in the golden summer of '38. My cousin Cresson Kearney, a Rhodes Scholar, had introduced me to Dana Bailey, also a Rhodes Scholar. The three of us had had glorious, carefree fun rowing on the Thames. Now, all night, every night, the attacks were so brutal that it seemed all of England might be bombed into a pile of smoking rubble.

A few weeks ago, I had listened as CBS's commentator Edward R. Murrow had broadcast a grim description of a walk in London streets. "It was one of those nights when you wear your best clothes," he said, "because you're never sure that when you come home, you'll have anything other than the clothes on your back." Murrow was clearly trying to bring the war to America and America into the war, and in spite of the opposition—Charles Lindbergh and his America Firsters—I was sure it was only a matter of time before that happened. Murrow had signed off that evening as he always did, as the British did now, when they said a somber goodbye to each other: "So long—and good luck."

So long and good luck. When I heard this, I thought of the men I knew, young men just my age—Cress and Dana and Tony and Rudi— all of whom had already gotten their draft cards and would be called up when there was war, if not before. *So long and good luck.* It made me want to cry and beat my fists against the wall.

Or go back to England, put on a uniform, and volunteer to drive for the American Ambulance organization I had read about just yesterday.

Or retreat from the war with O'Keeffe in the New Mexico desert. Which was where I was going. At least for now.

So long and good luck. I would need it.

CHAPTER TWO

Santa Fe
Maria

Perhaps someday I will just love you for being you—and that alone
will matter. I can't believe in the firmness of any human relationship
at the moment—in friendship, in love—as anything but tempo-
rary—a bit of joy while it lasts and education when it ends.
                                        —Maria Chabot to Dorothy Stewart
                                          San Antonio, December 9, 1941

I know why tourists often said that their first sight of Santa Fe takes
their breath away, especially in the days before the war, when the City
Different was still different from other cities.

But different in a way that fitted naturally into the landscape,
instead of standing out against it. The town was built of earth-colored
adobe clustered around a sunbaked, earth-colored plaza, the whole of
it cupped in a wide bowl crosshatched by *acequias*—irrigation ditches fringed with cottonwoods and poplars. The tawny desert plateau
surrounding the town was rimmed by cedar-blanketed foothills and
farther, ringed by red palisades and purple mountains, still snow-
capped in mid-June. The piñon-scented air, thin and intoxicating at
seven thousand feet, was so dry it pinched your nose. And domed over
all, the luminous, infinite, unforgiving sky. From a distance, the city

seemed serene and impersonal, although I had learned that the business of living and working in it could also be somewhat . . . different.

I was on my way to see Dorothy, who lived with her sister Margretta on Canyon Road, a dusty unpaved street in what had become the artist-colony section of town. A muralist, painter, and printmaker, Dorothy came to Santa Fe in the middle 1920s after studying in France and Italy and at the Pennsylvania Academy of the Fine Arts. Margretta, an energetic organizer of women's suffrage groups and the widow of a governor of Nebraska, arrived a couple of years later. Both had independent incomes that allowed them to do pretty much as they chose.

And since Santa Fe prided itself on being the City Different in as many magically eccentric ways as anyone could imagine, there was complete freedom of choice. Dorothy was a generous supporter of the arts community and mothered every young artist who came to town. Margretta (Sister Piggy or just Peeg to those who loved her) was devoted to Indian issues. Currently, she was badgering the federal government to reject the proposed dams on the Rio Grande and the Rio Chama that would destroy several ancient Indian villages and flood their fertile lands. Both sisters cared about preserving the old adobes that made Santa Fe such a remarkable place, so they had asked their friend Kate Chapman to manage the restoration of Dorothy's and Margretta's Canyon Road houses. In her restorations, Kate preserved the thick walls, packed earth floors, and other elements of classic Territorial architecture. I loved what she had done and studied it carefully. Years later, when I started to work on O'Keeffe's Abiquiu house, I would realize just how much I owed her.

Dorothy and Margretta lived in the old Juan José Prado House at 519 Canyon. Next door was Margretta's historic, restored El Zaguán, another one of Kate's renovations. It was a larger, sprawling adobe divided into a half-dozen apartments that Margretta and Dorothy rented to their friends, usually women artists. On the same block: Dorothy's smaller studio, the Galleria Mexicana, a charming adobe where she hosted performances and parties, always parties. If Canyon Road was the cultural center of Santa Fe, Dorothy's Galleria was the social center of Canyon Road and surely a seductive danger for serious artists, I've always thought. The practice of art here tended to be more of a community project than an individual expression. It had certainly been difficult for me to settle down to writing when I was living at El Zaguán. There was always another story to hear, another party to go to, another adventure to join. Not the best situation for someone as distractible as I am.

I got off the bus, stowed my luggage in a locker at the bus station, and walked to the Galleria. I found Dorothy reading at a table in the studio's little walled garden, beside a frilly pink rosebush and a flush of indolent peonies. There was a pitcher of iced lemonade on a silver tray at her elbow.

"Hi, Ducks," I said, bending to kiss her cheek. "I am just off the bus. Don't take a deep sniff—I've been riding for days."

Dorothy's smile lit her square, pleasant face. "So glad you're here, Pet." It sounded as if she meant it, but that's how Dorothy always sounds. Well-rounded and shorter than I by half a head, she was wearing a loose Mexican *huipil*, white, embroidered with gold and brown sunflowers. "You're staying, I hope. A few days, a week, even?"

"Not quite." I flopped into a chair. "I need to take the afternoon bus to Española. O'Keeffe writes that she's been at Ghost Ranch since the end of May and is in a mess. The house is torn up and the girl who cooked and cleaned for her turned out to be pregnant and got the boot. I expect I'm needed." I suppose I was name-dropping, maybe even boasting a bit, but it gave me pleasure. Dorothy had Agnes. I had O'Keeffe, although not in the same way.

"I expect you are," Dorothy said drily. "You always seem to make yourself indispensable." There were several glasses on the tray—Dorothy was forever expecting drop-ins—and as she poured lemonade, her tone became big-sisterly. Or motherly, if you like. I was twenty-some years younger, and she had always been as much mentor and mother as lover and friend.

She pushed the glass across the table. "I'm still not sure what interests you in O'Keeffe. Those costumes of hers are so strange. Does she want people to think she's a nun? And all that insistence on privacy, hiding herself away out there in the desert. You might almost think she doesn't like us." A sidelong glance. "Is it her painting that attracts you, Pet? I've heard that those giant flowers of hers bring in a lot of money. Ten thousand for that jimson weed she painted for Elizabeth Arden's salon."

"Meow," I said.

Dorothy laughed. "Do you blame me?"

"Of course not." I sipped the sweet-tart lemonade. She could be forgiven a twinge of professional jealousy. Her art went for peanuts, compared to O'Keeffe's. It wasn't just the jimson weed, either. There were the notorious calla lilies that had sold for twenty-five thousand dollars a dozen years ago. Some people said the sale was a hoax, perpetrated by Stieglitz to jack up the value of his wife's paintings. If that's what it was, it had obviously worked. Not only did the paintings bring an astonishing price, they generated an astonishing amount of publicity. And they were astonishingly beautiful. All of O'Keeffe's work had a mystical, spiritual beauty that couldn't be measured against price, I thought.

Dorothy smiled. "If it isn't the painting, it's infatuation?" Another smile, a little lighter. "A crush?"

Infatuation. Yes, perhaps—but not the kind Dorothy meant. I shook my head. "Not that. It's not like that at all."

At least, I didn't think so. I considered before I spoke again, trying to answer honestly. "It's her discipline, I think. Her clarity. Her ability to pay attention to the thing she's working on. Her aim to live and work alone, out there in the desert, away from people." Was that it, all of it? Or was there more?

"Not a crush." Dorothy chuckled, skeptical. "Well, we'll see." She eyed me over the rim of her glass. "If things don't pan out with O'Keeffe, Pet, you know you're welcome here. Margretta would be delighted if you'd come back to work for her. Her Indians always need help. And there's an empty room, just for you."

"Room for me?" Pointedly, I glanced around. "Agi's out reading the rocks again, is she?" Dorothy's current partner had become fascinated by prehistoric desert petroglyphs, a passion reflected in her painting, sculpture, even her textiles.

"She'll be back this evening. I'm sure she'd love to see you."

"Oh, without a doubt," I said.

Dorothy regarded me. "How did the writing go while you were home? Make any progress on your novel?"

I sighed. "You would have to bring that up." Dorothy knows I'm prone to distractions. "I finished the Chabot House apartments, which didn't leave a lot of time for my own work. But I expect to have a lot more free time this summer. Just O'Keeffe and me—and there can't be that much to do out there on the ranch."

I changed the subject. "What's been going on here? How is our little Marie? And what's happening with Olive these days?" Marie

Armengaud, a French teacher, sprightly and gamin. Like so many others, she had come to Santa Fe to recover from a lung ailment. Olive Rush was a painter and muralist.

"Marie is still smitten with that Sarton woman," Dorothy said ruefully. "May has gone back East and there haven't been any letters lately." She waved a hand. "As for goings-on, Olive Rush and I are doing some lithographs together. Agnes has started a new sculpture. Kate just began another adobe restoration. And Margretta says to tell you that if you have time, she'd love your advice on a problem with the Indian Market. I don't think it's terribly urgent."

A few years before, I had proposed holding regular markets on the central plaza, where Indians from the nearby pueblos could sell their pottery, weaving, baskets, jewelry, and other art. A highly successful idea, as it turned out—and even more successful when I arranged for buses to pick up the artists at their pueblos. An immediate hit, the market had become an important tradition. I was proud of it.

"I'll stop by Sister Piggy's on my way to the bus," I said. "If I miss her, tell her to write. She can send it care of O'Keeffe, at Ghost Ranch. There's no telephone, of course."

"No telephone." Dorothy wrinkled her nose. "You poor dear. You really *will* feel marooned." She gave me a meaningful smile. "But perhaps you won't mind. You and O'Keeffe will have all that time to yourselves."

All that time to yourselves. I knew what Dorothy was thinking— what all my lesbian friends were likely to think—and I shook my head emphatically. "No, Ducks. It's not like that at all. And it won't be."

Both skeptical eyebrows went up. "You're sure about that?"

"I'm sure."

And I was. The O'Keeffe I had met was a small, slender woman, stern-faced, her steel-dark hair constrained in a tight bun, with eyes that looked through you and a half-smile that suggested some sort of occult knowing. She was entirely to herself, contained and nun-like, nothing at all like the bare-breasted woman with the seductive hips and neat, dark patch of pubic hair that her lover Stieglitz had photographed and displayed twenty-some years ago, while he was still married to another wife. And nothing at all like the rumors of an unrestrained O'Keeffe who had enjoyed herself a decade before in Taos, with Beck Strand and Mabel Dodge Luhan's stalwart Native American husband Tony. As far as I could tell from our brief acquaintance, *that* O'Keeffe—the sensual, sexually uninhibited woman Dorothy was imagining—was gone, abandoned, a cast-off persona that no longer fit. Or it was only the fictive stuff of legend and rumor. Both were possible, I supposed.

Dorothy raised her eyebrows again but she only said, "Well, that's too bad," without saying exactly which of my pronouncements was too bad. And then she went on to other topics. She knew everybody in town and she was always full of news.

But after a few more minutes of chitchat, I glanced at my wristwatch and stood to go. "If I want to talk to Peeg and still catch the Chile Express to Española I'd better be on my way." I leaned forward and whispered. "*Te adoro*, Sweetness."

"Come back whenever you can," Dorothy said, rising. She slipped an arm around me, but her lips brushed my cheek only lightly. "In fact, come next weekend, if O'Keeffe can spare you. Piggy and I are having a party Friday night—the usual suspects, all your friends. But remember, you're welcome any time. *Mi casa es tu casa*. I would love to have you nearby. Always."

Yes, of course, I thought, not quite resigned and only a little bitter about Agnes. That's me. Always nearby.

❖

The Chile Line was a 125-mile narrow-gauge railway with Santa Fe on one end and San Antonito, Colorado, on the other. It took its name from its passengers' culinary preferences and from its customary cargo: chiefly New Mexican chile peppers, along with beans, corn, pigs, and goats. The railroad had been losing traffic to truck haulers and was scheduled to be closed in September, which was a shame. It was faster than the bus and more convenient—and chugged through a spectacular landscape of river and desert.

I got on at Union Station. The line ran up the middle of Guadalupe Street, crossed a couple of trestles and paralleled Rio Grande Boulevard, heading north to Buckman and Embudo and across the river on the iron truss bridge at Otowi, where Edith Warner had a little tea room and served the most delicious chocolate cake in the world. Then on to the village of Española, halfway between Santa Fe and Taos, where I got off, thinking that local folk would miss the Chile Line when it was gone. It was always crowded with moms and kids, old Indian grandmothers with baskets of chiles and sometimes a cage of live chickens, and workmen with their toolboxes. The engineer and fireman liked to shoot jackrabbits along the way, and passengers sometimes brought their guns and joined the fun. Then there was the big yellow dog at Tres Piedras, who famously waited for the engineer to toss him a rolled copy of the *Santa Fe New Mexican*, which he carried home to his owner.

I had missed lunch in Santa Fe, so when I got off the train in Española I walked across the dusty street to Garcia's Diner for a satisfyingly greasy hamburger and a grape soda. Then I climbed onto a rickety bus that smelled of hot diesel oil, cigarette smoke, and garlic. There were only a half-dozen passengers: three Indian women from the San Juan Pueblo, a Spanish-speaking priest carrying a bottle of homemade chokecherry wine, a Navajo woman with a baby goat, and me. The bus was headed north and west to Tierra Amarilla—in a rather pokey fashion, because the driver was also the postman and stopped to deliver a sack of mail to the post office in Bode's Mercantile and General Store in Abiquiu and leave mail at the ranch mailboxes along the road. He would let me off at the gate to Ghost Ranch, along with O'Keeffe's mail (two envelopes from Stieglitz and one from Claudia O'Keeffe, her sister). It was a two-mile hike up the lane to the house, but I'm a strong hiker and that was easily doable. If my suitcase and carry-all got too heavy, I would leave them beside the lane and come back for them later with O'Keeffe's car.

I was looking forward to walking through the desert again, after a frustrating winter of stewing over Dorothy, tending to the parents, and trying to fit my writing time around my hours with a hammer and paintbrush at Chabot House. Here, there would be none of that. I could manage O'Keeffe's small, neat household in the mornings, leaving my afternoons free—gloriously free—to write. I would be spending the next five months with a fascinating woman whose clear-eyed vision and strength of purpose I deeply admired. From whom I might learn how to deal with my mess of muddles and confusions. Might learn how to look, how to see what is really there, and put the art of seeing to work in my writing. Perhaps, if I studied O'Keeffe carefully enough, I could learn to use words in the same way she used paint: to show how it *feels* to see what is there.

The Ghost Ranch gate was marked by a bleached buffalo skull impaled on a fence post. I said goodbye to the driver, the priest, the woman, and the baby goat and climbed off the bus. As it chugged away, I took a deep breath, picked up my luggage, and began to walk. The afternoon sky was clear and cloudless, the warm breeze was scented with sage and piñon, and the magical desert of the Piedra Lumbre made my heart sing.

THE PIEDRA LUMBRE

The countryside of New Mexico is not a static background for the story of its people. The landscape, and the geophysical forces that have created and continue to re-create it, *is* the story of New Mexico. The topography underfoot offers a continuous journey backward and forward through millions of years of creation and destruction. This region is as dramatic to geologists as it is to artists. The skeleton of the earth is stripped clean of a pastoral hide in much of the country, and the fractures, scars, and bruises of eons of uplift, erosion, and volcanic activity are exposed. This is a primal landscape where "the very floor of the world is cracked open," as Willa Cather put it.

—Lesley Poling-Kempes
"A Call to Place"
Georgia O'Keeffe and New Mexico: A Sense of Place

I am the child of Changing-Woman—come! Come, come!
Sunbeams make a moving trail over it—come! Come, come!
On top of Pedernal Mountain—come! Come, come!
Where Changing-Woman was born—come! Come, come!

I arrive there too—come! Come, come!

—Navajo chant, Hosteen Klah, ceremonial singer
Recorded and transcribed by Mary Chabot Wheelwright
Navajo Creation Myth, Santa Fe, 1942

The land that inspired Georgia O'Keeffe's paintings and sang in Maria Chabot's heart is called the Piedra Lumbre, the Valley of Shining Stone. It is roughly a hundred square miles of high desert basin, held in the stern embrace of four rugged mountain ranges: the Tusas to the north, the Sangre de Cristo to the east, the Jemez to the south. Sixty-some miles to the north and west of Santa Fe, the multicolored landscape is diagonally cut northwest to southeast by the Rio Chama, zigzagging its downward way from the Continental Divide to the Rio Grande Rift. During the 1920s and 1930s, there was talk of a dam across the Chama that would create a flood-control and recreational lake, but World War II tabled that discussion, and then other issues arose. A lake, for instance, would inundate the rich river-irrigated bottom lands that belonged to many small Native American and Anglo farmers, as well as hundreds of archeological sites. But the dam won. Construction was begun in 1956 and finished in 1963.

It wasn't the first time this basin has seen a lake. The Piedra Lumbre is an eons-old succession of shallow equatorial seas and swampy flood plains and deserts and seas again, home to duck-billed dinosaurs, half-ton coryphodons, flying reptiles the size of small airplanes, mastodons, and giant ground sloths. Currently, it is home to antelope, coyotes, jackrabbits, mountain lions, lizards, and snakes (watch out for that little green prairie rattler—it's deadly) as well as ravens, hawks, bald eagles, and a handful of hardy humans and their sheep, goats, horses, and cows. The southern horizon, shaped by eons of exploding volcanoes and scoured by wild rivers, is crowned by a high mesa with a narrow blade of a summit, three thousand feet above the basin below. The first Native American visitors called it Tsee p'in. The later Spanish, Cerro Pedernal. Both names mean "flaking stone mountain." Flaking stone, both the doing of it and the thing done. Flint.

It is the precious flint of Pedernal that first drew humans to this place, perhaps ten thousand years ago. Nomads, they came to its eastern and western slopes to quarry the flint for their tools: knives, scrapers, blades, arrow and lance points. Centuries later, descendants of the Mesa Verde Anasazi journeyed down the Chama River and settled here, building pueblos of stone and adobe on the mesas—including the one at Abiquiu—and on wide ledges high in the cliffs. These Tewa Indians supported their settlements with fields and gardens in the floodplains of the river and creeks, where they cultivated corn, beans, melons, squash, and (naturally!) chile peppers. An industrious and energetic people, they made pottery from local clay and baskets from river reeds, as well as tools from Pedernal's flint.

But these Indians were above all a people of spirit, celebrating the movements of the sun, moon, and seasons across the landscape that became their spiritual home. To them, Pedernal was the sacred Woman-Who-Changes, The-Woman-Who-Is-Transformed-Again-and-Again. In Navajo creation stories, Changing Woman is the Mother of All the People. She is born on this mountain every spring, grows into a young woman during the summer, becomes the mother of twin warriors in the autumn and a wise elder in the winter, and is born again with the coming of the new spring. Pedernal, Changing Woman, is the heart of their story, the sacred heart of the land to which they belong.

Over the centuries, Changing Woman has seen many changes at the foot of her mountain. The Apaches and Utes—trading, raiding, enslaving tribes invading from the north—put an end to the relatively peaceful Tewa settlements along the Chama. By the mid-sixteenth century these were abandoned, their inhabitants retreating downriver to larger, more defensible pueblos along the Rio Grande and in the mountains beyond.

In 1598, the first Europeans, the Spanish, moved northward from their conquests in Mexico with their horses, their sheep, and their guns. They came looking for gold and land, establishing themselves in what they called Nuevo México—until 1846, when American troops marched in over the eastern mountains, and took possession of the land. The Piedra Lumbre became part of New Mexico Territory. And then, in 1912, part of the state of New Mexico. Santa Fe was named as its capital. Santa Fe—home to a rich mix of cultures, to those seeking health in the dry, clear air, and to a vibrant community of writers and artists.

And this is where a young artist named Georgia O'Keeffe visited with her sister Claudia in the summer of 1917, on a vacation from O'Keeffe's teaching position at West Texas State Normal College in Canyon, Texas. On that trip, they rode the Chile Line up to Taos and southern Colorado. O'Keeffe's imagination was captured by the infinite skies, the vast, open desert, the storms and sweeping winds.

It would be another dozen years before she returned. But from then on, she would say, "I was always coming back."

CHAPTER THREE

Changing Woman
Georgia

I have bought this house—paid $3,000 dollars for it—cost $1,400 to build seven years ago—I would rather come here than any place I know. It is a way for me to live very comfortably at the tail end of the earth so far away that hardly any one will ever come to see me and I like it.

—Georgia O'Keeffe to Alfred Stieglitz
July 27, 1940

Georgia stands on the *portal* of her house at Ghost Ranch and looks across the orange and red and purple badlands toward Pedernal, firm and angular, anchoring the faraway horizon. She has begun another painting of the mountain, which Maria told her is sacred to the Navajos. For them, Pedernal is Changing Woman, transforming herself with the seasons and the natural rhythms of life.

Georgia thinks of this often, seeing herself in Changing Woman, especially now, with so many major transitions in her life. And especially now that she owns this house, with its spectacular view of the mountain and the feeling of a vast infinity lying beyond the horizon. She has the profoundly mystical sense that Pedernal itself—the spirit of the ancient mountain that wears the shape of a deer on its flank—

has brought her to this place, in the same way that a harbor beacon lights the way to refuge.

"It's *mine*," she said to Maria as they stood on this spot the previous autumn, looking out across the desert. "God told me if I painted it enough, I could have it." She has the feeling that the mountain takes care of her, takes care *for* her. And when she dies, her ashes will be scattered there. She will be truly of this place then, as the sun and wind and rain and changing seasons are of it. The steadfast presence of Pedernal on the horizon always calms and centers her.

But not now, not today, at least, not at this moment. Up on the roof, one man is hurling curses at another in a language she doesn't understand. At the end of the porch, someone is noisily sawing a length of cedar, while the rapid-fire pounding of a hammer comes from the dining room. The air is heavily laced with the oily odor of hot roofing tar, so heavy that Georgia can taste it on her tongue.

She turns back into the house, fighting off a feeling of utter helplessness. The place is in an appalling mess, the floors and furniture thick-furred with adobe dust, every room in complete chaos, with no hope of restoring order any time soon. Chaos isn't something she is used to. It makes her feel queasy, uneasy, unsettled.

Life in New York is nothing like this. For the first dozen years of their marriage, she and Stieglitz lived a tidy, well-ordered life at the Shelton Hotel, where housekeeping was provided and they took all their meals in the cafeteria. For the past five or so years, they have lived in an East Fifty-Fourth Street penthouse with a full-time cook-housekeeper who keeps things spick and span and puts lunch and dinner on the table. Even at the Stieglitz family vacation home on Lake George, where she and Alfred spend the summer months, there is always kitchen and household and garden help.

Here—well, it isn't just the repairs. Finding the right person to manage the cooking and cleaning is proving to be an unexpected challenge. For the first week, she had had a little Spanish girl named Bernice, recommended by Mr. Bode, who owns Abiquiu's general store—its *only* store. Bernie, as she liked to be called, was neat and quiet and did things just the way Georgia wanted them done. But it was quickly apparent that she was pregnant, quite far along under the loose dress she wore, and no husband. Georgia fired her, assuming that it would be easy to find someone else—a mistaken assumption, as it has turned out.

Finding help wasn't a problem in the years before she bought this house, when she rented it or a cottage at Ghost Ranch, as a guest. Then, she took her meals along with the other guests in the dude ranch dining room, so there was no shopping or cooking to bother with. A maid from the ranch did the cleaning and laundry. And Arthur Pack, owner of the ranch, sent his ranch manager Orville Cox to start the balky generator, fix the water pump, and unclog the sink drain.

Now that this house is truly *hers*, though, she can't ask for help from the ranch. And finding the right person among the locals is proving to be a headache. For one thing, she doesn't speak Spanish and isn't inclined to learn, which makes communication rather a challenge. For another, there are the ghosts. It seems that the place was first settled by a pair of outlaw brothers named Archuleta who corralled their stolen cows and horses in a nearby box canyon and stuffed their robbery victims down a well. The ghosts are said to make such an infernal clamor that the superstitious Abiquiu folk call the place El Rancho de los Brujos, the Ranch of the Witches. They are afraid to come anywhere near the place after dark. And most help will have to live here during the week, since almost none have cars.

Georgia understands their reluctance, because—while she's not superstitious in a silly, spooky way—she believes that places have a sacred, spiritual dimension. When the wind blows in the canyons of the shining cliffs, she can hear the earth speaking. And when she stands barefoot on the roof of her adobe house, she herself is that mystic bridge between the earth and the sky.

Bernie spoke decent English, came from Colorado, and was quite sensible about witches. After Georgia let her go, Mr. Bode recommended a bouncing, gum-chewing Anglo girl—Mamie—who didn't mind witches but couldn't boil water and didn't know one end of a broom from the other. Mamie was followed by a young man, an artist, sent from Santa Fe by Vernon Hunter, an artist Georgia had met in New York. She thought at first that the young man might work out. He was quite nice-looking (she enjoys having attractive young men around) and could be trusted to do the shopping and run errands in town. But the boy couldn't cook and wasn't interested in learning, so Georgia sent him back to Santa Fe. Which means that she has to do everything herself—at least until Maria Chabot arrives. Soon, she hopes. Maria seems quite competent and even eager, offering to do her best to make Georgia's life simple and productive in return for bed, board, and time to write. Maria, who knows her way around the area, can probably find a local girl to do the cooking and cleaning. But until then . . .

Feeling tied into knots, Georgia goes back to her easel, where she is working on a painting of the stunning red and yellow cliffs she can see from the studio window. The first Spanish explorers, awestruck by the way the setting sun turned the sheer cliffs to brilliant fire, called them Piedra Lumbre, Shining Stone. She has already painted them several times, loving the way their colors change with every cloud that drifts across the sun.

But as she picks up her brush, she hears a warning shout, a loud *crash*, and the sound of breaking glass from the breakfast nook, where Mr. Peabody's crew is putting in the new window. She drops the brush. Her head is aching dully. Her temper is dangerously frayed, and she has to admit that Stieglitz was right when he said that the renovations would be too much for her, that she would end up in bed with a sick headache or some other ailment that would keep her away from her easel for a week. That's what happens back in New York whenever she experiences severe emotional stress. In fact, she has been seriously ill at least once a year from the time she began living with him.

Now that she owns this place, however, Georgia knows that there are things that need to be done if she means to live here after her husband— twenty-two years her senior—is gone and she is independent. Increasingly frail, he has complained of angina for nearly a decade, so while it might sound cold-hearted, she knows she has to think ahead. She loves the desert. And she dislikes New York, especially these days, with everyone on edge about the terrible news from Europe and the possibility of America getting involved in another foreign war. She has already made up her mind that after Alfred is gone, she will leave the city and come to the desert. She will come *here*. Immediately.

So when Mr. Peabody brought the Indian men from San Juan Pueblo to repair the leaks in the roof and plaster cement on the outer adobe walls of the house, she told him to go ahead and knock out a bigger window in the dining room and another in the little corner porch that looks out toward the cliffs, as well as install a skylight in the bathroom and open up a doorway between her studio and the adjacent bedroom. Unfortunately, she didn't anticipate the amount of adobe dust created by these renovations. It fills the air and settles on every surface (including her still-wet painting). And the men track it everywhere and drop things and shout and bang and scrape from first light until sunset. And the place is a thicket of construction materials: stacks of wood and rolls of stucco netting and cans of hot tar and tanks of lime and bags and bags and *bags* of cement. The men have been at the job for nearly a week and will probably take another ten days. If the rest of the summer is like this, she *will* be sick. She will never get any work done, and work is what she's here for. It is the reason she comes—that, and the need to get away from the city. From Alfred. And from Mrs. Norman.

Alfred. She presses her lips together. Yesterday's mail had brought another fevered letter from her husband, the third in two days, each filled with complaints of ill health (his angina probably real, the rest of it prompted by a chronic hypochondria), petty grievances against the new cook-housekeeper, and deliberate mentions of Dorothy Norman, with whom he is still carrying on a romance. Georgia often thinks that her husband is much more wonderful in his work as an artist and a supporter of other artists than he is as a human being. And that she has had to put up with an *extraordinary* amount of contradictory nonsense during the twenty-five years they have lived together—not to mention having to endure his self-involved, fractious family, famous for their feuds and perpetual petty jealousies. Stieglitz's letters are a blinding sandstorm of sometimes painful words, reminding her that she is still tied to him and will be until the end. It is hard not to feel sorry for herself. Sometimes she even feels sorry for young Mrs. Norman.

But it has always been the public humiliation of the affair that galled her, even more than the implications of Mrs. Norman's rivalry for Alfred's affections. "I do not for one moment accept the idea of your going about publicly making love to someone else," she told him angrily. "We can't control what we feel, but we can control the public exhibition of it."

In full retreat from her husband, his mistress, his family, and his friends and disciples, Georgia began spending summers in New Mexico a dozen years ago, when she and Beck Strand had come to Taos to stay with Mabel Dodge Luhan. She fell in love with the desert that reached to the distant mountains under the arch of infinite sky, realizing even then that her life as an artist depended on what this place might give her. She knew she had to come back.

And so she had, first to Taos again—although not to Mabeltown, which was clotted with Mabel's devotees. Georgia didn't like Mabel and she refused to be thought of as *anybody's* devotee. So the next year she had gone to Marie Garland's H&M Ranch on the Rio Grande, where Marie entertained notables. And then to Carol and Roy Pfaffle's San Gabriel Guest Ranch. But even in those places, she had found the social life was too distracting.

"I must be someplace where the people do not run me crazy," she wrote to Beck in desperation—Beck, who knew almost all her secrets. "I don't see anything to do about that but to have a house of my own." And at that moment, she knew what she had to do.

As a girl, Georgia was known for her determination—her ability to decide what she wanted and plot a course to take her there, even when it meant managing other people. (She once asked a classmate, "When so few people ever think at all, isn't it all right for me to think for them, and get them to do what I want?") Her career as an artist felt secure, but she longed desperately for a house of her own, somewhere out in the desert. She had seen a ruined adobe in the village of Abiquiu that intrigued her. But most of the roof was gone, the walls were melting back to the earth, and the asking price (the Catholic Church owned it) was six thousand dollars—too much, given what it would cost to resurrect the place. Adobe building was an art, and she didn't know anyone who could manage a project like that. Even if she could somehow manage to buy the place, rebuilding it was out of the question.

In the meantime, she discovered remote Ghost Ranch, even more remote than the guest ranches on the Rio Grande. There, she made a few friends among the guests—the Hardings and the Johnsons and David McAlpin, special people she continued to see back East because they have a place in her art life there. But for the most part, she avoided the evening social gatherings and kept to herself, hiking and painting in the red hills and under the cliffs, basking in the landscape of brilliant light, strong forms, and pure color. But no people. "If only people were trees," she once told an interviewer, "I might like them better."

To be fair, she suspected that most of the guests at the ranch didn't like her any more than she liked them. They thought her blunt (she was, and prided herself on it) and often rude. (She wasn't, she told herself, just disinterested and willing to let it show.) They also thought her unconventional, even bohemian, because she came to the ranch alone, leaving her elderly husband—seventy-something and frail—for a full six months every year. What kind of wife did that? An uncaring wife? A neglectful wife?

A *resolute* wife, she wanted to shout at them, for they couldn't know what courage it took to leave Stieglitz, who raged at her like a madman as she prepared to leave. But these people's opinions were no more important to her than those of the art critics who insisted on seeing her giant flowers as something they weren't. She simply paid no attention.

For several summers, Georgia came back to Ghost Ranch, staying in one of the cottages until Arthur and his new wife, Phoebe, moved to the ranch headquarters. Brownie, Arthur's first wife, had eloped with their children's tutor, and the house Arthur built (Rancho de los Burros, named for the children's burros and a wordplay on Rancho de los Brujos) held bitter memories for him. He had been glad to let Georgia rent it—until the year she forgot to let him know she was coming and he rented it to someone else.

There had been a heated argument, quite an awful fracas, actually. Her tongue had got the better of her and she had lashed out with several cruel things she shouldn't have said. But she had gotten what she wanted, which made it all seem quite reasonable. Arthur sold her the house and the surrounding several acres for $3,000. It had been more than she wanted to pay, but at last, she has a house of her own.

An uneasy cease-fire prevails after that, and Arthur obligingly tells people that Georgia tries to be a friend. But their argument about the house is only the opening hostility in what seems likely to be a long-smoldering conflict. Now, help from Ghost Ranch is rarely forthcoming, even when the pump refuses to work and the kitchen sink drain clogs up again. And when she wants something out of the Ghost Ranch garden—fresh lettuce or corn or cucumbers or a melon—Phoebe (Arthur's new wife) is likely to put up a fuss. Georgia is beginning to realize that a house of her own in the desert isn't the easy retreat she hoped for. And Stieglitz's hysterical responses to her absences make the arrangement even more difficult.

Alfred has gradually gotten used to her annual departures, but he still lets her know that he is deeply hurt and very angry. It is his way of attempting to control her life, she thinks, just as he has always controlled her work: when and where and how often she showed it, who bought it, as well as her subjects and the medium—even the interpretation, that awful Freudian nonsense he had come up with. When they had begun their affair, she hadn't known even the first thing about the *business* of art, hadn't imagined that an artist might be able to earn a living by selling her work. He sometimes claimed that making art for sale was little more than prostitution, but he was very good at selling—so good that she had been glad to cede him that authority. She'd had no idea then that he would extend his authority to her life, even refusing her a child.

"Your paintings are your children," he'd told her, not realizing how brutal those words were. He'd said that if she had a child, she would never paint again. What if he was right? She had picked up her brushes, then, and made another painting.

Ironically, Dorothy did have the time. The wife of a wealthy Sears and Roebuck heir and already a mother, Mrs. Norman was almost twenty years younger than Georgia and *forty* years younger than Stieglitz when they met. She had appeared at his gallery (then the Intimate Gallery, known as the Room) and within months had become an ardent follower, answering the phone, managing the rent fund, and making cash contributions when the money ran low. She plainly, publicly adored him and Stieglitz was publicly foolish about her. He suffered sympathy cramps with her second pregnancy and speculated to friends that the child—a boy, Andrew—might be his, which Georgia knew could very well be true. There were the interminable telephone calls and the daily impassioned letters to "Darling Dorothy my dearest" (one letter mailed accidentally—or was it?—to Georgia), as well as photographic sessions in the nude and embarrassing public displays of affection.

Georgia isn't a prude. She has loved other men before Stieglitz and she's had one or two brief flings after they were married. She occasionally thinks with pleasure of Tony, Mabel's Indian husband, and

Jean Toomer and that fellow in Hawaii, the one who managed the sugar plantation, and she feels a special satisfaction when a handsome young man lets her know that he finds her attractive and interesting —Eliot Porter, for instance, or Orville Cox. But that's different, and she is always (she feels) discreet. Not so Stieglitz. His affair with Mrs. Norman is a torch he proudly holds high. Their friends know that the pair have been lovers and wonder aloud (loud enough for Georgia to hear them) when she will finally have enough.

It finally happened. Through most of her married life, Georgia has suffered regular bouts of depression. She underwent breast surgery twice and has been plagued by such a variety of illnesses that she often spends whole days in bed. Humiliated by her husband's flagrant infidelity and by the failure of a widely publicized mural project she undertook for Radio City Music Hall, she suffered a nervous breakdown and was hospitalized. For the first month, her doctor refused to allow Stieglitz to visit. In the second, his visits were strictly limited. And still he clung to Mrs. Norman.

When she recovered, Georgia did not return to her husband but instead went with her friend Marjorie Content to Bermuda, considering whether she should go back to Stieglitz or leave him and end the marriage. She had loved him passionately once, but how long had it been since they had slept in the same bed or even in the same room? She will never admit to anyone but herself that she owes her career to him (and to herself only with pain and great reluctance). She knows he is still crucial to the success of her work—that is, to its commercial success, which is the way the world values art and the means by which she has to live.

And she knows that her work might not have been recognized at all if he hadn't been such a zealous supporter in their first years together.

If he hadn't hung her photographs in his gallery—those nudes that make her cringe even now, twenty years later. "It made a stir," art critic Henry McBride had written. "Mona Lisa got but one portrait of herself worth talking about. O'Keeffe got a hundred. It put her at once on the map. Everybody knew the name. She became what is known as a newspaper personality." *Newspaper personality.* That hurts, although of course it helped draw attention to her work.

She knows something else, too. That she is no longer the woman Stieglitz made. That she has to keep some of herself to herself or she will have nothing left to give to her work. And that she has to work and sell her work if she is to continue to support the two of them, as she has done for the past seven or eight years. More, she has to work—and *sell* her work—so that she can afford what she needs for herself: for this house in the desert, where she can live half the year while Stieglitz is alive and all the year once he is gone and she can finally leave the city. Work is not only her life in the present, the act that defines who she is. It is her investment in the future. In *her* future.

Hence the house at Ghost Ranch, which she bought as soon as she had the money—money she put into her account at Bankers Trust, not the account she shares with Stieglitz.

Hence these inconvenient renovations, which she tolerates, even welcomes, because they make the house *her* house. And every day and every night in her house will belong solely to *her,* and not to her and Alfred.

Except, of course, that somebody else has to cook and clean and fix the sink drain and start the power generator, or there won't be time for her work. And if there isn't time to paint, she won't be able to afford the house and all it represents.

She sighs. There is nothing she can do about Alfred and still less about Mrs. Norman. But really, something has to be done about the household help. What, though? *What?* She is hoping that when Maria Chabot comes, she will have an idea or two. She is acquainted with the people at Abiquiu. She will surely know someone who lives nearby and is willing to come.

So Georgia is relieved when the same afternoon bus that delivers the mail (two plaintive letters from Alfred and a peppy one from Claudia) also delivers Maria, who appears at the door with a cheering smile on her face, a suitcase in one hand, and an immense canvas carry-all over her shoulder.

Georgia recognized Maria's potential usefulness when they met the previous October at Los Luceros, where the girl was helping Mary Wheelwright edit her collection of Navajo chants. Maria is one of those young women who make themselves known when they come into a room. She is dark-haired and broad-shouldered, handsome in an energetic sort of way and hearteningly cheerful. She has a boundless stock of ideas and more than enough vitality to carry them out. She can be boisterous, as Georgia observed when they drove up to the Toadlena Valley to watch the Navajos dance the Mountain Chant. And she can be blunt. She speaks what is in her mind, just as Georgia does, and she speaks it emphatically, with conviction. Best of all, she likes to see that things are done, and she is infinitely resourceful when it comes to the doing. Out here in the desert, that capability could be a lifesaver. Georgia thinks of people in terms of their usefulness, and Maria plainly intends to make herself useful.

"Hullo, Georgia," Maria says, in that loud, clear, Texas-flavored voice of hers. She glances at the tools on the floor, the drifts of adobe dust, the broken glass under the window. "Looks like you're doing a little renovating. Good plan. Get it all done and the mess out of the way so it doesn't interfere with your painting any longer than it has to."

And in the first half-hour after her arrival, Maria has disposed of her bags, exchanged her denim skirt and blouse for jeans and a plaid shirt, and conducted a business-like conversation with Mr. Peabody, whom she knows from some remodeling work he did for Mary Wheelwright. Then she finds brooms, mops, and buckets for two of the men, instructing them in firm, fluent, voluble Spanish while Georgia looks on, bemused and immeasurably relieved.

By the end of the second half-hour, she and Georgia have discussed meals for the next week and have gone through the pantry and the small refrigerator to see what is there (not much).

And then she climbs into Georgia's station wagon and heads for Mr. Bode's general store in Abiquiu. She is back a couple of hours later with everything on the list: eggs, bacon, beans, cheese, apples, and a pair of thick steaks for supper, along with a bottle of wine from the cantina across the plaza from Bode's. She also brings a large basket of garden vegetables, a *ristra* of dried chiles and garlic, a jug of milk, a pot of fresh butter, and the assurance of more where that came from— supplied by her friend Flora Brunette, who keeps a cow, a flock of chickens, and a large vegetable garden in Barranco, a tiny village a mile or so west of Abiquiu. Best of all, she has located a woman who has agreed to a trial week of cooking and cleaning and is sensible about witches.

"If this one doesn't suit," Maria says, "Flora knows of one or two other possibilities. I told her we wanted somebody who will stay until you go back to New York, if you like her. Somebody we can *count* on." Which is exactly what Georgia would have said herself.

By this time, Mr. Peabody's workmen have cleaned up the broken glass and shoveled and swept most of the adobe dust out of the house. Feeling that things are finally under control, Georgia returns to her easel while Maria sautés a fresh squash in butter and garlic, makes a salad, and broils the steaks over an outdoor fire. They take their plates out to the *portal* and sit on either side of the large tree stump Georgia uses for a table.

"It looks delicious," Georgia says.

"Thank you." Maria raises her wine glass. "To a successful summer of painting—and writing." She glances across the desert at Pedernal. "And to Changing Woman."

Georgia touches her glass to Maria's. "To Changing Woman," she echoes. And quickly corrects herself. "To changing *women*." She smiles. "Two of us."

It feels like an auspicious beginning.

GHOST RANCH

The history of a place is, in the truest sense, a jumbled pile of stories that finally come to settle and rest one upon another until the ending of one is indistinguishable from the beginning of another.

—Lesley Poling-Kempes
Valley of Shining Stone

Georgia O'Keeffe was not the first woman to arrive at Ghost Ranch with the intention of freeing herself from someone else's story about her.

In the spring of 1928, Carol Stanley Pfaffle's gambler-cowboy husband walked away from a high-stakes poker game with the title to a chunk of the Piedra Lumbre in his pocket. It wasn't a very attractive or habitable chunk, if you believed the locals (they refused to be caught dead there after dark). But it came at the best possible time, at least as far as Carol Stanley was concerned. Fate played a hand in that game, you might say. Or maybe it was Changing Woman who dealt the cards, and the players were merely along for the ride.

The 157-acre piece that Roy Pfaffle won was originally home-steaded by the outlaw Archuleta brothers—but not for long. They disagreed, one murdered the other, and the murderer-brother ended up on the gallows. The spirits of their many victims were left to haunt the cliffs and canyons, so convincingly that the place became known as El Rancho de los Brujos, the Ranch of the Witches. Ghost Ranch.

At the time of that fateful poker game, Carol and Roy owned the San Gabriel Guest Ranch, a few miles from the village of Alcalde on the east side of the Rio Grande. But even before she bought the San Gabriel, Carol had already lived an unconventional life. Born in 1880 and raised in a family with connections to the prestigious Massachusetts Cabots, she studied classical piano at the New England Conservatory of Music, taught in Boston's South End Music settlement school, fell in love with a musician her family didn't like, closed that unfortunate chapter, and changed her story by going west—in 1914, an audacious choice for a woman of her social class. Exploring the desert with Natalie Curtis, an ethnomusicologist studying Native American music, Carol rode astride, slept in a bedroll on the ground, cooked over a campfire, wore breeches, and stopped worrying about her hair. Three years later, she changed her story again, marrying (much to her friends' surprise) Roy Pfaffle, a handsome cowboy and trail guide. Using an inheritance from her mother, she bought the scenic San Gabriel Ranch, a dozen miles north of Santa Fe on the road to Taos. She and Roy would turn it into a dude ranch.

During the Roaring Twenties, the San Gabriel prospered. Guests came—and came back, drawn by Carol's efficient hospitality, Roy's amiable congeniality, and the allures of the Indian pueblos and the bohemian art colonies of Santa Fe and Taos. The ranch attracted the likes of the Rockefellers, Pulitzer winner Oliver La Farge, Willa Cather and her companion, Edith Lewis, Mary Cabot Wheelwright (a Bostonian Cabot who bought nearby Los Luceros). And Georgia O'Keeffe. O'Keeffe spent her time to herself, painting. The others fished and hunted and took photos, climbed mountains, rode onto the desert, and watched Indian dances at the nearby pueblos, San Juan and Santa Clara. In the evenings, they played cards by the light of kerosene lamps while Carol played the Steinway Roy gave her for their anniversary.

But Roy's gambling and alcohol addictions undermined the

marriage and the Crash of 1929 did the rest. The ranch collapsed and Carol got a divorce. Now fifty but still plenty energetic, she also got the deed to the haunted 157 acres of the Piedra Lumbre that Roy had won at that poker table a few years before. She and her Steinway moved into the dilapidated adobe the Archuleta brothers had built at the mouth of the canyon: Ghost House. She sold some family property back East and used the money to buy an adjoining 17,000 desert acres, launched a fledgling cattle business, and constructed a half-dozen guest cottages and a corral. She wrote to the many people who had been her guests at San Gabriel Ranch, letting them know where they could find her and inviting them to come for a visit.

And they did. Ghost Ranch got off to a strong start in the early 1930s, attracting many of Carol's friends from her years at San Gabriel, and more. Among them were Arthur Pack and his vivacious wife Brownie, a photographer. Arthur, a wealthy conservationist who had founded *Nature Magazine* and the American Nature Association, was smitten with the badlands landscape and the vast blue sky. The Packs purchased a three-acre parcel from Carol and built an adobe-brick U-shaped house with a *portal* that offered a fabulous view of the fabled Pedernal.

But the Depression bit deep and the next five or six years brought a severe drought to Changing Woman's desert. Carol's cattle operations fell on hard times, and Arthur rode to her rescue with a generous offer to buy the ranch and carry on the tradition of hospitality she had created. Carol accepted the offer, fell in love with one of her cowboys, married him, and moved on—another story.

Things happened fast after that. Arthur's wife Brownie was an adventurous woman who was aiming for a career as a wildlife photographer. She and Georgia became great friends and often walked and rode up the canyons and into the hills. But Brownie decided she didn't want to live on a dude ranch at the far edge of nowhere. (Changing Woman again?) Like Carol, she moved on too, decamping with Frank Hibben, her children's tutor and a Princeton archaeology graduate student twelve years her junior. Arthur Pack was left with the ranch, stunned and alone.

But not for long. The next summer, Phoebe Finley, the attractive young daughter of one of Arthur's colleagues in the conservation movement, came to work at the ranch. Just out of college, the free-spirited and feisty Phoebe had grown up camping in mountains and deserts with her family. She too was smitten by Ghost Ranch, and by Arthur. They were married as soon as Arthur's divorce was final and moved into Ghost House, now the ranch headquarters. Phoebe discovered a talent as a dude ranch manager, and she and Arthur settled happily into life with their well-off guests, offering friendship and intellectual conversation, as well as ranch meals, riding lessons, and guided automobile and horseback trips to Navajoland, Canyon de Chelly, and the Grand Canyon.

One of those guests was Georgia O'Keeffe, who had *not* come for friendship or riding lessons or even intellectual conversation. O'Keeffe came to paint. For the first three or four years, she stayed in the Garden Ghost Cottage, taking her meals in the ranch dining hall but keeping to herself as much as she could. When the Packs moved out of the house at Rancho de los Burros, she rented it. As soon as she could, she bought it.

The house was built in 1933 of adobe bricks handmade on the ranch. The floors were pine planks, while the ceilings were constructed of *latillas* of aspen and cedar laid diagonally over *vigas* (log rafters) of pine and fir. Like all traditional adobe dwellings, the roof was flat (perfect for outdoor sleeping), slightly sloped to drain melting snow and rainwater. And yes, it does rain in the desert, especially during monsoon season, and sometimes very hard. *Canales* drain the water off the roof.

Originally ten rooms, the house was constructed in a traditional U-shape around a rectangular unpaved patio filled with whatever happened to grow there—sagebrush, mostly, but also chamisa, a gray-green shrub that bloomed bright yellow in the fall and was used by the Navajo as chewing gum. An untidy green mound of jimsonweed sprawled beside the *portal*, covered with fragrant white trumpets that bloomed from dark to dawn. A buffalo skull, bleached bone-white, hung on the parapet.

O'Keeffe's studio was in the long living room at the back of the house, with her easel in front of a window that looked out on the multicolored cliffs, constantly changing color and form as the sun and cloud shadows moved overhead. Several hundred feet high, the cliffs dwarfed the low, flat house. With its earthen colors and natural contours, it fit simply, naturally, into the landscape—as if it had always been there, as if it belonged, in the same way the rocks and cliffs and sage and chamisa belong.

❖

O'Keeffe belonged there under the cliffs too, and in the same way that sage and chamisa belonged. She did not, however, relate comfortably to most of the people who lived or visited Ghost Ranch and who—in her opinion—did not belong there. Over the years, this became something of a challenge for both her and the Packs, her closest neighbors.

"I had to stay right there and see that Georgia didn't kill some-one," Phoebe Pack would remark to one of O'Keeffe's biographers. "She hated strangers." In his 1966 memoir, *We Called It Ghost Ranch,* Arthur Pack remembered, "Chary of her friendships, she carefully avoided the common variety of dudes, rejecting all celebrity hunters with a firmness and finality that left them gasping." Faced with her often peremptory demands for service or requests for food from the kitchen or garden, Phoebe usually decided it wasn't worth arguing. "With people like Georgia," she sighed, "it's a heck of a lot easier to do what they want."

Once, though, she stood her ground. As she told biographer Laurie Lisle, Georgia had come into the kitchen of the dude ranch one day and noticed a large cake on that table. "I'd like that cake," Georgia said. "My housekeeper's having a birthday and it'll do just fine." But Phoebe had twenty-five guests to serve that night and had to say no. Georgia stared at her for a moment, then slammed out of the kitchen in a rage. "Such audacity," Phoebe said. "And so like Georgia."

The challenges intensified over the next few years. When war came, the guest-ranch business couldn't survive the combination of gas rationing, difficult cross-continent travel, and labor shortages. During the war, it was used as a vacation retreat for scientists from Los Alamos. When the war ended, Arthur and Phoebe moved to Tucson, leasing it to friends, Hollywood film crews, and paleontologists in search of dinosaur bones. (A major fossil discovery was made there in the summer of 1947.) In the early 1950s, the Packs began looking for an organization that might be interested in turning the ranch into an educational center. In 1955, the Presbyterian Board of Christian Education accepted their gift of the property and began transforming it.

And then it was war again, of a different kind. As Arthur tells the story in his memoir, O'Keeffe burst into his meeting with Presbyterian board members. "What's this I hear about your giving the ranch away?" she shouted. "If you were going to do that, why didn't you give it to me?" Turning to the dumbfounded church officials, she snapped, "Now I suppose this beautiful place will be crawling with people and completely spoiled. I never had any use for Presbyterians anyhow!"

Arthur had forewarned the new owners about their prickly neighbor, but as he remarks in his book, nothing could have prepared the Presbyterians for such a "frank and conclusive rejection of the institution they stood for." Later, O'Keefe would tell an interviewer, "You know about the Indian eye that passes over you without lingering, as though you didn't exist? That was the way I used to look at the Presbyterians at the ranch, so they wouldn't become too neighborly."

O'Keeffe never became neighborly, either at Ghost Ranch or in Abiquiu. But she eventually came to recognize that life in the desert is more livable when you're on speaking terms with the people on the other side of the road. When the ranch headquarters burned in 1983, she donated fifty thousand dollars and loaned her name to a fundraising campaign to replace the building and add a social center and a museum—although it is likely that Juan Hamilton (another "someone always nearby") had something to do with this generosity.

The people who have lived at Ghost Ranch have come and gone, and the communities that humans have built on the land have changed. But the shining cliffs still stand, silent sentinels, looking out across the high desert basin to Pedernal, serene and entirely to itself. Changing Woman, ever and always the same under the infinite sky.

CHAPTER FOUR

The First Year
Maria

I want to thank you for the many many things you thought of for me—Your real kindness—and freshness—You made so many things so easy for me. . . . I hope that you find being alone very pleasant.
—Georgia O'Keeffe to Maria Chabot
New York, November 17, 1941

Georgia! How wonderful it is to be alone. It's as good as being in love. Do you know the little pink hill by the turn in the road that you painted with the yellow cliff behind—the one that curls into deep red brown at its north end and is buttressed up by a violet affair at the south? It was so good today I felt ashamed to be looking at it.
—Maria Chabot to Georgia O'Keeffe
Ghost Ranch, November 21, 1941

Dear Maria—When you leave wire the mailbox shut so the skunk will not sleep in it.
—Georgia O'Keeffe to Maria Chabot
New York, December 1, 1941

That first year, 1941, we settled into the ranch in June. In November, Georgia took the plane back to Stieglitz and New York—her other life. I stayed on at the ranch for another month to work on my writing and enjoy a few days with Dorothy, who came for a visit. I also undertook to make the house weathertight for the winter, which wasn't an easy job. It was so cold that Thanksgiving that my undies froze stiff on the clothesline and frost crusted the windowsills until midday. Even the cat was cold (El Gato, a Siamese, had been loaned to us by Georgia's friend Richard Pritzlaff to manage the mice that plagued our pantry) and Pedernal was covered with snow—Changing Woman in her finest winter garb.

Overall, it had been a successful summer, I thought. The ranch was in a bit of a mess when I arrived, but it hadn't taken long to size things up and figure out what had to be done to make us comfortable and get the place running efficiently. Mr. Peabody just needed a little encouragement to get his Pueblo helpers to clean things up at the end of the day. Having worked on the Chabot apartments all winter, I'd learned quite a bit about construction and could see what needed doing. After the job was finished and the men got things cleaned up, it took another week to set the place to rights.

I had spent a fair amount of time in the area over the past seven or eight years, so I knew where to go for what we needed and who to ask for advice. By the middle of August, things were running pretty smoothly. But the ranch was remote, so most trips to town involved several hours of rough driving over desert roads designed for horses and mule trains, not automobiles. And there was no guarantee of getting back the same day if an up-canyon thunderstorm flooded one of the several arroyos that crossed the road. Instead of having afternoons free for writing, as I had hoped, there were always things waiting to be done—so often and so many that Georgia began calling me the "hired man." She meant it as a compliment, I think, although with O'Keeffe, it was always hard to tell. I found out quickly enough that she could be sarcastic.

Lucia, the woman Flora recommended, turned out to be an excellent cook and quite a capable housekeeper, but she got crosswise of Georgia over the way she stacked the wool blankets in the storeroom and was gone by the first of August. I took over her duties until I enlisted Benina, a pretty, brown-skinned teenager who wore her dark hair in two thick, shiny braids—less skilled than Lucia, but tolerant where witches were concerned, and eager to learn.

Which, as Georgia points out, is the important thing. It's better to have helpers—slaves, she called them—who are willing to do things the way you want, rather than people who expect you to put up with work habits they've learned somewhere else. The word *slave* implies ownership and I wasn't very comfortable with that, but I had to agree with the general idea. When you're paying someone a salary, she or he, whoever, should do what you want.

Of course, since I wasn't getting a weekly paycheck, I wasn't a slave—at least that's what I told myself. And while I enjoyed Georgia's little joke about being her "hired man," I considered myself a friend, doing what I did because I admired her and wanted to learn as much as I could from her. And *about* her, too, because I was still thinking about that feature article.

Or book. I was sure there was enough for a book—more than enough, really—if I could only find the time to write it. I was beginning to imagine what might be in it, what shape it might take. I was making notes, too, although this made Georgia uncomfortable. She preferred that I work on my novel about Mexico, which was only half-finished. To encourage me (and since she felt sorry—and a little guilty—that I didn't get more writing time during the summer) she sent me a check for $300 at the end of the year. Her note said that the "quality and vitality" of my spirit were "remarkable" and that she wanted me to use the money for time to think and work on my own thing by myself.

I protested that I didn't want her check, but not very hard, I'm afraid. I was torn: it's true that I had very little writing time at the ranch this summer (nothing like those agreed-on half-days), and I needed the money. Of course I needed the money. But I was a *friend*, not one of her slaves. Taking the check compromised me. It also had a certain note of finality about it, especially since she hadn't yet said whether she wanted me with her again next year. And yes, to be utterly honest (and in spite of my protest to Dorothy), I was probably a little smitten with her.

A little? Perhaps more. But who wouldn't be smitten by this astonishingly successful woman, who was able to live where she chose and how she chose, who made a living doing what she loved to do, and who insisted on meeting life on *her* terms, absolutely and without compromise and with apologies to no one, ever? There wasn't another woman like her anywhere.

And for me, the summer was important because I'd gotten to know her, at least a little. She didn't talk much about herself, although Stieglitz and their marriage were on her mind and she talked readily about him and about the two of them. And about her husband's mistress, whom she hated, passionately—and with good reason, if you ask me. While the Norman affair might no longer be physical and even though Georgia said she was still fond of Stieglitz, she hadn't shared his bed for some time. And except to hang shows, she said she stayed away from the gallery because Mrs. Norman was always there.

Her great gift, I decided, was as a listener. She listened to me in a way that no one, not even Dorothy, had ever listened, all the while holding me with that extraordinary gaze, fixing me with those wise eyes of hers—old eyes, it seems, although her face, while sun-lined and wrinkled, was young. She listened and watched with a focused intensity that made me feel seen and heard, *fully* seen and heard, for the first time in my life. It led me to say things I haven't said to anyone, not even to Dorothy, about sex and women and men and books and writing. It led me to want—yes, if I'm honest, to want more from her. To want something of what Dorothy and I had, once. What Dorothy and Agnes had now.

But O'Keeffe was so utterly to herself that I simply could not imagine approaching her in that way. And of course she didn't approach me, either, although the night before she left for New York, when I finished reading to her, she reached out and touched my face.

"You are a very handsome young woman," she said. "I hope you know that."

I caught her hand. "Handsome?" I've never wanted to be pretty, not in the girly way my mother would like. But handsome? It was a good word, I thought. It had dignity, weight, substance.

"And with such health and strength and vitality." She drew her hand back. "You're fortunate to have such strength, Maria. I admire it, and your competence. You've made things easier for me this year. I'm grateful for your help."

My help had been needed daily, as it turned out, hourly even. And if Georgia felt the contradiction between her insistence on her need for a solitary life and her need of someone always nearby to make that solitary life possible, she never appeared to see it.

For one thing, the ranch required a hired man's full attention, just to keep it operating. There was no city electricity or water or gas, of course. Every time we wanted to fill the water tank, I had to crank the old Fairbanks Morse diesel generator that powered the pump (Georgia couldn't—she wasn't strong enough). Even after the damned thing got started, it would die after ten minutes and had to be cranked again. The well water was mineral-laden and Georgia considered it nonpotable, so once a week, I drove to Abiquiu and brought back a dozen five-gallon jugs of spring water for drinking and cooking. I also hauled gasoline for the generator and kerosene for the lamps, the three-burner stove in the kitchen, and the portable heaters we used in the bedrooms on cold nights.

And there was the shopping. Staples and canned goods came from Mr. Bode's store in Abiquiu, but he didn't stock the fresh vegetables Georgia craved. When she bought the house, she planned to have a garden. But the soil under the cliffs proved to be sand and gravel and the well didn't produce enough water to irrigate. So every few days, I drove to Barranco to pick up whatever was available in Flora's garden: fresh corn, beans, onions, squash, lettuce, melons, raspberries—and always the garlic and chiles Georgia loved. (She ate them at every meal, even breakfast.) On Saturdays, I drove to Española to shop for beef, pork, and chicken and pick whatever fruit was ripe in the orchards at Los Luceros.

The shopping became even more of an issue when company arrived, which happened often—and which O'Keeffe hadn't mentioned in our discussions about the summer. (In fact, she often said she planned for a "solitary" summer, and that's what I had been looking forward to.)

The guest situation was a strong source of friction between Georgia and me, especially since I was supposed to have half-days for writing. Holger Cahill (the director of the Federal Art Project) came for a week, with his wife, Dorothy Miller, the curator at the Museum of Modern

Art. Henwar Rodakiewicz and his wife Peggy Kiskadden (he a film-maker, she a Philadelphia heiress) arrived with her two teenage children, Tissie and Ben. Artist Cady Wells, who lived in nearby Jacona, dropped in frequently, usually unannounced and sometimes with a friend or two. Johnny Candelario, another photographer, drove out from Santa Fe frequently. Richard Pritzlaff—who bred Arabian horses at his ranch under Hermit's Peak, on the eastern side of the Sangre de Cristo mountains—came bringing El Gato. All interesting people, yes, and I enjoyed them, individually. Some more than others.

But extra people meant extra food on the table, extra dishes to wash and beds to make, and extra feet tracking in extra sand and dust, not to mention extra pickups and drop-offs at the Lamy train station or the Albuquerque airport. Benina met the challenge with an admirable equanimity, but I'm not made of such stuff. I often had to grit my teeth behind my smile, especially on weekends, when Benina wasn't there. Of course, I didn't expect Georgia to give up her friends, but she could tell them to let her know when they were coming (isn't that just plain courtesy?). And to come a few at a time, rather than in groups.

I had two guests of my own that year: Tony Long, whom Georgia (who liked to play matchmaker) called my "beau" and who drove out from Santa Fe for an occasional evening. And Rudi Staffel, once. But Georgia was exceptionally cranky the day Rudi came—she could be a tiger when the painting didn't go well or when something upset the routine. She sent him away before I even knew he was there. He had been drafted and was on his way to report for duty, but he'd gotten off the train at Lamy and hitchhiked all the way out to the ranch. I was angry and disappointed when I learned what had happened, but she just shrugged. O'Keeffe never apologized. Ever. For anything.

There's a funny story to be told about matchmaking, though.

Things had barely settled down from a previous batch of company when Bernice Velasquez (the pregnant maid Georgia had sent away) got off the afternoon bus and walked up the lane to show us her new baby boy—a sweet little guy who immediately won our hearts. A thunderstorm blew up, so Georgia invited Bernie to stay overnight. At supper, she told us that the baby's father knew nothing about the birth of his son.

O'Keeffe put on a frown. "That isn't *right*, Bernie," she said, quite sternly. "A father ought to acknowledge his baby. And take responsibility for him. You mustn't do it all yourself. Who is this fellow? Where does he live?"

Bernie was reluctant, but Georgia insisted. Finally, we learned that Max—the father—lived in the mountains of western Colorado, where he and Bernie had grown up. He was working in a timber camp there.

That was all O'Keeffe needed to hear. The next morning, we packed Bernie, the baby, and his diapers and bottles into Georgia's Ford and headed north, with me at the wheel. After a long trip, we dropped Bernie off at her mother's house and took the baby up the mountain in search of Max. We found him at the timber camp, and Georgia told him the full story—in English, which I translated into Spanish. He tried at first to deny responsibility (the real father, he claimed, worked in a nearby Civilian Conservation Corps camp). But when Georgia made him take a look, the baby won his heart. The little boy, he agreed, was his.

A few hours later, all five of us—Bernie and Max and their baby crowded into the back, Georgia and I up front—were headed back to New Mexico for a wedding. The bride and groom hadn't a dollar between them, but from the guests at Ghost Ranch, Georgia collected ("extorted," Phoebe later joked) a ring, a wedding cake, a bottle of wine, and $22.50, a handsome wedding gift. We drove Bernie and Max to the priest in Tierra Amarilla. He married them and christened the baby, whom Bernie named Maximiliano Alfredo, for his father and Alfred Stieglitz. Little Max slept through the whole shebang in my arms. He didn't even squall when his head was splashed with cold water. When it was all over, we gave a little feast for Bernie's local relatives, with cake and blue crepe paper decorations. It was quite an affair.

Thinking about this afterward, I wondered whether the episode—which showed Georgia's truly human side in a way nothing else had—might have grown out of her unhappiness at not being able to have a child of her own. Stieglitz had adamantly refused to allow her to have a baby, saying that he was concerned for her health (she was so often ill) and warning that she wouldn't have time to paint if she was puttering around with babies. Getting pregnant by "accident" wasn't possible, either, she said. He kept track of her menstrual cycles. He knew when to expect "the curse" and used the dates to schedule travel and days off from painting. He blamed it for her moods.

When we talked about this, Georgia said she thought he refused her wish to have children because he wanted to manage her life in the same way he managed her art. That's what it sounded like to me, but I had another thought. Stieglitz's gallery earned him and Georgia no income. For their first half-dozen years together, they lived on an allowance from his family, in a rent-free apartment in his brother's home—acceptable to him because he was an artist and artists lived in garrets. But it emerged that his wife was one of the very few artists who had the ability to earn a good living from her painting. (If that notorious $25,000 calla lilies sale proved anything, it proved that.) Having a child might compromise her ability.

Unfair? Perhaps. Disrespectful? Certainly—especially since Stieglitz was known for his intense scorn of commercial art: art made for money and therefore "sullied" by the "demonic" urge for financial gain. It was something he talked and wrote about constantly, while at the same time he demanded the highest prices for his wife's art. Yes, my thought was certainly disrespectful. But it would come back often. If it occurred to Georgia, she didn't share it with me.

The Bernie-and-baby excursion wasn't our only trip that year. In August and September, we drove to a painting site O'Keeffe calls the White Place, deep in the badlands north of Abiquiu. It's a hidden spot at the head of a canyon, a barren amphitheater just a hundred paces across, half-enclosed by sky-high bone-colored sandstone cliffs. There's no road, but the station wagon was high in the rear and tough enough to climb up the arroyo, zigzagging around tumbled boulders and jutting ledges of white rock. We took enough food and water for an overnight stay, sweaters and blankets, and Georgia's large painting box, easel, and stretched canvases. And El Gato, who liked to stalk lizards but was smart enough to stay away from snakes. That canyon is a treacherous place when it rains—it can fill wall-to-wall. We always chose a day when there was no threatening weather and the sky was perfectly blue—a White Place day, we called it.

In late October and early November, we also drove to O'Keeffe's favorite painting site—Black Place—in the Bisti Badlands. It was a four-day, 150-mile trip, requiring another full day of preparations. The roads were abominable and there were no services, so I began by checking the Ford—oil, gas, water, four tires and the spare. The back seats of the car came out, leaving a four-by-six-foot space into which I packed our supplies. Water for two people, two gallons a day for four days. Split piñon for a cooking fire and to ward off inquiring animals. Jackets and blankets. A pup tent large enough for two, in case it rained (otherwise, we slept under the stars). Food, of course: dried beef, Spam, canned beans and canned corn, spinach and lettuce, fresh-baked bread, fruit, oatmeal, canned milk, coffee, sugar, salt. Each of us had a tin cup, knife, fork, spoon, and plate, packed into a small collapsible table that became the work table for our camp. Cooking pot and coffee pot. Lantern, axe, and canvas sacks with a change of shirts and socks, in case we were rained on. O'Keeffe's easel, of course. Canvases and painting equipment. And the cat.

The Black Place is a wild landscape of alien, undulating shapes— "like a mile-long parade of elephants," O'Keeffe said. "Grey hills all about the same size with almost-white sand at their feet." Otherworldly mounds and pillows and pillars of yellow and red and black sandstone and shale, laced by labyrinthine mazes and studded with towering, weirdly capped stone spikes called hoodoos. It's barren, austere, un-inviting—forbidding, even. It's like nowhere else I've ever been, and I wondered why O'Keeffe wanted to come here.

"What attracts you to this place?" I asked her one night. The fire was dying down, the high desert air was getting cold, and we were about to crawl into the tent.

"It's the strangeness, I suppose, the mystery." She was silent for a moment. Then, very quietly: "It's . . . what I don't know. When I paint, I always feel that I'm making the unknown known, not just in what I'm painting, but in myself. This place holds more unknowns than anywhere else. And it pulls them out of me. I'll never quite get it, of course. It's the reaching that counts." With that crooked smile of hers, she added, "Half the work is done for me here. All I have to do is paint how it feels. How it feels to *me*, not anybody else. Just to me."

How it feels to me. I needed to hear that, and think about it, in my own work. I wrote it down on the cover of my notebook, so it would be right in front of me, whenever I had the time to write.

There were other good things, especially when we were alone at the ranch, no guests, just the two of us (and Benina, of course). Early walks among the warm red hills and chalky yellow cliffs, just looking, saying nothing. Breakfasts on the *portal*, with Pedernal draped in its blue morning mists, anchoring the distant horizon. Evenings when I read to Georgia beside the fire: *The Adventures of Marco Polo*, whose journeys we traced on a map, occupied us for several months and Witter Bynner's splendid translations of T'ang poetry, *The Jade Mountain*. Nights when we slept on the roof under a dome of infinite, wheeling stars, the almost narcotic sweetness of the night-blooming jimsonweed heavy on the air.

And Georgia introduced me to the Mensendieck exercise program. We practiced daily, nude in front of a mirror. The exercises, designed to strengthen the spine and correct the posture, required visualizing each pose before we executed it slowly, slowly. The practice was built on the premise that movements are best guided by intentional, disciplined thoughts—an idea that was central to almost everything O'Keeffe did, even in her painting. She often said that she saw the whole thing in her mind before she put a brush to the canvas.

I had to smile to myself, though, imagining what Dorothy (Agnes, too!) would think if they saw us stretching and bending and reaching, neither one wearing a stitch of clothes. But they would be wrong, for even in this very intimate physical practice there were no hints of intimacy in O'Keeffe's voice or manner. She was all ordered shape and deliberate movement, nothing else. It was as if she were outside her body, disconnected from it and simply arranging its various placements in the way she arranged shapes on canvas.

And I? I was thick and bulky where O'Keeffe was thin and agile. I was critical of myself and could never execute the movements with her serene detachment. While we were exercising, I often thought of the nude photographs Stieglitz had taken and wondered if Georgia had developed a similar sort of displacement while she was posing for him. Did she understand that while he told her he was turning her body into art, he was really transforming her into an artful object of sexual desire? Not just his desire, but the desires of the many men who would wander through the exhibit, staring endlessly, longingly, lustfully at the photos, imagining having that body—having *her*—to themselves. In those long hours of posing, as she was the passive object of his passionate camera, did she abstract herself from her body, as if she were not present *in* it?

I dared to ask her once. She didn't speak for a moment. Then she flipped a hand and said without inflection, "Those photographs had nothing to do with me—with me personally, I mean. When I look at them, I wonder who that person is." I wanted to ask why she said "person" and not "woman," but she had already changed the subject so I didn't. And anyway, I already had my answer.

All this barely begins to sum up my first summer with O'Keeffe. When I took her to Lamy to catch her train in November, the next summer was still up in the air. She said she was uncertain about Stieglitz's health and felt quite helpless about it—she just didn't know her plans yet. She had spoken of inviting Cady Wells' friend Jean to stay at the ranch. Did that mean she didn't want me? Or was she simply assuming that I would be back, without committing herself to asking me. (Which was like O'Keeffe, who put every decision off as long as she could, and made and remade it two or three times over, leaving everyone to wonder what she intended to do.)

And of course it was very hard for either of us to plan anything, given all the worries about war, only a dark cloud on the horizon in November. But the cloudy uncertainty exploded into certainty in December, and by the time I got home, the *San Antonio Express* was screaming JAPS BUTCHER AMERICANS AT PEARL HARBOR! and people were panicking, afraid the next bombs would drop on our heads.

Events unrolled swiftly, propelled by a frantic, frenzied momentum. Congress declared war on Japan the day after Pearl Harbor. On Thursday, December 11, Germany and Italy declared war on us, although the *Chicago Tribune* buried the story on page 4, behind the news that the navy had sunk a Japanese battleship off Wake Island and that American car and truck production would be cut by 75 percent because of the need to put factories to work making tanks, planes, and ships. Everybody in the country seemed ready at last for war, even Charles Lindbergh, who declared that we must meet it as "united Americans"—quite a reversal for him and the America First Committee, which speedily dissolved itself. In the face of such fearsome enemies, it seemed we were finally to be united.

The war had already come to San Antonio, which—because of its military bases—was considered one of the six major potential enemy targets in the country. Civilian flights had been cut dramatically but the sky was filled with military aircraft. Soldiers were everywhere. The highways were a stream of fast-moving military convoys: heavy equipment, big guns, trucks filled with uniformed boys who looked like children playing soldiers. The city went completely dark for its first blackout test, trying to eliminate any trace of light that might give away our location to enemy planes. Planes? I wondered where they might be coming from, since neither Japan nor Germany claimed to have any long-range bombers. But everybody was possessed by the war fervor and we threw ourselves into the spirit of the exercise. The night was satisfactorily dark and certainly noisy, with factory and railroad whistles blowing and fire and police sirens shrieking—a stand-in for air raid sirens, which wouldn't be installed until the summer.

All my friends wanted to talk about was military service—who had been drafted, who was enlisting, where they were going for basic training or deployment. Men aged twenty-one to thirty-five had to sign up now, and men eighteen to sixty-four would be coming up soon. And there was more talk about needing women. The previous year, a congresswoman from Massachusetts had proposed a bill to establish a women's Army corps; this year, it was likely to pass. Every war poster I saw (and we saw them on every window and wall) urged me to do my part for the war effort, so enlisting was something I knew I would have to consider. I was healthy, single, childfree, literate, and I could add and subtract, which made me exactly the kind of woman the military wanted.

But if I did that, I would have to give up my dream of becoming a writer. And of spending another summer with O'Keeffe, if that was in the cards. So for the moment, I signed up to give blood as often as the Red Cross would put a needle in my arm, volunteered for the neighborhood scrap drive, and began watching the newspapers to see what happened to the women's Army corps bill.

Dorothy and I had spent some time together before I left New Mexico. She came to the ranch for a weekend, and I stayed with her in Santa Fe for a few days. She was rather put out with Agnes, who had gone back East to visit the novelist and poet May Sarton. She and Agnes were still officially but not exclusively a couple, and the two of us had several wonderful days—more like the old days, the good days. Our pleasure in one another had changed because each of us had changed, yet we were still together and would be always, somehow. If I had learned one important thing in 1941, it was that there was nothing fixed or permanent about a friendship—with Dorothy, with Georgia, with anyone. That it was always fluid, always in flux, always and entirely mutable. That it never quite ends, it simply becomes something else, and then something else again.

That was my winter life in San Antonio the first year of the war— while Georgia was in New York, fighting on her own front.

PART TWO

The Faraway

1942–1944

CHAPTER FIVE

A New York Life
Georgia

Are you coming to the ranch again—? I never knew whether you wanted to come or not—With the war as it is going I may have to walk if I want to return east in the fall trains may not carry mere artists. When I ask you if you want to return to the ranch I must add that I cannot afford to pay a good hired man like you unless something unexpected turns up—

—Georgia O'Keeffe to Maria Chabot
New York, May 8, 1942

You never knew whether I wanted to come to the ranch or not—Do you think you could keep me away (—even if I weren't invited—) only it's pleasanter being asked. As for this afterthought of yours about my being or not being paid. Don't you know that you don't pay for the good things of life—an O'Keeffe canvas excepted? Skip it, Georgia—if I'm fed and housed and enlightened what more?

—Maria Chabot to Georgia O'Keeffe
San Antonio, after May 10, 1942

Hunching her shoulders against the icy wind, Georgia sets her black felt hat firmly on her head and turns up the collar of her black wool coat. It is only a six-block walk from their Fifty-Fourth Street apartment to Stieglitz's Madison Avenue gallery, but she is already chilled, and no wonder. The February wind whips through the deep, narrow street canyons, the skies are weighted with leaden clouds, and the pavement is slushy with dirty snow—a bleak and gloomy contrast to the remembered brilliance of sun and sky and cliffs in faraway New Mexico.

Georgia has long ago admitted to herself that the months she spends in the city are largely obligatory, a tribute rendered to her elderly husband less out of love and more out of gratitude for what he did for her in those early years. If it weren't for Stieglitz, there'd be no reason to be in New York. Most of the artists in his orbit no longer impress her, and their work seems disheartened and predictable. The events of the city's art community have become a chore rather than a pleasure, especially when it involves courting potential buyers for her paintings. There is little in her daily life here that awakens any great passion, and even the canvas she is currently working on is only a pale copy of the vivid desert landscape that fires her heart: all the vital, life-giving energies are out there, in New Mexico. Here, there is only the lassitude of the must-do and the constant, grinding, growing worry about war.

About to cross Second Avenue, she steps away from the curb to avoid getting splashed by the M15 bus, but not far enough to escape the belch of diesel fumes. This dull, dispirited feeling—it surely isn't *her*, she tries to tell herself, and perhaps not even the city. It is the war, which for the past two years has hung over the distant horizon like a summer storm far out to sea, heat lightning forking from the clouds, thunder rumbling distantly. America is shielded by two vast oceans, east and west. The country is safe, most Americans believed. They could stay out of it.

No longer. The storm is here, at home. The strike at Pearl Harbor two months ago is still a sickening blow, daily relived in the newspapers and on the radio. Singapore has fallen—the "worst capitulation in British history," Churchill calls it—and the Japanese are making headway in the Philippines. Here at home, Mr. Gallup says that 97 percent of Americans approve of the declaration of war. Young men are being called up by the hundreds of thousands, handed a Springfield rifle that last saw service in France twenty years ago, and sent off for rudimentary basic training while they wait to be shipped out. Almost a million men were inducted in 1941, and the military is aiming for three times that number in 1942. Congress is lowering the draft age again and is about to pass a bill to create a Women's Army Auxiliary Corps. Georgia wonders if Maria will enlist and frowns, hoping she won't. That's selfish, of course. But when it comes to managing the Ghost Ranch house, Maria was enormously helpful. Where could she find anyone else quite so competent?

She passes a sign that says SHELTER with an arrow pointing down a flight of stairs. New Yorkers are understandably jittery. The *Times* reports that Hermann Göring, the head of the Luftwaffe, is building a fleet of long-range bombers—the Amerikabomber—designed to drop five-ton bombs on New York. Mayor LaGuardia has ordered two hundred thousand air raid sirens to be installed as soon as possible. Boys in uniform fill the streets in army green and navy white. The Defense Bonds that went on sale in the summer of '41 have been re-named War Bonds, and people are being urged to buy a bond out of every paycheck. Posters are everywhere: *Are You Doing All You Can for Uncle Sam? Stamp out the Japs! Defend Your Country—Enlist Now!* Dark-to-dawn blackout is not yet mandatory, but there are worries that the city's lights are silhouetting offshore ships and making them easy targets. So a "dimout" is in effect. Times Square is dark. High-rise buildings are required to curtain windows on the fifteenth floor and higher. There's no night baseball at Ebbets Field or the Polo Grounds, and the Statue of Liberty's torch is turned off.

The war touches everyone in big ways and small. Men are being called up, so there are plenty of jobs—good jobs—for women. Sugar and coffee will be rationed in the next month or two and anybody with any sense is buying up whatever they can afford. The troops have to be fed so meat and fish are already hard to get. The airlines and railroads are converting passenger service to troop transport, and gasoline and tires will be rationed as soon as somebody figures out the best way to do it. Assuming that Georgia can find a way to get to New Mexico, will there be any gasoline for her Ford when she gets there? She has read that the rubber shortages are causing tire thefts everywhere. Will she still have tires on her car? Life at the ranch was difficult enough last summer, and she'd had both a car *and* Maria to handle the errands and manage the help. It will be impossible without gas and tires, and Maria hasn't volunteered anything about her plans.

As if that weren't enough, when Georgia went to the Rembrandt exhibit at the Metropolitan last week, she discovered that a great many of her favorite paintings were gone. The glow of the museum's five-and-a-half acres of gallery skylights was thought to be a tempting target for Göring's bombers, so the Met leased Whitemarsh Hall, a Pennsylvania country house built of steel and concrete. More than fifteen thousand paintings, tapestries, and even a few mummies were being surreptitiously moved there—ninety truckloads, each accompanied by an armed guard and insured at a million dollars—with the hope that they could escape the bombing.

Stieglitz prefers to stay in the city, but whenever Georgia can get away, she drives across the river to New Jersey, where she stays with Esther and Seward Johnson (of the Johnson & Johnson pharmaceutical family), at their dairy farm. Essie and Seward—whom she met at Ghost Ranch—are splendid hosts and their farm is a welcome escape from the bleak ugliness of the winter city. It is also a necessary escape from Stieglitz, who is increasingly despondent these days. Just being around him is a drag on her spirits. Born to a wealthy Jewish family, Alfred was educated and began his career as a photographer in Germany. Hitler's rise to power and his brutal treatment of the Jews is sending him into the depths of black despair.

Escape. Georgia knows that anyone looking at her life from the outside sees a successful career and a well-governed, well-groomed existence. When her work began to sell in the mid-1920s, she and Stieglitz moved from their apartment in his brother's house to a two-room suite on the twenty-eighth floor of the new high-rise Shelton Hotel. The hotel cafeteria and cleaning services freed her from cooking and housekeeping. By the mid-1930s, Stieglitz had begun asking (and getting) a record-breaking five thousand dollars for one of her paintings, and they could afford something larger and nicer—the penthouse apartment on East Fifty-Fourth.

But the move hasn't been a happy one for Stieglitz. He complains that it is too far from the gallery and taxis cost too much. The windows make the rooms too bright and too cold; he must wear his woolen long underwear all year long. Worse, since Georgia is paying the bills, she has put both the lease and the telephone in her name, and—not wanting to be bothered with meals and household chores—she has hired a full-time cook-housekeeper, Saga. Stieglitz can never remember her name. He calls her the "sour Swede" and complains that she can't cook.

But Georgia enjoys the penthouse, which is both an aerie above the clamor of the city and a statement of her success as an artist. Wide windows (curtained now to meet the wartime requirements) fill the rooms with natural light and afford a fine view of the East River and the Queensboro Bridge over the rooftops of Sutton Place's mansions. A brick-paved terrace is bordered by a trimmed boxwood hedge. The brilliant white walls are hung, gallery-like, with her paintings and Stieglitz's photographs. The dark oak floors are relieved by a pair of striped black-and-white Navajo rugs. The lighting is severely minimalist-modern, some of it just bare electric bulbs without shades. Their few chairs are simple in design and covered in black or white. There are three bedrooms, so they sleep in separate rooms now, and she doesn't visit his bed except for the goodnight kiss. The third bedroom is her studio, her escape—her *necessary* escape—into the world of work.

At Madison Avenue, Georgia turns the corner, catching a blast of wind that snatches at her hat. It is just one more block to Fifty-Third and Madison, where Stieglitz's third art gallery, An American Place, opened twelve years before. The location was right, just a few blocks from the Museum of Modern Art and the Fifty-Seventh Street art district. So was the space: a seventeenth-floor corner suite in a modern office building. But the timing of the opening couldn't have been more wrong: December 1929, with the stock market in free fall and the gala twenties diving into the calamitous thirties. Stieglitz's friends and the artists he exhibited—Marin, Dove, Hartley, and Dorothy Norman, of course—rallied around him, managing to keep An American Place open during the dark years of the Depression. Now, as the world slides into yet another war, the Place clings to life, fragile and diminished, like Stieglitz himself.

Suite 1710 is a small but beautifully designed exhibition space. The main room is high-ceilinged and large, some eighteen by thirty feet, with three windows on the west end, shaded for light control. The ceiling lights have blue reflector bulbs, replicating daylight. The floor is glossy gray. The white walls seem to recede, so that the art works, foregrounded, appear to hang suspended in space. At the east end of the room, doorways open onto a smaller exhibition space and Alfred's tiny office. A cubicle near the entrance serves as a darkroom. On the walls now: the work of Marin, Hartley, and Dove, with a few of Stieglitz's photographs and several Picassos from his collection.

This morning, the suite is empty. At the entrance, Georgia takes off her coat, hat, and galoshes. She is dressed as usual in a straight black skirt and a white blouse with a black knitted sweater, her dark hair skinned into a tight bun at the back of her neck. Since the advent of Mrs. Norman, who manages the gallery and spends most of every day there, she avoids the Place until it is time to hang a show. She has told Alfred she plans to work there today so he can warn the woman to stay away. He won't be there, either. He is in the apartment, nursing another cold. But the pictures she is to hang for her show are there, already uncrated, waiting. She takes down the things on the wall and sets to work.

This is her annual show, which always features her new canvases of the previous year, as well as a few of her best things. She knows that she is fortunate to be able to show so often, something few other artists can manage, especially women. It has proved to be the spine of her career. But it is a challenge, too, for she must always have something new to hang, which carries the risk of being criticized as "overproductive"—too much work can lead to its devaluation. This is a special problem for her, since she likes to work in series, each painting of the same subject show-ing her something new about it, and about painting, and about herself.

The pictures she is hanging today—*Black Hills with Cedar*, *Red Hills and Bones*, *Cliff Chimneys*, *My Front Yard*, a dozen more—are the work of the previous summer in New Mexico, sights she could see from the ranch house, places she and Maria had gone together, shapes and lines and bands and mounds of brilliant color, rich and intense.

For her, the images provoke powerful memories of folded and pleated and layered rock, of vast skies and unbroken silences. Georgia smiles as she remembers the days she spent in the desert, the resinous scent of cedar and sage, the blazing heat of a noon sun on bare skin, the stars wheeling overhead through the infinite night.

Alone in the gallery, she works quickly, assuredly, with a measuring eye. She has always enjoyed hanging a show, feeling, seeing, *tasting* the way the experience of one picture feeds the experience of another, the individual pieces coming together to tell a story with a beginning, a middle, an end. But nonlinear, too, less like a narrative and more like the echoing sounds and rhythms of a poem, elements of one painting foreshadowing or recapitulating or recalling elements of another.

The satisfying and pleasurable work takes several hours. She has just stepped back to survey it when the entrance door opens and Dorothy Norman comes in, calling eagerly, "Alfred, dear, I'm here." The woman is lithe, willowy, pretty, and younger even than her years. She stops abruptly as she sees Georgia.

"Miss O'Keeffe." Her dark eyes, doe-like, widen. "I'm sorry. I didn't expect—I didn't know—"

"You can clean up," Georgia says shortly, gesturing toward the empty crates and the tools on the floor, the paintings and photographs she has taken down and stacked against the wall.

Nothing more is said. There is nothing more to say.

❖

It is mid-afternoon when Georgia returns to the penthouse. She looks in on Stieglitz, who is propped up in bed with a gray shawl about his shoulders, round-rimmed spectacles perched on the end of his beak of a nose, reading a book. He has turned up the electric heater and the air in the room is hot as a sauna and redolent of VapoRub. Every week, every day, he seems to lose more energy and vitality. Georgia feels helpless about it—about his becoming less and less—but of course she cannot say this to him, nor agree with him if he says it to her.

So instead, she says, "You look well this afternoon," although he doesn't. His sparse white hair is uncombed, his bristly white mustache coffee-stained, his face as gray as his shawl. Often now, she thinks back to the beginning, wondering if she ever really loved him. Or merely loved being loved by him, praised by him, her career shaped by him. She has no answer to the question.

"How was your lunch?" she asks.

"There was boiled egg in the salmon salad." His voice is querulous. "I wish you would remind our sour Swede that I cannot tolerate boiled egg. Next time, she should leave it out."

Georgia doesn't remind him that there might not be a next time for salmon, that canned fish is going to the troops instead of the grocery. But arguing with Alfred only provokes his harangues.

"I'll let her know," she says, and pauses. "The hanging is done. I left Mrs. Norman to deal with the pieces I took down. I suppose you've told her what's to be done with them."

He glances up sharply. "She was there?"

"Yes," she says. "I wish you would remind her that I cannot tolerate her." She blunts this acid remark with a slight smile. "I won't be home this evening. Henwar and I are going to see *Arsenic and Old Lace* at the Fulton."

"Ah," Stieglitz says, almost wistfully. "One of my favorite theaters. As I recall, we saw *Oscar Wilde* there, didn't we? Several years ago. And

The Jazz Singer, the year after we were married, wasn't it?" He pauses. "Perhaps . . . perhaps I could join you and Rodakiewicz."

"Your cold," she reminds him. "And the weather. I'm not sure it would be wise."

He considers that for a moment. "I suppose you're right," he says. "You two enjoy yourselves." He returns to his book.

She closes the door behind her as she leaves his room.

❖

Georgia's show disappoints both of them. As usual, Stieglitz keeps track of attendance and in March, when her paintings come down, he tells her that fewer than two hundred people saw them. The low attendance isn't much of a surprise. The war takes up so many column inches that newspapers have little space for art announcements, and the war news is so overwhelming that people have no heart for anything else.

But this show aside, Georgia's career as an artist is clearly on the up-swing. *Life* magazine recently proclaimed her "America's most famous and successful woman artist." The paintings she did on the Hawaiian trip paid for by the Dole Company are still being prominently featured in advertising campaigns in the *Saturday Evening Post* and *Ladies Home Journal.* And the Art Institute of Chicago, where she had studied as a young woman, has offered her a solo retrospective—a major triumph. As usual, Alfred balked at the idea of shipping the precious paintings all the way to Chicago (in wartime!) but relented when the Institute agreed to buy a canvas, *Black Cross, New Mexico*—at the astonishing price he set. The agreement made him jubilant and surprised Georgia, who wondered how many patrons had been required to fund the purchase. That's how these things worked, of course. The Institute informed their wealthy supporters that it had an exclusive opportunity to acquire an O'Keeffe and several stepped forward, eager to contribute —and each one eager to be known as the most generous donor.

Stieglitz's relentless brokering no longer embarrasses Georgia or even makes her uncomfortable. She's gotten used to his contradictions: he's a master salesman and a vocal critic of the commercialization of art, both together. At her first one-woman show, she was astonished when he sold one of her Texas pictures—a railroad train moving through the dawn—for four hundred dollars, then an outrageous price for a watercolor by an unknown female artist. He did this by first being unwilling to sell a work, then putting such a ridiculous price on it that when the would-be buyer finally broke down his apparent reluctance and managed to walk away with the painting, the purchaser believed that he had acquired a rare and uniquely precious thing. Until then, she had thought that teaching was the only way to earn a living in art. The sale had shown her that she was wrong, and throughout the years, her husband's sales strategies have established the highest possible market value for her art. Every time his infidelity gives her pain, she thinks about his belief in her work and is grateful.

The show's disappointment is only another evidence that there is nothing for her in New York. She is more determined than ever to go to New Mexico, even though the war is likely to make life at the ranch difficult. And there is the cost to think about. The income from her painting has dropped, and there is nothing coming in from the gallery. The lease on the penthouse is going up, which suggests that it's time to make a move. Saga (the "sour Swede") is asking for more money, and last year's renovations at the Ghost Ranch house cost a good deal more than she expected. She has money in the bank but she grew up in a financially straitened family and always feels better when she has a substantial reserve. So if Maria wants to work that summer, the girl has to know that she won't be paid.

"When I ask you if you want to return to the ranch," Georgia has written, "I must add that I cannot afford to pay a good hired man like you unless something unexpected turns up"—which she certainly cannot expect, given the war.

And Maria—who loves the desert and clearly enjoys being in charge of things at the ranch—has agreed to come without pay, as a friend. Which definitely complicates things. All her life, Georgia has tried to avoid being indebted to anyone in any way—except for Stieglitz, of course, to whom she owes loyalty. And love. She draws a firm line between her few friends and the people who work for her. It's a helpful distinction, since the workers, her slaves, come and go so often.

Still, even with that complication, Georgia is relieved that Maria will be with her this year. The young woman is volatile, restless, somewhat untidy, often stubborn, and always forceful, opinionated, and ready to speak her mind. In fact, she seems to feel especially free to tell Georgia exactly what she thinks, which is not always what Georgia expects to hear. Her friends don't presume to take that kind of liberty and her hired helpers don't dare.

But Maria is also an invigorating intellectual companion. They share many common interests, and their conversations are always thought-provoking. Best of all, she knows how to get things done out there in the desert. She is strong, skillful, inventive, a self-starter, a problem-solver. Whatever the job, she gets it done handily, with a minimum of fuss. And Georgia is a pragmatist to the bone. Without Maria's competencies, life at the ranch would be very difficult and there would be little or no time for painting. She supposes that she should be grateful that Maria isn't asking for money. She couldn't pay her anything like what she's worth.

❖

In early June, Georgia takes the train to her native state to accept an honorary doctorate from the University of Wisconsin. Three of her younger sisters—Anita, Catherine, and Ida—join her in Madison. All three are their usual chatty selves, trading sisterly tales and reminiscences about times past. But as in most families, there are topics they can't talk about: their father's alcoholism and his ill-fated business ventures; their mother's painful and lingering death from consumption; and their own corrosive disagreements. The sisters have come together on this occasion not just to celebrate Georgia's achievements, but to bury a long-simmering quarrel.

When they were girls, Georgia had brooked no rivalry. Her sister Catherine once told a friend, "She was It. She had everything about her way, and if she didn't she'd raise the devil." A few years before, she had raised the devil with Catherine and Ida. Both sisters had begun painting, and Georgia had encouraged them. After all, painting was a pleasant pastime for a woman.

But painting was one thing while exhibiting was something else entirely. When Catherine and Ida began showing their work, Georgia saw it as an attempt to trade on *her* professional reputation. The *New York Times* reviewer saw it that way, too, headlining his review ANOTHER O'KEEFFE EMERGES. He pointed out that five O'Keeffes (two grandmothers, Georgia, and now her two sisters) had occupied themselves with art.

"Presumably the saga is now complete," the critic added with a hint of dry mockery, "although you never can tell." Perhaps, he insinuated, yet another too-prolific O'Keeffe was picking up her paintbrush. There were already a great many O'Keeffes (too many, perhaps?) on the market. Now there would be still more.

Infuriated by the idea that her sisters dared to become her rivals, Georgia wrote to Catherine, threatening to tear her paintings to pieces. Catherine, who had been painting flowers, quit in utter despair. "Her letter was death against me," she would tell someone years later. Ida, the more original and imaginative artist, kept on painting, at least for a while. But she didn't have a Stieglitz to sell her work, she had to make a living, and the Depression made that even more difficult. Unwilling (or unable) to brook any rivalry, Georgia refused to communicate with either of her sisters for four long years.

Now, during this rare family get-together, they deal with the disagreement in time-tested O'Keeffe fashion, pretending it had never happened. It is the way Georgia manages all of her relationships. There is no apology for the four-year break. The quarrel and its lingering resentments will not be forgotten, it just won't be mentioned. By the time the sisters trade kisses and leave Madison, they have tacitly agreed that bygones must be bygones.

After the ceremony, Mike Harding—a good-looking, dark-haired young man whose parents were guests at Ghost Ranch and who made it a point to see Georgia whenever he was in New York—drove her to Taliesin, the famed house and studio of architect Frank Lloyd Wright. Georgia is intrigued by Wright's "organic architecture," which he says is built on the principle of "the harmonious union of art and nature." The structure of his buildings is integrated into the space of the land in something like the way Georgia imagines structure and space in her paintings. She has admired Fallingwater, a house Wright designed and built in Pennsylvania and which has been featured, with his photo, on the cover of *Time*. Now, admiring Taliesin, she is glad to listen to him, and he is delighted to talk to her.

Tall, white-haired, and flamboyantly dressed, Wright resembles Stieglitz in more than just appearance, Georgia thinks. He is an incessant talker, a wily publicist, and—when it comes to claiming public attention—a masterful showman who is creating his own celebrity. (Less charitably, many of his fellow architects see him as a showoff playing every trick in the book to get his work noticed.) He's had only a few commissions during the Depression but remains in the public eye by exhibiting his drawings wherever he gets the chance. And by hosting visitors at Taliesin, which is not just a studio but a showcase for his work—and for himself. The architect has transformed himself into artist-as-icon, a public personality. And Taliesin is his autobiography.

Boarding the train for the trip back to New York, Georgia realizes that Wright has given her a great deal to think about. She is increasingly conscious of the fact that her art will have to support her when she moves permanently to New Mexico. Could she use her adobe house at Ghost Ranch as Wright uses Taliesin—as a way to stay in the public eye? Of course, she isn't an architect, but adobes are inherently quite interesting, certainly different, even remarkable. And people have already evidenced an interest in her unique life—a well-known artist, a woman, living simply and independently in a remote corner of nowhere. Like Wright, artist-as-icon, but with Pedernal and the open desert on one horizon and the shining cliffs on another.

It is a tempting idea. But even though she tucks it into the back of her mind for more consideration, she knows it won't work. The house at Ghost Ranch is too remote, too hard to find, too small to host more than a few people at a time. And her privacy there is precious. The solitude and seclusion give her the time and space she needs to work, and while she recognizes the absolute need for publicity, she wants to control it. She might invite a photographer or two—Johnny Candelario, for instance, quite a good-looking and charming young man—to photograph her and the house and the desert. She thinks the magazines will be glad to have the photos and the story. But she can't have strangers traipsing in and out the way Wright does at Taliesin.

No, she concludes. No, not the ranch.

But the *idea* is still there.

❖

Back in New York, she gets to work. She has decided to find a cheaper place to live—not an easy task, but she manages it. Available in early October, the new apartment is at 59 East Fifty-Fourth, between Madison and Park, across from the Hotel Elysée and just around the corner from the Place, which makes it ideal, in Stieglitz's view. His family objects that the rooms are small and dark, with low ceilings, narrow windows, and no view. But the lease is less expensive than the lease on the penthouse, a major consideration, now that Georgia has two residences to support. Stieglitz heartily approves because his new bedroom has its own heater and he won't have to take a taxi to the gallery. Taxis are a vanishing species these days, for their drivers are wearing khaki and gas and tires are hard to get. People have to walk or take a bus—and the buses are always late and crowded.

"Alfred is very pleased with the change," Georgia writes to Claudia, "I am not so pleased but I don't really care." Which is true, since she expects to spend at least six months of the year in New Mexico, where her heart comes alive. In New York, she is only marking time.

The new apartment won't be available until the fall, but she has paid the lease and matters are settled. She can begin packing for her trip to New Mexico. As she does, Alfred suffers yet another angina episode (almost a routine occurrence when she is about to leave), although he is such a hypochondriac that even his doctor finds it hard to tell what is real and what is exaggerated. Still, she delays her departure, thinking to ease his mind.

But when he is somewhat recovered, he produces another worry. How can she leave when the world, the *whole* world, is going so completely, so irretrievably to hell? In the Pacific, Corregidor has fallen, Burma is gone, and Guadalcanal. In North Africa, Rommel is poised to take Tobruk. Much closer to home, a German U-boat has sunk a British freighter at the mouth of the St. Lawrence. Good heavens, *the St. Lawrence*! The next thing you know, the Nazis will be sailing up the Hudson! They will bomb all the railroads and bridges! If she leaves, she might not be able to get back. New Mexico is out of the question this year. Why, even the assistant secretary of the navy has said that we are losing this war, period. And that we should damn well understand it, period.

But Georgia is undeterred. The family is nearby if he needs them. Saga can manage his laundry and if he doesn't like her food, he can walk across the street and eat in the hotel dining room. Mrs. Norman, his friends the Beaumonts, and a half-dozen others will drop in at the Place every day, so he will be well looked after. With a smile, she pats his arm and tells him not to worry. She finishes packing, leaves a half-dozen sweetly reassuring notes scattered around the apartment for him to find after she is gone, and takes a taxi to the train.

Two days later, on June 13, she steps off the Santa Fe Chief at Lamy, where Maria is waiting, her broad face wreathed in smiles, with the station wagon. They stop in Española for meat, in Abiquiu for staples, in Barranco for fresh milk, eggs, and a few vegetables.

And in another few hours, a fine supper finished, she is sitting on the *portal* at Ghost Ranch, gazing across the vast desert of the Piedra Lumbre, watching the wind unspool a shimmering drape of evening clouds from Pedernal's flat crown. Maria pours them both a glass of wine as she reports on the things she's been doing to get the ranch ready for their summer. Evicting the snakes that have come in for the winter, replacing the spark plug in the generator, fixing the garage door, seeing to a roof repair, stocking the pantry, arranging with Benina and a new girl, Orlinda, to do the cooking and housekeeping and with Flora for garden vegetables and Mary Wheelwright for fruit. Oh, and borrowing El Gato from Richard Pritzlaff to keep the mice at bay.

"Thank you," Georgia says, amazed as always at the things Maria thinks to do, without any prompting. Things that she will not have to do or even *think* about, so that tomorrow morning, she can go straight to her easel.

"The war is going to make things tough," Maria says matter-of-factly. "Gasoline and tires will be hard to get, probably food, other things, too. But we'll get through, if we just keep our heads." She raises her glass. "To us, Georgia. Getting through."

"Yes," Georgia replies. "To getting through." She looks toward the horizon. All winter, Changing Woman has been so far away. Now she can almost reach out and touch her. "I think I'll paint her again," she says.

"Nothing's keeping you," Maria replies, leaning back comfortably in her chair.

And so, that summer—and the next, and the one after that—Georgia paints the Pedernal. Not just once, but many times.

And every time, the mountain becomes a little more *hers*. Or she becomes a little more mountain. She's not sure which.

CHAPTER SIX

Women Who Rode Away
Maria

The ranch is closed up, deserted, sitting out on the plain in the moonlight. I am no longer a part of it. Tomorrow noon I catch the bus for Texas—and I say to myself "This is the end of a life."—I am sad—nor can I help it. I think how I worked at the ranch—how I tried—how I learned. The butane tank—I know all its whimsies; the cracks under the windows needing putty in the springtime—are my cracks—the goddamned old pump—the shelves and shelves of food I helped to can. I can't believe they will be eaten by someone I don't even know—have never seen. Life wasn't easy there, but it was good. There was something clean about it—and—I gave it my heart. I am a wretchedly faithful person and I hang on like a dog. Going to-morrow will be severing something: four years of something I don't yet—probably never—will altogether understand.

—Maria Chabot to Georgia O'Keeffe
Santa Fe, November 4, 1944

We have nothing of our own, Nicolas Poussin writes. "We hold everything as a loan."

So, too, with time, and with my summers with O'Keeffe at Ghost Ranch, which I still count as months well spent and happy, even if I didn't entirely appreciate them in that way then. It was all a loan, you see, the time, the place, the life. But it was a path, too—a path into a new way of living, of knowing, of being.

Years later, after articles about Georgia began to appear in the national magazines, I often shook my head at the calm serenity with which she was depicted: Zen-like and enigmatic in that black belted kimono-style wrap dress she wore for the photographers in those later years. Self-possessed, imperturbable, as dispassionately composed and mannered as one of her abstractions, portrayed as living an idyllic solitary desert life.

That wasn't the way it was during the New Mexico summers of the early 1940s. There was nothing even remotely Zen-like about either of us, and our desert life was neither idyllic nor solitary. The problems we faced were often insoluble, given the limits of our resources. The challenges came one after another, some of them due to the war, some to the remoteness of the place, some to our own rather thorny personalities. We were two independent, strong-willed women trying to live together in a difficult time in an inhospitable desert, neither of us very tolerant of missteps, our own or the other's. We were like the woman in D. H. Lawrence's story, who left her husband and children and rode into the mountains to join an Indian tribe. We went into the desert and never returned.

And nothing there was easy, made even more difficult by the fact that we both responded to frustration with sudden bursts of anger. Afterward, I was given to abject and repeated apologies for what Georgia liked to call my "tantrums." Apologizing was a destructively self-deprecating habit I learned from my mother, who continually apologized to my father for her imagined infractions. If anyone reads the letters I wrote to Georgia during those years, they will notice my frequent apologies and think I was the one always at fault in our disagreements. Not so, by any means, but we displayed our angers differently. My childish tantrums rattled the windows but were quickly done with, like a ten-minute thunderstorm, lots of flash and noise and then gone over the horizon. Afterward, I felt like a worm. I needed to talk about my misdeeds. A compulsive penitent, I groveled, confessing my sins and declaring my guilt over and over.

Georgia's furies, on the other hand, were volcanic. They simmered sullenly for hours and then erupted with an earth-shaking suddenness. Her anger was usually aimed at the hired girl or the hired man, but sometimes at an acquaintance or even a friend, who might stare at her in utter bewilderment. When it was over, it was over. It was as if it had never happened—and as if the other person had never been confused or saddened or hurt by her violence. She was constitutionally unable to admit that she had acted badly or that she was wrong, and she was wrong just as often as the rest of us. And she refused to apologize, always, for anything.

At the time, her refusal was a trait I admired. I saw it as an unyielding belief in her own rightness, a defense that must have served her well when she had to barricade herself and her art against Stieglitz and the critics. But it certainly made life difficult when it came to finding and keeping the hired help. Word got around quickly in the tight little local community that Miss O'Keeffe had a temper and wasn't afraid to use it.

And I would come to see this as deeply corrosive when it came to friends and friendships. "The first time I was ever frightened by you," I wrote her once, "was that June in 1941 when you came out of your studio and screamed at Star, a workman on the roof." It was an epic event I never forgot, and one that would be repeated, often, with me (or Benina or Frances or Flora) as the target. It would eventually be one of the things that separated us.

But that was in the future. In those years, we simply got along as best we could. Our first year at the ranch, Flora Brunette had supplied all the fresh vegetables, eggs, milk, and butter we could use. We had been able to get meat and poultry from Mr. Bode in Abiquiu or at the Saturday farmers' market in Española. Benina and Orlinda and I learned to bake bread by Georgia's recipe, using the whole wheat flour and wheat germ that her friend Esther Johnson sent from New York and honey that I got from the hives at Los Luceros. Whole wheat is much healthier than processed white flour, according to another of Georgia's friends, Adelle Davis, whose book, *You Can Stay Well*, was her well-thumbed bible. Davis had also given Georgia her recipe for something called yogurt: fermented milk that we made from two quarts of fresh milk and a can of evaporated milk. And granola, a breakfast cereal made from Quaker oats, pecans from the tree in my parents' San Antonio yard, wheat germ, coconut, sunflower seeds, raisins, dried milk, and honey. And soy flour, when Esther Johnson could find it for us.

Back in 1941 and 1942, most people weren't thinking of *healthy* eating. Given the Depression during the 1930s and the war in the '40s, just putting something on the table took a lot of effort and planning. But I could see why the right diet had become so important to Georgia. She had spent whole months of her life in bed with one plaguy thing or another: headaches, stomachaches, menstrual cramps, sinus infections, colds, flu, nerves. She'd had breast surgery and was hospitalized for several months for a nervous breakdown. She was convinced that the right food and essential vitamins would help her celebrate her hundredth birthday. (She would be proved almost right.) Eating well was a top priority for her, almost as important as her painting. We spent a lot of time thinking and talking about food and trying to find what she wanted.

But that was never easy. Flora had gotten a wartime job at the hospital in Santa Fe and wasn't home to take care of her garden. Her cow was dry and a fox had raided her chicken coop, so milk, butter, and eggs had to be found elsewhere. Mr. Bode was rarely able to get any meat, and I considered myself lucky if I could round up a chicken or some fresh-caught Rio Grande catfish or trout at the market in Española. Meat and cheese were rationed, as well as cream, cottage cheese, and even canned milk. We ate a lot of Spam and canned corn beef in those years, and dried beans, which we bought by the twenty-pound sack. And oatmeal, which was Georgia's favorite supper dish, especially good when we could get fresh fruit or berries.

So both Georgia and I longed for a garden—a longing that was at least partly fueled by the government's Victory Garden campaign, which was blazoned in every newspaper and illustrated with photos of a beaming Eleanor Roosevelt harvesting baskets of lettuce and to-matoes grown on the front lawn of the White House. The soil in the corral where the Packs had kept their kids' burros seemed to have at least some organic material in it, so that first year, I spaded it up and planted some experimental rows of lettuce, corn, and beans. But the rats and the rabbits—who loved fresh green things just as much as we did—nipped every stem as it poked its head out of the ground. We needed a rabbit-proof fence, but fencing was impossible to find. "The war, you know" was an apologetic phrase everyone heard everywhere.

Georgia was already thinking ahead to the time—after Stieglitz was dead, although neither of us wanted to put it that way—when she would leave New York and live year-round in New Mexico. But would she *really* be able to live at the ranch all winter? The Piedra Lumbre typically got three feet of snow between December and early April, and sometimes it snowed as late as May. The county might not be able to get the gasoline to keep the road to Abiquiu clear. And since the Packs spent their winters in Tucson, Ghost Ranch would be closed and nobody would be available to plow the two-mile ranch road. The hired girls couldn't get in or out, and I would be in San Antonio with my parents. O'Keeffe would be really alone and seriously stuck for weeks at a time—without a phone. It just wasn't safe.

That was when she began to think seriously about finding a place closer to town, where she could live and work while the war was going on and gas was rationed. If the place had a garden and a well (or a spring or an irrigation ditch), she could raise the food she needed. Ideally, such a place might have room for strawberries and raspberries and a few acres for fruit trees—I've always loved peaches, which were grown in my cousin's family orchards in Texas. In blossom, the trees are pure delight, and there's nothing quite as wonderful as a ripe, juicy peach. When I was working for Mary Wheelwright at Los Luceros, I walked every day in the orchards there and learned that peaches, apples, and apricots did very well in the area, at least where irrigation could be counted on. They were a reliable cash crop.

And so I began to think seriously about an orchard as a way to support myself. Having seen the orchards in Texas and those at Los Luceros, I was under no illusions about the work involved. I knew that farming would mean embarking on a difficult journey, but I was strong and healthy and energetic, and it felt like the right challenge. If I could find a place that suited me and one that I could afford, I could manage the orchard during the growing season and write—and meet my obligations to my parents—during the winter, when the trees were at rest and needed no care.

The idea had another advantage, too. It might be hard to understand this, now that the urgency of war is long past, but I felt increasingly guilty every time I heard one of the "do-your-bit" jingles on the radio or glimpsed one of the many posters that urged women to take a war job. Those posters were everywhere in those years, some of them truly heartening—for instance, the woman in overalls fitting an airplane part, with the caption: "The more women at work, the sooner we win." Others were patronizing, like the one where the muscled munitions worker is saying to a diminutive coworker, "Good work, sister. We never figured you could do a man-sized job."

The jingles and posters were supposed to prod us to become Rosie the Riveter or Mabel the Mechanic, or join the USDA's Crop Corps or the Women's Land Army and help grow the nation's food. By the end of 1942, more than two million men had left farming for the military, and women were being urged to find a job on the "farm front." War work was an idea that appealed to every woman's patriotism, of course. Mine, too. Guys I knew—Tony, Rudi, Dana, Johnny—were serving. Girls I went to high school with had become nurses or ferried airplanes from factory to airfield or did secretarial work for the government in Washington.

And I had my chance. Back in Santa Fe, I had already heard from Dorothy McKibbin—Dink. She was the liaison for the super-secret project on the Pajarito Plateau west of town, which was siphoning off most of the available labor in northern New Mexico. Dink wouldn't tell me what devil's brew they were cooking up there on the Hill, as Santa Feans called the place. But she offered me a good job in what she called their mysterious "inner sanctum."

I almost said yes to Dink, both because she was such an enthusiastic recruiter and because I knew I should be doing something for the cause besides giving blood and (when I was in San Antonio) donating a day a week to the Red Cross. But I would be doing my bit if I was involved in work the government considered "critical to the war effort"—work like farming or raising fruit trees. And I would rather be out in the fields than sitting behind a desk at an Army post. Or even at Los Alamos, where interesting people seemed to be working on something important.

The more Georgia and I thought about finding a place where we could have a garden and I could work on the "farm front," the more compelling the idea became, so we began looking. We started in Barranco, where Flora was home for the weekend and could show us around. The property we liked best was a piece she called "La Tapia," a three-and-one-half acre square of flat, walled garden space with a tidy little peach orchard and access to the Barranco springs. (In Spanish, a *tapia* is a space enclosed by a wall.) It also had a little three-room adobe house—just three bare rooms, but it had a sound roof and could be expanded and modernized. Flora thought it might be for sale, but she wasn't sure. Nobody in Barranco had bought or sold property in many years. She gave us the names of the absentee owners so we could check and suggested several other irrigated sites up and down the river.

We didn't stop there. Over the next months we considered over a dozen possibilities between the ranch and Española. Our favorite was a site in Abiquiu that O'Keeffe had stumbled across when she first visited the village eight or nine years before, and which had hovered in the corners of her mind like an impatient ghost. It was a nearly three-acre property at the very edge of the mesa overlooking the green valley of the Rio Chama. There was a ruined adobe hacienda, once the largest and most splendid house in the village, with a spacious walled garden and a few old peach and apricot trees, and—importantly—water rights to the Abiquiu *acequia*, the local irrigation ditch. Georgia-the-artist was drawn to a weather-worn wood-slat double door recessed into the wall that led to the patio. Georgia-the-pragmatist knew that when she made a permanent move to New Mexico, Abiquiu would make a more habitable winter residence than the ranch.

I was drawn to the history of the old hacienda, which was built by the Chávez family in the early 1800s, and to the hidden symmetries of its elegant adobe structure. But even more than that, I was drawn to the challenge of restoring both the house and the garden to their earlier splendors. I had this crazy idea (well, it seems crazy now, looking back on the work it took to make it happen) that I could rebuild it. I told Georgia that if she bought that house, I would restore it for her. I could already see it in my imagination, a low, earth-formed, earth-colored dwelling, rising organically out of the Abiquiu mesa. And I knew just who to consult on the project—Kate Chapman, who had done such beautiful work rebuilding Dorothy's and Margretta's adobes in Santa Fe. She and Dorothy had even written and published a booklet together: *Adobe Notes or How to Keep the Weather Out with Just Plain Mud.* If Georgia would let me work on the house, Kate and Dorothy would be glad to lend their experience and expert help.

But that was a pipe dream. Old José María Chávez had died in 1902 and the once-splendid adobe had stood empty for decades, falling into greater and greater decay while it passed to José María's son and then to his grandson (both of whom lived elsewhere). The roof had fallen in, the walls were melting back to the earth they were made of, and a neighbor was using the old *tepeste*—the corral—and several of the rooms as a pigsty. At one point, the property might have been purchased for six thousand dollars, but Georgia had thought that was too much. Now, it belonged to the church, for when the last Chávez heir died, it had been deeded to the Archdiocese of Santa Fe. The donor stipulated that the house be rebuilt as a school for village children and a residence for the nuns who would teach them. It wasn't for sale. We could only dream about it. And dream we did, often.

But the planting season was beginning and if I was going to try my hand at farming, I needed to get started. I found several irrigated acres near Silvestres, a village not far from Ghost Ranch. The land had been producing pinto beans, so I ordered seed and got it planted in time to make a fall crop. There's a ready market for beans throughout New Mexico, and I could find field help in the neighboring pueblos. I was only renting the land so I couldn't plant the peach and apple trees I dreamed about. But I could grow beans—I thought.

I had been looking for a challenge, and I found it. Once I got the seed into the ground, I had to cope with voracious Mexican bean beetles, untoward weather (drought, hail, flood, an early freeze), and problems with the *acequia*, which had to be cleaned out and new gates built and installed before I could irrigate. While the small garden I planted for Georgia on part of the acreage (lettuces, broccoli, green beans, melons, squash, corn) gave us what we needed, my bean crop was an embarrassment. Humbled, I had to join Georgia in laughing at the pathetic outcome.

But what I learned in the hours I spent in the fields was worth more than mere beans—or even mere money. The summer taught me that while I didn't yet have enough experience to be a competent farmer, I had the strength, the commitment, and the interest—the passion, really. This discovery surprised me and pleased Georgia, who had a high regard for disciplined dedication to a project. She encouraged me to go on, because the project clearly suited both of us. She even said that if I found a piece of land large enough for a garden (for her) *and* an orchard (for me), she would buy it for me or loan me the money to buy it. I could pay her back out of my earnings from the land. That was exciting, especially because Georgia wasn't known for her generosity.

Over the next two summers, I would spend quite a bit of time looking for the right property in the area around Abiquiu and eastward, toward the Rio Grande—but fruitlessly, as it turned out. Until out of the blue . . .

But that's still a couple of years in the future. I don't want to get ahead of my story.

There were so many challenges to meet that summer that I didn't get much writing done and Georgia didn't paint as many pictures as she had hoped. However, gas rationing wasn't as severe as it would become later, so we were able to take several day trips to the White Place and—in October—a longer trip to the Black Place.

We also drove to Los Luceros to visit Mary Wheelwright and then on to Taos to see Georgia's friend Beck Strand. She and Paul Strand were divorced and—now calling herself Becky—she had married William James, a wealthy Colorado businessman who operated the Kit Carson Trading Company in Taos. Like Georgia, Becky wasn't beautiful but striking, with straight, shoulder-length gray hair pulled back from a strong face, deep lines etched between dark brows, pale eyes, watchful and knowing. I liked her blunt, no-nonsense directness but was struck by what seemed to me a wary, conflicted admiration when it came to O'Keeffe. It was as if Becky knew and understood Georgia, but what she knew both pulled her close and pushed her away. I wondered at this push-pull—what it was and why—but couldn't ask. I doubted I would ever know.

In early October, returning El Gato to his owner, we drove across the mountain to Richard Pritzlaff's ranch at Sapello, where both of us enjoyed a full day looking at Richard's art collection. While we were there, he gave a party for a group of young soldiers from the Army base near Albuquerque. Some of them got a little drunk. I confess: I did, too, and ended up jabbing a soldier's arm with a fork when he made a pass at me. The party ended in a glorious melee, which became the stuff of legend. Georgia herself enjoyed retailing the story. "Maria actually *stabbed* him!" she would tell friends, although she said I used a knife. (I wasn't *that* drunk.) She commemorated the event with a painting of a pair of pink flowers called "Maria Goes to a Party," which she included in her 1943 exhibit.

That fall, O'Keeffe had made plans to move from the New York penthouse to a smaller apartment, so she took the train back to the city in October. We wrote often over the winter. Her letters were always a pleasure to read, with unfinished, unpunctuated sentences that flitted swiftly and breathlessly from one thought to the next and the next, very like the way she talked. They were written in that oddly stylized handwriting that reminded me of a medieval manuscript. The letter that touched me most was memorable because Georgia was almost as grudging with her thanks as she was with her apologies: "I must always say thank you for many many things," she wrote in a letter that she signed "Sincerely and fondly." And there was one that made me smile because it sounds like a joke but isn't: "When you leave wire the mailbox shut so the skunk will not sleep in it." (Nobody wants the mail flavored with eau de skunk.)

As 1942 came to a close, I stayed on at the ranch through mid-December. I visited Mary Wheelwright at Los Luceros, attended an Indian dance at Taos Pueblo with Becky James (whose genuineness I enjoyed), and spent some delicious time with Dorothy in Santa Fe, just the two of us. Agnes notwithstanding, it was like before, like always. Like forever.

But mostly I wrote, shoveled snow, and did various end-of-season chores: taping newspapers over the garage windows so curious visitors couldn't look in, draining the pipes so they wouldn't freeze, wiring the mailbox to keep out the skunk, and bidding farewell to Changing Woman, out there on the horizon.

And thought long and longingly about orchards.

❖

The next year (1943) began with O'Keeffe's January retrospective at the Art Institute of Chicago. It was the first such show the Institute had given to a woman, so it was an important event. She invited me to come. I waffled, but at the last moment, I bought a train ticket.

I got there just as the exhibit opened and found her in bed at the Blackstone Hotel, ill with the flu—and exhaustion, I thought, and probably nerves. She had hung the show herself (of course) and it was stunning: sixty-one pictures from 1915 to 1942, flowers and churches and crosses and landscapes and the bones of New Mexico. It drew a thousand people a day—a thousand!—and everyone said how beautiful it was. "Remarkably popular," the *Chicago Tribune* sniffed, in a classic understatement. And the art critic for the *Chicago Sun*, Dorothy Odenheimer, confessed that she hadn't expected to like O'Keeffe's work: "I dismissed her, as have many others, as a merely decorative painter," Odenheimer wrote. But she changed her mind when she saw the exhibit: it was "disciplined, dramatic, unforgettable." When the reviews came out, we celebrated in Georgia's hotel room with a room-service tray of decadent French pastries and a pitcher of milk.

I spent four days in Chicago, some of the time with Georgia at the Institute, some with Emily Edwards, my favorite cousin, who was teaching art at Hull House. Emily had broken several ribs in a fall and was in the hospital. I had booked a room at the Hotel Atlantis, but Emily insisted that I stay in her apartment. I drank wine with some of her Greek neighbors and bought a little jar of pine resin in a neighborhood Greek deli to make retsina for Dorothy the next time we were together—a reminder of a memorable retsina the two of us had enjoyed in Athens.

When I got back to San Antonio, I found both my father and mother seriously ill with pneumonia. Two days later came news that my half-brother Fred, just fifty-three, had died in Mexico of uremic poisoning, likely the result of decades of alcoholism. A historian who specialized in Texas and Mexico political and social history, Fred was living with a friend in San Luis Potosí and working on four different manuscripts. I was the only family member available to go to Potosí, deal with his executor (in Spanish), gather up his papers (such a mess), and deliver them to the historical society in San Antonio, where some of his work had already been published. His death was a bleak end to a challenged and generally unhappy life. And a difficult time for me, with ill parents to care for and Fred's business and professional affairs to conclude.

In New York, Georgia's homecoming had been no easier. When she got back from Chicago, she went straight to bed with a sinus infection. Stieglitz had had another heart attack while she was gone and there were day and night nurses to manage. She wrote me that she was already dreaming of a garden in New Mexico. "You had better count on growing chilies and beans enough," she wrote. "I see myself drying chilies like the Indian woman at Barranco."

In March, after I had done the best I could with Fred's estate and had seen my parents much improved, I took the bus to Santa Fe, where I stayed with Dorothy for a few days. Agnes was out of town, so there was plenty of time to enjoy the retsina and our little reunion.

Then on to Barranco, where I stayed with Flora and went hunting for land for a garden and space for a cash crop—ideally, land for a small orchard, although I didn't hold out much hope of success. I was right. I spent several days with the land records in Tierra Amarilla, checking for clear titles before I began talking to owners. But one after the other, the possibilities all led to dead ends. I might rent some land for the growing season, but there was no property for sale, and no orchard in my future.

The old hacienda at Abiquiu was still there, of course, still empty, still waiting for someone to come along and resurrect it. Archbishop Gerken had died, which gave us some hope that perhaps the church might be persuaded to sell it. But when Mr. Bode (speaking on Georgia's behalf) discussed the possibility with the parish priest, he was told that the old place wasn't for sale—to anyone, at any price. What's more, it would *never* be for sale so please stop bothering him about it.

That's when I began to see just how difficult it was for an outsider to try to buy property in the area. These were close-knit rural communities where the dwellers had once held the land communally and where, in the first raw decades of the twentieth century, wily land traders had cheated them out of it. Over the past several years, I had become acquainted with many people in Barranco, Abiquiu, and Española. I counted Spanish, Genízaros, and Indians among my friends. I had attended weddings and confirmations and the blessing of an *acequia*.

I had even been invited to visit the Abiquiu *morada* when Penitente ceremonies were taking place—sacred events that was almost never shared with outsiders. But through the quiet courtesy of the people I knew, there ran a dark thread of suspicion of Anglos. They were not going to sell me any property—or Georgia, either. One of the elder Abiqueños told Flora that they didn't want any strangers living in their town. And by strangers, they meant us.

I was discouraged. And while Georgia was still supportive, she reminded me that life was full of obstacles, even for the persistent and impassioned. "As you go on," she wrote, "you'll be discouraged again and again. And even if you get the land you want, the worms and wild life will be against you." That practical observation made me smile—a little. She was right. The worms and the wild life were always there, waiting.

In the end, I succeeded in renting another piece of land and tried another cash crop, this time with a more varied menu for the bugs: beans, melons, corn, and cabbage plus the vegetables Georgia wanted. The work kept me out in the field for most of the summer—I was as brown as a Navajo—and impressed the Rio Arriba County Rationing Board enough to get extra gasoline and recapped tires for Georgia's station wagon, which she loaned me. Problems with the irrigation ditch, insects and rabbits ("the worms and wild life"), and a sharp drop in the price of beans right at harvest time made for another frustrating season.

But it had its pleasures, too. There was a small house on the property so I often took a bedroll and camped out there overnight. I kept our table supplied with the food Georgia wanted, and I was at the ranch often enough to deal with the usual hired man's problems: the balky sink drain, the recalcitrant generator, the persistently leaky roof, the hired help. When Benina left after a series of escalating spats over housekeeping matters, I found a new cook-housekeeper named Frances who could speak enough English to take Georgia's orders. She would prove to be a mainstay over the next year or two.

An interesting thing happened that summer. We hosted the usual flurry of summer guests—usually unexpected, difficult to accommodate, and the spark for several heated quarrels between O'Keeffe and me. But we were also (and unexpectedly) visited by a pair of blue-suited, fedora-hatted FBI agents who were doing what they called "background checks." They interviewed both of us and the Packs and their employees at Ghost Ranch. It was all very mysterious, until we understood that whatever the government was building at Los Alamos required the hard work of some high-powered scientists. The FBI was looking for a remote and highly restricted weekend vacation spot for them—a place where they wouldn't become the targets of curious spies and where they weren't likely to visit a neighborhood cantina, drink a little (or a lot of) booze, and spill their military secrets.

Of course, these mysterious VIPs would be staying in the cottages at Ghost Ranch and taking their meals in the dining hall there. But Georgia and I were the nearest neighbors and would likely be invited to various doings. So we were investigated as well and apparently found not to have any suspicious connections. The agents told us that we could chat with these mystery guests about anything—except who they were, where they came from, and what they were doing up there on "the Hill." We went to several of the Ghost Ranch barbeques and enjoyed the people we met. They were quite obviously well-educated people who enjoyed literate conversation, good music, and bridge. But it wasn't until the bombs were dropped at Hiroshima and Nagasaki that we figured out just who they were and what they had been working on.

For O'Keeffe, the summer of 1943 was one of her most productive.

She did twenty-some paintings, beginning her pelvis series and producing more pictures of the cliffs behind the house and the red hills nearby, as well as green and yellow cottonwoods along the arroyo, a skull that Johnny Candelario gave her, and an impressive ram's horn I found in the irrigation ditch near my bean field. We made several painting trips to the White Place and one, in mid-October, to the Black Place. There, we built our small cooking fire and ate oatmeal and fruit and crawled into our blankets inside the little tent. And then it got cold, and colder, and a torrential rain poured down. I was wrapped in double blankets and wearing every stitch of clothing I had brought. Georgia was cocooned in her bedroll with pajamas, robe, sweaters, scarves, and two woolen hoods. The tent blew away and we were *wet*— but the dawn found us undaunted.

When we got back to the ranch I wrote to Stieglitz about it: "One of those typical Black Place nights where you battle all the sky and all the wind, and water runs underfoot, and the fire is a thing almost impossible to keep alive. There was a moon somewhere—and every time it came out we thought it was the dawn and hoped it was the dawn—but it never was. The dawn was as dark as the night, and the tent fell in, and we laughed like fools and loved it." When I thought of the painting O'Keeffe began on that trip, I often wondered whether the people who saw it could have possibly imagined that storm.

When Georgia got back to New York, she found that Stieglitz seemed more frail than when she had left—but better after her return, as he always was. She also learned that her housekeeper was leaving. She went through three "slaves" (a Finn, another Swede, and a Russian) before she finally found one that suited: young and quick, she wrote, pretty and Irish. She was very hopeful that the girl would work out, but this one didn't, either. She had to keep looking.

Meanwhile, her New York life was busy. She wrote that she had gone to see Paul Robeson in *Othello* ("awful and wonderful") and that she had turned down an offer of $10,000 for the large *Black Iris* that was shown in Chicago. And then she reminded herself (and me) that she might have used the money to buy and renovate the Abiquiu ruin, if only it were for sale. She asked me to ask Mr. Bode, once again, if there might be a chance of that happening. "It is good to have your letters of the good life and good place," she wrote. "As I look at this world I am always thinking how good it is to have so much of that one—and how very good that one is—even when it rains all night at the Black Place."

But it seemed to me that having another conversation with Mr. Bode wasn't likely to change the situation. Instead, when I went to Santa Fe to spend some time with Dorothy, I looked up one of our friends, Katherine Ferrally. Katherine handled many of the real estate transactions in northern New Mexico. Irish Catholic herself, she was devoted to the church and (more to the point) personally acquainted with the newly installed archbishop, Edwin Byrne. I told her everything I knew about the Abiquiu house and asked her for her ideas. She offered to take the matter directly to Archbishop Byrne and tell him that the old hacienda was a complete ruin and of no possible use to the church. Much better to sell it and use the money to establish a health clinic in the village—something the archbishop was interested in—or perhaps a parish house. She would tell him that O'Keeffe was willing to rebuild the house in Spanish Colonial style (an architectural favorite of the church) and that—when it was finished—it would be an asset to the entire community. She wasn't sure what good this would do, but she was willing to make the effort, when the time was right. I thanked her and gave up thinking about it.

I stayed on at the ranch until December that year, doing chores, buttoning the place up for the winter, and listening to the war news on my portable radio. The Allies had taken Sicily, the Italians had surrendered, and Roosevelt and Churchill had met Stalin at Tehran. Scattered progress was being made in the Pacific, while on the home front, Victory Gardens were providing almost half of the vegetables on the American table and women made up more than a third of the American workforce.

Back home in San Antonio, life was all about the war. The Andrews Sisters gave us "Boogie Woogie Bugle Boy," the Vagabonds "Comin' in on a Wing and a Prayer," and Vera Lynn "The White Cliffs of Dover" and "We'll Meet Again," which always made me cry. To forget the war we watched *The Great Dictator* and *Casablanca* and *The Grapes of Wrath*. To forget everything else, we drank: Ramos gin fizz, Zombie, Mai tai. When we weren't drinking, we danced. Glenn Miller and "Pennsylvania 6-5000." Benny Goodman and "Ain't Misbehavin.'" Duke Ellington and "Take the A Train."

And the war ground on, endlessly, endlessly, with no end in sight.

I spent that winter doing some writing but mostly thinking about what I had learned during the year. Given my lessons in worms, wildlife, and weather, I better understood the challenges of farming, although the jury was still out on whether that made me a more competent farmer. I had certainly learned something important about the difficulties of joining the local community: I might be welcome as a friend of a resident—Flora's friend, for instance. Because everybody knew me, I might even be welcome at the *morada* or at the Abiquiu *cantina*.

But I would always be an Anglo. An outsider.

❖

I knew myself to be an outsider in another, even more hurtful way. Left to ourselves, O'Keeffe and I were comfortable housemates. Our ongoing disagreements were created almost entirely by the unexpected arrival of her friends, which made it a challenge for me to keep enough food in the house (especially the food Georgia preferred) and the household running smoothly. But something else was bothering me, something that went deeper than mere inconvenience.

Most of the visitors during the past several summers had been men—artists Cady Wells and Maurice Grosser, filmmaker Henwar Rodakiewicz, photographers Ansel Adams, Johnny Candelario, Eliot Porter, and of course Richard Pritzlaff. They came to enjoy a few pleasant days in a scenic corner of the Southwest with a fellow artist who could talk books and painting and the art business. Some of them came, I suspected, because O'Keeffe was married to Stieglitz, and between them wielded more power and influence in the art world than almost anyone else. An ambitious young photographer or artist could see them as holding the keys to the kingdom.

All these men were young, dark-haired, and quite good-looking. Georgia was flirty with each of them—exceptionally flirty, it seemed to me. Outrageously flirty. It was something she did with her husky voice, her smile, one eyebrow, and a certain deliberate invitation in her eyes. Ansel Adams had even documented that coy, raised-eyebrow glance in a photo a couple of years before: O'Keeffe standing next to Orville Cox, a younger, good-looking cowboy. Her expression was so obviously seductive that when the photo began making the rounds, the local gossips decided that she and Orville were lovers—simply had to be, they said, no doubt about it. Just look at the way she's looking at him. When Orville's wife saw the photo, that was her impression, too. Enraged, she ripped it in two, kept her husband's half and tore Georgia's to bits.

Since Georgia was in her late fifties by now and all these men were a couple of decades younger, her flirtations might have seemed harmless and even rather foolish. That's what one of the neighbors thought. She told me that Georgia flirted "conspicuously" with one of her relatives, good-looking forty-two-year-old Uncle Winfield. "It's so obvious," she said. "All of us think it's pretty funny." She paused, considering. "Except for my mother. She says Mrs. Stieglitz is too old for that sort of thing. She says it isn't . . . becoming."

That was one view. Richard Pritzlaff, on the other hand, enjoyed watching her flirt. He told me he'd been amused by what he saw when we attended the party at his ranch, where Georgia was coyly dallying with a couple of good-looking young enlisted men.

"It's even a little cute," Richard said with that lazy grin of his. "I didn't think the old girl had it in her."

But it wasn't always innocent or amusing for those who were involved. O'Keeffe could be obviously, overtly seductive, to which Maurice Grosser (whom I had heard was living with composer and music critic Virgil Thomson) responded with a teasing, good-natured banter. But her attentions made both Henwar (who was recently divorced from Peggy) and Johnny (young, quite good-looking, but inexperienced) squirm uncomfortably. Henwar was concerned enough to speak to me about it, and Johnny—a friend from Santa Fe whom I had introduced to Georgia—asked for my advice in his shy, tentative way. He was an up-and-coming photographer who frequently visited the ranch to take photos. He hoped that O'Keeffe and Stieglitz would support his professional work and had even taken a portfolio of prints to New York to show to Stieglitz. He wanted to remain friends with both of them, but her attentions were putting him into a vulnerable position. "In New York," he told me, "I hear people say that she can be . . . well, vindictive. When she doesn't get what she wants, I mean. I'm afraid of ending up on her bad side. Can you do anything? Talk to her, maybe?"

I tried, but it didn't go well. At first she got huffy, as only O'Keeffe could get huffy—and then coldly angry—with me. She was just being friendly, she said, and accused me of being jealous of "her young men," as she called them. She could see I wanted them for myself, which was laughable, given that I had just come back from a lovely weekend with Dorothy.

She also charged me with being afraid that one of them—Maurice, especially—might replace me as her hired man and leave me with no good reason to stay at the ranch. I had to admit that there might be some truth in that. Still, while Maurice was a good-looking young man with a great deal of Southern charm, he had zero interest in doing the shopping and he didn't know diddly about water pumps and power generators. If it was a hired man she was after, I didn't think Maurice was up to the job and I was pretty sure he didn't want it. I told her so. If he wasn't to be the hired man, what was he?

That's when her cold anger became volcanic. "Just who do you think you are?" she cried, stamping her foot. "You have no right to criticize me. I don't take that from my friends. And you're *not* my friend. You're not the kind of person I would choose for a friend. Ever!"

I felt as if she had socked me in the stomach, hard. I wasn't . . . *what* kind of person? Was it my education? The way I looked? The fact that my family had no money, that I had no connections with people in her New York art world? That I sometimes drank too much? That I preferred women? What kind of person would I have to be, to be her friend? And if I wasn't her friend, what was I? One of her slaves?

But there was no point in asking. I could fire questions all day and never get an answer. Or I would get a dozen answers as her mood changed.

About jealousy, though, she was right. And wrong, at the same time. I was jealous, but not in the sense she meant it, and certainly not jealous of her young men. I was certainly possessive about the ranch, which for me was a very special place. I had helped her make it—the house, that is. I loved the cliffs and the desert and the Pedernal. I loved being there. I even loved working to maintain it, most of the time, anyway. I didn't mind sharing it with a few people, but not with gangs.

A personal jealousy of Georgia, based on a romantic or physical attachment to her? No, nothing like that. But I admit that I *was* jealous—of the image I had of her in my mind. I wanted her to act like the accomplished, confident woman she was, not like a silly ingénue whose seductive intentions were caricatures of the real thing. It wasn't . . . it just wasn't worthy of her.

And worse, it might even be dangerous, if the wrong man moved in and took advantage of her—which might well happen, I thought, given the kind of help she needed out there on that remote ranch. She liked to think she could take care of herself, but she couldn't, not really. Not then, and certainly not as she got older. Long after this episode was over, when she was sightless and in her eighties and invited the young, handsome, dark-haired Juan Hamilton into her life, I would remind her of the day thirty years earlier when we argued about this. She would refuse to hear it then, too. But I would know that I had been right. And that I had been the only one brave enough and *friend* enough to tell her.

Georgia went back to New York in late October. Her letters were exactly as usual, with no indication that she remembered her repudiation of our friendship. Perhaps she didn't. But *I* did, although in an interesting way, I didn't resent her for it, or even blame her. I knew she had spoken out of anger because I had told her something that no other person in her life would dare to say. I had told her the truth about herself, and it was not O'Keeffe's way to accept that.

But because she had said what she'd said with such seeming assurance, it had come with the force of a blow that I could not evade. I had to believe her. O'Keeffe would never consider me a friend, but as her hired man, I was helpful. I was available and convenient. I enabled her to stay comfortably at the ranch and take painting trips in the desert. What I had been to her for the past three years amounted to little more than utility, for which she mailed me, after the new year, a check for three hundred sixty dollars. She paid me what she paid her other slaves. Fifteen dollars a week—and they got weekends off. Unlike them, I might feel rewarded by her constant company and whatever enlightenment I could wring out of our relationship. But I wasn't the kind of person she would ever choose as a friend.

The jagged edge of this knowledge was blunted a bit when Richard Pritzlaff—again—offered me a job as his ranch manager. He was planning to expand his Arabian breeding program and was looking for some responsible management.

"You're wasting yourself on O'Keeffe, you know," he said, quite seriously. "I'll pay you double what she's paying."

"Ha ha," I said. "Twice peanuts is still peanuts."

"Then I'll pay you more. Three times, four times. Hell, I'll pay you what you're worth." He scowled. "Look, Maria. I admire Georgia's art. She is genuinely gifted. I respect her ability to make a paying career of it when so many artists can't. She's an amusing friend and I enjoy being with her. I can see that she needs a great deal of looking after and it's very good of you to spend half the year doing it. But she's taking advantage of you. Come over the mountain and work for me. You're smart, skilled, competent—just what I need. I'll pay you every nickel of what you're worth and be glad to do it."

When I told Georgia about Richard's offer (but not the "taking advantage" part), she laughed. "He probably wants to marry you," she said. "You should think about that, you know. It would be just right for you, Maria." Georgia could be naïve about people, but this made me roll my eyes. Didn't she know that Richard was gay?

I tabled the Pritzlaff offer for the time being, but I continued to think about my little orchard, which was now only a shimmering mirage on the distant horizon of my imagination, even farther away than ever. I considered all of this with resignation as I prepared to leave the ranch for the winter. I taped newspapers over the windows, tacked tar paper over the pantry door, drained the water pipes, wired the skunk out of the mailbox, and said goodbye to Changing Woman, her distinctive peak now covered with a dusting of fresh white snow.

Looking back now, I wonder if I might have been happier over the next year if I'd had a crystal ball and could have guessed that, within the next year, I would have that orchard, and more. Much, much more, along with all the pleasure and pain it would bring me for more than a decade.

Yes, happier, I think. Or perhaps not.

❖

I returned to San Antonio as usual and, in the early months of 1944, put things in order for my parents and continued to grapple with Georgia's blunt rejection, trying to find a context that it might fit into.

I had heard her make cruel remarks to others. She had told me about slapping Stieglitz's three-year-old niece, Sue Lowe, for calling her "Aunt Georgia" and about the "country manners" that sometimes made her "behave rather badly," as she put it, half-smiling. And once, after one of her arguments with Arthur, she told me that she had spared the poor fellow nothing. "I drew all the blood I wanted to and wiped my knife clean on what was left of him." These, I thought, were sudden cruelties, unplanned, even unintended. Anyone else, thinking it over afterward, might have apologized to the victim. But O'Keeffe was never anyone else. She was . . . herself.

And so I apologized (my habitual way of dealing with such awkwardness) for reminding her that she was human. For her part, she never once remarked on it—her way of pretending she hadn't said it. And, I suppose, a kind of apology in itself.

Anyway, it was at the top of my mind when she wrote that I was "welcome" to be with her that summer as long as I didn't do anything but work at the ranch. I was told not to farm. I liked the idea of having time to spend on my writing (I had laid my novel aside and was working on yet another book, this one about our life in New Mexico). And I loved the ranch—the cliffs, the red hills, and Changing Woman on the horizon. I was still hanging onto the dream of my out-of-reach orchard, but the beetles had taught me that beans were not an acceptable substitute. I kept reminding myself that while I was important to O'Keeffe only because I was useful, this was true of nearly all the people she had dealings with, even her sisters. And yes, even Stieglitz. Her arrangements with others were what, in another decade or so, would be called "transactional." I was welcome at the ranch because of what I could do for her. I would never forget that, although I suppose I was operating in the same way. I did what I did for her because

I admired her and wanted to make her comfortable—and because I wanted to learn from her and from the experience. Which is transactional, but in a different way.

While I attempted to hold onto the clarity of that realization, Georgia seemed to intentionally blur it. In March, Alice Brayton visited San Antonio and we had lunch. A small, white-haired lady with the energy of a contained cyclone, Alice and I had been introduced by Mary Wheelwright at Los Luceros. A generous soul, she was headed back to her summer home in Newport and invited me to go with her to New York, offering to pay my train fare and put me up at the Colony Club, the famous women-only social club on Park Avenue. It was a chance to see Georgia's 1944 exhibit (still hanging at the Place) and take in a few Broadway shows. Who says no to that kind of invitation?

When I phoned O'Keeffe to let her know that I was in town, she insisted that I check out of the Colony Club and stay with her and Stieglitz. She temporarily forgot that I wasn't a friend—perhaps (I thought) because the wealthy Alice Brayton (who also collected art) had befriended me and Georgia wanted to establish a connection with Alice—perhaps she wanted Alice Brayton to know that *she* was a friend of mine. Whatever her reasons, O'Keeffe gave me a private showing of her previous year's work at the Place, introduced me to members of the Stieglitz circle and even the ill-famed Mrs. Norman, and invited me to help her hang the Marins that were going up in the gallery after the O'Keeffes came down. Together, we went to see *The Cherry Orchard* and *Carmen Jones* and twice to hear Beethoven's Ninth, which was glorious.

But the unexpectedly best part of that unexpected trip was the time I spent with Stieglitz, an old man now and slow but benign, very genuine, and deeply appreciative of the support I offered Georgia at the ranch. "It comforts me to know you are with her," he said, "and that you are looking out for her. She *needs* to be looked after, you know. She is delicate and so often ill. There are so many things she simply can't do for herself."

In that remark, I could hear the controlling Stieglitz who liked to believe that Georgia couldn't survive without his constant attention. (I could also glimpse the Georgia who sometimes preferred, for her own reasons, to seem helpless or even inept.) But in a quite contradictory way, it was also tender and sweet and I couldn't help liking him for it.

For several days, Stieglitz and I looked at photographs together, including the nudes he took of Georgia. Those startled and, yes, shocked me. I hadn't expected anything so frankly, forthrightly erotic, especially given the era in which they were taken and (even more startling) publicly displayed. I thought again that the curiously mannered, nunnish costumes she wore in New York—black, white, and unrelentingly severe—had to be a declaration that she was *not* the woman who posed, unclothed and uninhibited, for those photographs.

Looking at them also reminded me of her provocative behavior with her "young men" at the ranch and I wondered about that, too. She had given me to understand that she had been reluctant to pose nude for Stieglitz and had agreed only to please him. Now, looking at the actual photographs, I couldn't see any evidence of reluctance. It seemed to me that she loved the camera's lingering voyeuristic glance at her naked body as much as she had loved the man behind the lens. Was the unmistakable erotic urgency so evident in the photographs still with her, while the photographer himself was now a very old man? Did she miss that part of her life and want to revisit it, with someone young and virile? Did she long to be the object of sexual desire again, as she had been when she stood naked in front of her lover's camera?

I thought of all this as I helped Stieglitz sort through his Picassos and Matisse drawings for the upcoming Philadelphia show and bring some order to the untidy files he was working on. When I was ready to leave, he said, quite earnestly, that he was sorry to see me go, that I represented something very "healthy and health-giving." And when I got back to San Antonio, he wrote, "My love to Maria. Yes we are friends. True ones."

Which made me smile, thinking that I was the type of person whom Stieglitz could accept as a friend, even if his wife could not. But then I thought again, and wondered. Am I his friend because I am Georgia's slave and keep her comfortable and safe at the ranch? A Stieglitz stand-in, as it were? Ah, well . . .

❖

Since I wasn't tending beans, I picked up my camera more often, making photos of the ranch, O'Keeffe, her visitors, the White Place and the Black Place, where we went several times on painting trips. I took her picture on the back of Maurice's borrowed motorcycle, a1936 Harley-Davidson. My title was the prosaic "Hitching a Ride to Abiquiu," but somebody later called it "Women Who Rode Away," after Lawrence's story. I liked that, because Georgia and I had read that story together. It ended in tragedy, as I saw it, and perhaps Lawrence did, too. But Georgia admired the woman, willing to leave everything and journey into the unknown, even if she lost her life in the process.

I loved that photo because it revealed O'Keeffe as I so often saw her, at her most human and *real*, not coyly flirtatious, as in Ansel Adams's photograph of her and Orville Cox. And not coldly nunnish, as in the many photos taken of her in costume. Stieglitz (who hadn't read Lawrence's story) also admired the photo—ironic, I thought, since Georgia wasn't smiling so winningly because she loved riding on a motorcycle. It was because she loved riding on that motorcycle with Maurice. They went riding almost every day and sometimes late at night. She didn't get much painting done. And since Maurice wasn't the only guest (in any given week, there might be four or five), I rarely had a moment to sit down at my typewriter.

But something of material consequence did get done that summer. There had long been a recognized need for a health clinic in Abiquiu—something that Katherine Ferrally and I had discussed when we talked about the ruined hacienda Georgia wanted to buy from the church. Two of my friends—Alice Marriott, a Red Cross worker from El Rita, and Augustine Stoll, a Santa Fe County nurse—had been urging me for a couple of years to enlist Georgia's support for a health clinic in Abiquiu. It was sorely needed.

The Red Cross backed the project and there was federal funding available, if the community showed an interest. I brought it up to Mr. Bode and we hatched a plan to raise enough money to get the federal funding. O'Keeffe pledged five hundred dollars and agreed to pay the rent on a vacant house on the Abiquiu Plaza to hold it until the clinic could move in. (Another transactional arrangement. She hoped that establishing a more neighborly connection with the Abiquiu community would soften the church's adamant position on the house. It certainly helped.) I wrote to a Santa Fe doctor who was retiring, suggesting that she donate her clinic equipment and furnishings. Arthur and Phoebe pledged a thousand dollars toward the project, and so did Mr. Bode and a neighbor on the Chama River. We were on the way.

Not surprisingly, however, the clinic idea wasn't universally popular among Abiqueños. The elders practiced traditional medicine and many saw doctors and nurses as another Anglo threat to their native way of life. Father Bickhaus wasn't wildly enthusiastic, either, for he didn't like the idea of birth control advice being dispensed to his parishioners. But Augustine and Alice and I persevered. Despite the opposition, the clinic would become a reality shortly after the ending of the war.

But that small triumph aside, our summer at the ranch did not go well. The war was old news by this time, and even though gasoline and rubber rationing made travel difficult, people were resigned to it and eager to find a way to live "normal" lives, by which they meant taking vacations. O'Keeffe's friends began arriving early and kept on coming. Cady Wells and Johnny Candelario were now in the service, but Maurice Grosser came for a whole month, to Georgia's evident delight—she (to my chagrin) behaving like a vamp in a 1920s silent movie.

Maurice was still with us when Peggy Kiskadden and her two teenage children arrived. Then came Becky James with her husband Bill, Ansel Adams, a touring Chinese artist named Teng Chiu, Bernie and little Max, whose father was now fighting in the Pacific, and Henwar Rodakiewicz, Peggy's recently divorced husband. Henwar was another of Georgia's favorite young men.

Eliot Porter came too, but perhaps out of self-defense, brought his wife Aline. This was not felicitous. O'Keeffe did not appreciate the wives of her young men and Eliot's wife was young, attractive, and an accomplished artist. Georgia was outrageously testy when Aline was around and outrageously flirtatious—with Eliot—when she wasn't. (O'Keeffe's aversion to attractive wives was not an isolated event. Later, when I was in New York after Stieglitz's death, Nancy Newhall told me about something that had happened in 1940. Ansel Adams, Dave McAlpin, and Nancy's husband Beaumont were with Georgia at the

Stieglitz apartment in New York. On a whim, the four of them decided to go to the nearby World's Fair. Beaumont reached for the phone. "My wife would love to come," he said. Georgia replied carelessly, "Oh, that won't be necessary." Nancy wasn't invited.)

I liked most of Georgia's guests individually and some of them very much, especially Becky and Henwar. But collectively . . . well, there were just too many, given our remoteness, the size of the house, and the challenge of managing three meals a day. Georgia was even more short-tempered than usual, and there were more frequent blowups at the kitchen help and at me. I was irritated at having to make more frequent trips to town for food and supplies, organize and help prepare meals for often-unexpected guests, and arrange their entertainment. It was a damned good thing I didn't have a bean field to tend, I told O'Keeffe. It would be full of weeds and overrun by beetles.

We'd been at the ranch only a few weeks that summer when I wrote despondently to Stieglitz that I was on the brink of leaving Georgia even though she still had a houseful of guests. "I never can seem to get enough food into them!" I wrote. "I'm ready to boot them all out!" Finally, I had to tell Georgia that it was time for her to choose. She had to clear out the crowd by Saturday or I would leave. She actually seemed relieved that I was giving an ultimatum. She could tell them *I* was kicking them out when she was just as glad as I was when they were gone. But the disagreement had left its mark, and Georgia and I spent the next few weeks growling and snapping at one another like a pair of bad-tempered pit bulls.

At summer's end, I celebrated my thirty-first birthday, for me an important landmark. I knew it was time for a change. Much as O'Keeffe needed me (or someone like me) at the ranch and much as I might want to be a part of her life and her work, I knew we weren't going to live together another year. And she agreed. What's more, she had already invited Maurice to come back and stay for as long as he liked. I was welcome to visit, but she didn't think it was a good idea for the two of us—Maurice and I—to be there at the same time. I didn't have to be a Los Alamos scientist to figure out why.

Was I disappointed? Deeply, of course. In myself, in Georgia, in both of us. I would miss the ranch and the Piedra Lumbre and the shimmering desert, with Changing Woman anchoring the rim of the blue horizon. But I was learning to adapt and accept—at least, I thought (or hoped) so. And it was undeniably true that I needed to find a new life, new interests, something to pull me forward into my future. It wasn't with Dorothy, because Agi was still in the picture and I wasn't inclined to be a permanent third in a *ménage à trois*. But Olive Rush had a small casita in Santa Fe that I could rent for next to nothing, and Alice Marriott was looking for a housemate to share her tidy little Round Valley adobe in the foothills of the Sangre de Cristos—two viable options right there. When I came back to Santa Fe in the spring and began to look in earnest, I knew I would find others.

Georgia and I also agreed that, even though we would not be living together, we would do what we could to help one another. Or I would, at least. I knew it was healthy for me to go off on my own. I just wasn't sure how she would manage. She couldn't even start the water pump by herself. She needed someone always nearby, someone who needed to be helpful. Like me. Not like Maurice. As I wrote to Dorothy, he was "as civilized as they come." But he wasn't the type to do what had to be done.

On a Saturday in mid-October, I took O'Keeffe to Lamy to catch the train back East. That done, I drove back to Española to drop her Ford at Hunter's Garage, where we stored the cars (she now had two) for the winter. Then I picked up my suitcase and walked over to the Trailways station to buy a bus ticket for my annual winter trip back home to San Antonio.

But as things turned out, I didn't buy that ticket for several days. Instead of a bus ride, Changing Woman had a surprise for me, an amazing, utterly unpredictable surprise that would dramatically alter the direction of my life for the next fifteen years.

It was all about orchards, you see.

And Los Luceros.

Los Luceros

This is a splendid place. The house . . . was once the *estancia* of the great Spanish land owner of the region, a noble house of thick adobe walls white washed within, old brown ceilings laid over round beams, corner fireplaces that seem like an adobe oven sliced in half, and ancient Spanish furniture. And the country . . .

—Henry Beston
December 1925

The story of place is also, and always, a story of people.

In the beginning is the land, a fertile crescent embraced in a shifting arc of the Rio Grande and flanked by mesas and mountains and desert.

And then come the people passing through this fruitful place, each a story. Prehistoric nomads, hunting and fishing among the cottonwoods and willows along the river. Twelfth- and thirteenth-century Tewa farmers moving in from the western mesas to tend small fields. Then the colonizers. In the 1540s, the Spaniard Hernán Cortés in futile pursuit of the fabled Seven Cities of Gold. In the 1590s, the conquistador Oñate, eager for empire, planting his flag in what he calls New Spain. Spanish and Genízaro soldiers in their defensive outposts, followed by a century of farmers and shepherds working small acreages and living in one- and two-room adobe dwellings.

And then, in 1712, the powerful Spanish family of Capitán Sebastían Martín Serrano claims ownership of fifty thousand acres and builds a splendid *casa grande* of (eventually) two floors and twenty-four rooms with thick adobe walls, a pair of round towers, a chapel, and two neighboring adobe *casitas*, all of it surrounded by irrigated fields and peach, pear, and apple orchards.

Several generations pass and the vast land grant, parts of it parceled out among heirs, now belongs to the Luceros family. It is called Los Luceros, "The Morning Stars." When Mexico cuts itself loose from Spain in 1821, it becomes the important seat of the Prefectura del Norte, one of three political divisions of the province of Nuevo México.

In 1848, the Hispanos surrender to the invading Anglos, who claim all the territory west to the Pacific. The United States, from sea to shining sea, and Nuevo México becomes an American territory. The area is now called Rio Arriba County and the splendid Casa Grande— still the greatest in all that region—becomes the county courthouse, as well as the Luceros residence. A jail is added to the outbuildings.

Another seven decades pass. The title to the Los Luceros estate is handed from one Luceros heir to another, its expanse continually diminishing as pieces of its vast acreage are carved off through inheritance, sale, and foreclosure. By 1923, the Casa Grande stands empty, derelict, an adobe ruin. The remnants of its fields and orchards are bought by the owners of the adjacent San Gabriel Guest Ranch, Carol Stanley Pfaffle and her cowboy husband Roy. Time and trade have been good to the Pfaffles. They are making a name for themselves at their guest ranch.

And then fate steps into the picture—or perhaps it is Changing Woman, now in the unusually unconventional person of Mary Cabot Wheelwright, middle-aged Bostonian globetrotter and fervent admirer of Navajo culture and ceremony. The Cabot in her name bespeaks her connection with the Boston Brahmin lineage to which she owes her wealth and prestige. It is best remembered in John Collins Bossidy's famous ditty, which Miss Wheelwright occasionally recites, just to be sure you get the point:

> And this is good old Boston,
> The home of the bean and the cod,
> Where the Lowells talk only to Cabots,
> And the Cabots talk only to God.

In Miss Wheelwright's case, the description is apt, for what she might lack in humility, she possesses in authority and a strong sense of personal correctness. A friend says, "To put it bluntly, she could be bossy." Another friend remarks that she makes up her own rules and tolerates no dissent, but "her arbitrary ways were cushioned by so much generosity and kindness" that her "idiosyncrasies were easy to forgive." In a letter to her mother, Maria describes Miss Wheelwright as resembling a picture of Julius Caesar she remembers from a childhood book. She is "tall, thin, long-nosed, leather cheeked, kind eyes, wool clothes—and a hat that sits on the top of her head like a helmet." The Navajos call her "Stone Face," and intend the term as a compliment. But for all that forbidding exterior, Maria finds her "very liberal and kind as a thinking human."

Boston to the toes of her expensively serviceable shoes, Miss Wheelwright is a storybook old maid and proud of it, pointedly abstaining from tobacco, alcohol, or going, as she put it, "indecently clad." She is never at a loss for words, but her voice is shrill and high pitched, with an annoying intonation very like Eleanor Roosevelt's. She also has a habit of what another long-suffering friend calls "perpetual yackety-yack," much of it in an embarrassingly kittenish baby talk that makes her seem rather silly.

Mary lives an unrooted life. She spends part of the year at the impressive Wheelwright estate in Maine or at one of her Boston residences, and the remainder of the year traveling in America and abroad. Around the time of the Great War, she begins regular visits to New Mexico, where she develops a passion for Native art. She takes twice-a-year treks on horseback to the Navajo reservation northwest of the Piedra Lumbre to witness the Indian dances. There, she forges a quite remarkable friendship with a revered Navajo medicine man, Hosteen Klah. In collaboration with Klah and several translators, she undertakes the admirable but hugely daunting task of translating the spoken text of Navajo sacred rituals, which are in danger of being drowned under a rising tide—a flood, really, a tsunami—of unstoppable Anglo acculturation.

Now, as it turns out (Changing Woman simply must have had a hand in this, don't you think?), Mary Wheelwright and Carol Stanley were friends back in Boston, where both were active in the settlement movement. Because of that early acquaintance, Mary began using San Gabriel Ranch as her New Mexico home base and San Gabriel cowboys and drivers as guides for her forays into Navajo country. Given the condition of the primitive trails and the unpredictable weather, these rides are long and uncomfortable. But she perseveres. "I was determined," she says, "to convince cowboys that it was possible for a person to be a good sport and also drink tea."

One sunshiny afternoon in 1923, Mary and Carol are riding through the cottonwoods and poplars along the Rio Grande. They come upon the ruined Casa Grande of Los Luceros. The gardens and meadows have long gone untended, the adobe walls are melting back to earth, the wooden galleries and outbuildings falling to decay. But this derelict, clearly in need of being loved and lived in, appeals deeply to Mary, who can see in the ruin the shape of a home. She is accustomed to making decisions on the fly and following them up with money. She knows she has to have this house and its lands—130 surrounding acres of orchards and fields bordering the Rio Grande.

Carol respects this kind of decisiveness. She and Roy sell the property to Mary and Carol spends the next year restoring the Casa Grande in a blend of adobe Pueblo Revival and Spanish Colonial architectural styles. In 1924, Mary takes possession. Delighted with the historic estate and her splendidly renovated home, she fills it with Hispano furniture, *colchas* (embroidered bed covers), *santos* (religious statues), and art, as well as Navajo rugs, blankets, and silver and turquoise jewelry. She settles into a regular part-time residency—eight weeks in the spring, eight in the fall. It is a pattern that will continue until her death in 1958.

Mary does not enjoy solitude, so she ensures that she has plenty of company at Los Luceros. In addition to her year-round resident cook-housekeeper and housemaid, she employs a ranch manager, a chauffeur, and various field hands and cowboys. With her constantly as friend and traveling companion: her amiably compliant younger cousin, Lucy Cabot. And guests, always guests, among them some of the most celebrated in early-to-mid-century American and European art and letters: Aldous Huxley, Oliver La Farge, Thornton Wilder, Carl Jung, Ansel Adams, Henry Beston, Mary Austin, Leopold Stokowski, Willa Cather, D. H. Lawrence, Mabel Dodge Luhan, and Georgia O'Keeffe. Wealthy people, distinguished people, noted writers, artists, musicians. Like her Taos neighbor Mabel Dodge Luhan, Mary is known as a patron of the arts.

And Maria Chabot is there, too, not as a guest, but first as a photographer on assignment. In 1934, she visits Los Luceros to photograph its furnishings for a Works Progress Administration project directed by a friend of Dorothy Stewart's: a book documenting the design of traditional Southwestern furniture. Mary and Maria discover a shared interest in Native American culture and become friends. At the time, Mary is working with Hosteen Klah to document the Navajo creation story. Maria is working for the New Mexican Association on Indian Affairs to promote Pueblo art through the Indian Market, and later, for the federal Indian Arts and Crafts Board to investigate opportunities for promoting Plains Indian arts and Native artists.

Before long, Maria comes up with the ambitious idea of launching a magazine devoted to the indigenous arts of the world. Mary shares her enthusiasm for the project, and in 1939, the two of them look into funding possibilities for the magazine in New York, including the Guggenheim and Rockefeller Foundations and the Metropolitan Museum.

But the uncertainty of a European war hangs over the world and nothing pans out. Instead, Mary offers Maria the job of director of her recently established Navajo museum in Santa Fe. Maria gently refuses. She doesn't want a desk job. And she is coming to realize that (as one of Mary's friends delicately observes) "Miss Wheelwright has an open mind until it is made up—then it is closed to anything further."

In Santa Fe again, Maria returns to work for the New Mexican Association on Indian Affairs, surveying the harsh impacts of the severe federal livestock reduction program on Navajo livelihoods. After visits to 45 trading posts and 150 hogans, her survey is finished. Mary invites her to stay at Los Luceros while she writes her report. When that's done, and to repay the hospitality, Maria edits and types Mary's manuscript of the Navajo creation stories.

That finished, Maria is ready to go back to her own work, the novel about Mexico that she has been working on intermittently—and not very faithfully—for several years. If she is going to do anything with it, she ought to get to it. But Mary thrives on a busy social calendar, and since Maria has accepted her hospitality, she can scarcely refuse to join in.

One of those almost-daily social luncheons will change the course of her life. Among the guests is a friend of Mary's from New York: the artist Georgia O'Keeffe, famous for her oil paintings of giant flowers and infamous for the nude photographs her husband took and exhibited years before. She is accompanied by a much younger, good-looking man—the artist Cady Wells, a sought-after guest in Santa Fe and Taos art circles.

O'Keeffe says little at the lunch, but before she leaves, she invites Mary and Maria to tea at the adobe house she has just bought from Arthur Pack at Ghost Ranch, about twenty miles from Los Luceros. There, she asks Maria to drive her to Navajoland to watch part of the Yeibichai, a nine-night healing ritual considered to be the most sacred of all Navajo ceremonies, a ceremony that Maria has witnessed several times during her visits to the Navajo. It is a long drive—150 miles in inclement weather over terrible roads. On the way, they stop to explore an area of barren lava flows not far from Chaco Canyon, in the Bisti Badlands. O'Keeffe calls it the Black Place and tells Maria she likes to paint there whenever she can find somebody to go with her. She's not comfortable camping out alone. "I hate to admit it," she says, "but I'm not brave enough to camp out overnight by myself." Maria has no such fears.

Back at Los Luceros, Mary repeats her offer of a job at her Indian museum and when Maria declines (again) invites her to stay whenever she likes. And indeed, Maria will see Mary often, when she drops in to pick fruit or get honey or just stops to say hello. But she will spend the next four summers working as O'Keeffe's "hired man," keeping her Ghost Ranch household running smoothly and managing her painting trips.

Their time at Ghost Ranch holds many lessons, for both of them. Or perhaps Maria is the only one who learns. For O'Keeffe is like Mary Wheelwright in at least one way: she comes to most people and events with a mind fully formed, in the same way she comes to her canvas, the picture already firmly in her mind. She already knows what the person or event will show her and is rarely surprised. Or if surprised, unwilling to reveal it.

But whatever Georgia and Maria may have learned, certainly it is fair to say that the end of four years, both understand that it is time to move on from their arrangement. Time for O'Keeffe to find and train a someone-always-nearby who is more willing than Maria to cope with that constant parade of guests. Time for Maria to become more independent, to find a place where she can do more of the things she wants to do. She's still not sure what that is, though, except to hope it might involve more time at her writing desk. And an orchard. She hasn't forgotten that orchard.

And that's when Mary Wheelwright steps back into Maria's life. And makes her astonishing offer.

CHAPTER SEVEN

The Gift
Maria

After dinner Mary settled me down to the talk she had promised. She said promptly that she had made out her will—leaving all of Los Luceros to me. I was kind of weak in the stomach listening to her—the luck of it! And then she was crying, saying she "hoped I wouldn't mind," she didn't want it "to be a millstone around my neck," that I could sell it . . . or rent it or do anything I wished—only that I must be free with it.

—Maria Chabot to Georgia O'Keeffe
Los Luceros, October 13, 1944

I must also say that after my three times out with Mary this week I hold my head for you for what you will pay for Los Luceros—if you have to live in the house with her. —I rather think she has decided not to speak of you to me anymore—that we do not see eye to eye and of course she is right. That I have used you and she is now going to have you live as a lady as you should. She is making fine plans for you.

—Georgia O'Keeffe to Maria Chabot
New York, January 15, 1945

It was a shock, I tell you.

Georgia left in the middle of October that year—1944—so she could supervise Stieglitz's Philadelphia show as it was going up. I took her to the train at Lamy, garaged her car in Española, and was buying a Trailways ticket to San Antonio when Mary Wheelwright's chauffeur, Staples, found me. Mary had dispatched him to invite me to spend the weekend at Los Luceros, for a "little talk just between us girls." Out of the corner of his mouth, Staples added, "Better come. Old lady's got another bee in her bonnet."

Our talk happened in the *sala*, the grand hall where Mary received guests, played the Steinway that John D. Rockefeller had given her, and entertained the three Lhasa Apso dogs she adored. It was an appropriately formal setting for her pronouncement, which just about knocked me for a loop—especially because it came at such an important intersection in my life, when I had just left myself open to finding a new direction.

In fact, I was to wonder later whether Mary had made her decision when she learned that I wouldn't be returning to the ranch the following year, likely from Alice or Augustine, with whom I had shared my news. I would even ask myself whether Wheelwright and O'Keeffe might have cooked up this improbable offer between the two of them, each telling herself that she had my very best interests at heart.

But I don't think that's what happened. I know that at some point, O'Keeffe had mentioned to Mary that she had offered to loan me the money to buy an orchard. Mary likely recognized that she had it in her power to do Georgia one better by *giving* me a piece of land. Not only that, but it would be a far larger and all-around-better property than I could possibly purchase with a loan from O'Keeffe. The two women were deeply competitive, you see, and in some important ways, they were rivals—not just in New Mexico but in the New York social scene, where Mary was the wealthy art patron and Georgia the artist. I had already had occasion to feel like a piece of taffy being pulled between them. I would feel that way even more often in the months and years to come. But that was more my fault than theirs. I asked for it.

The story, in short. For years, Mary's cousin Lucy Cabot had been her devoted companion, as well as her designated heir to Los Luceros. A quiet, modest little woman, Lucy traveled with Mary from one residence to another and around the world, cheerfully seeing to her sixteen or eighteen pieces of luggage and looking after her as they boarded camels and elephants and trekked across wild terrain in the wildest weathers. I never once heard Lucy say a critical word about Miss Mary, as she called her cousin.

But Lucy had died a few months before, as Mary wrote to me—rather self-pityingly, I thought. "My *dear* playmate Lucy died yesterday morning from a heart attack brought on by overworking her d___ vegetables! . . . Poor lamb! . . . Well it's a chapter of my life closed and I hope I can go on playing alone!"

I thought it more likely that dear Lucy's heart attack had been brought on by something other than vegetables—perhaps by the prospect of managing the luggage for Mary's upcoming tour of Tibet. But her death had reminded Mary of the fragility of life, and she revised her will. I was to take the poor lamb's place as her designated heir, she told me on that memorable evening.

Los Luceros was to be mine.

"You may assume charge of the estate now," Mary said, with the conscious solemnity of a queen handing over the keys to her kingdom. "Or whenever it is convenient for you. I know you love the orchards and I am sure you will do a wonderful job. Los Luceros needs someone like you—someone who will always have its interests at heart."

Her heir? *Mary's* . . . *heir!* It was one of those breathtaking, jaw-dropping moments when all that you know and expect for yourself is knocked into a cocked hat. I was to inherit Los Luceros, one of the largest and most beautiful *estancias* in all of New Mexico. I was to have the orchard I had wished for—and not peaches only but apples and apricots and pears. And not just one small orchard, but acres and acres and *acres* of orchards!

I might have been struck by a lightning bolt, so stunning was the impact, and it took me several moments to get my breath. Seeing me utterly speechless, Mary filled the interval by bursting into tears. She cried and I cried and the Lhasa Apsos danced around us, barking joyfully, for a good four or five minutes.

Finally we exchanged hugs and I asked her if she was *sure* this was what she wanted to do, and she said yes, of course she was sure, very sure. She had given it a great deal of thought and I was exactly the right person to carry on at Los Luceros because I had stayed there often and knew and respected the history of the old place and valued her Native art collections and understood and even shared her passion for the Navajos and their rituals. She had heard of my experiments in farming (from Georgia, I was sure) and thought I might want to try my hand at making the old orchards and fields more productive, although of course she didn't expect me to do any of the actual work myself.

"Oh, no, my dear. None of that *work!*" She fixed her eyes on me and said, now quite sternly, that I, as a lady, a *propertied* lady, must depend on the men to do the physical labor. There were plenty of them and if the need arose, more could be hired. Oh, and if I needed any further enticement, she believed that taking on the role of ranch manager—even in the nominal fashion she proposed—would earn me a deferment if the National Service Act became law and I was threatened with the draft.

All of this made me a perfect candidate for Los Luceros, did it not? She had made the perfect choice, had she not? We would both be happy working together, would we not? She smiled triumphant-ly, one of those cat-that-ate-the-canary smiles. She was quite pleased with herself.

I was left with nothing to say to this incredible pronouncement but *how can I ever thank you* and *I am so grateful* and *I never expected* and *I'm sure it will take a few days to sink in.*

And in true Cabot fashion (talking only to God), Mary nailed down the details of my future. I should of course spend the coming winter with my parents in San Antonio, as I had planned. That I was such a dutiful daughter spoke well of their upbringing.

But when I returned to New Mexico in the spring I was to make Los Luceros my permanent home. I could choose to live in the Casa Grande with her or in the cottage that had belonged to Staples and his wife, who were retiring. I could let the land lie fallow and simply oversee its usual maintenance while I paid attention to my writing, a plan that she most heartily recommended. Or I could manage it as I chose with her three ranch hands: Joe, Polito, and Armando. There was of course no salary, but my living expenses would be nil and if I needed funds for new equipment or supplies, all I had to do was request it. She had told her Santa Fe lawyer, Mr. O. J. Seth, to ensure that I had access to the ranch records I needed and to substitute my name for that of the Dear Lamb in her will. I should go to his office in Santa Fe to confirm all she had said.

It was simply stunning, don't you think? The very best land in the entire upper Rio Grande valley, with a hundred and thirty acres of established orchards and fields of fine river-bottom soil and priority claim to the *acequia.* What's more, I knew it was the very best, bar none, because I had spent the last two years looking for land and was acquainted with every piece in the valley of the Rio Chama and along the Rio Grande. I felt exactly as Cinderella must have felt when she was transformed by her fairy godmother into the belle of the ball—except that this was life, real life. It was not a fairy tale.

And judging from Mary's satisfied look, I had no doubt that she was seeing herself in that magical godmotherly role. As she should, of course. She had made an extraordinarily generous offer to a young woman who had just closed one chapter in her life and was about to open the next, without a clear plan or a penny in her pocket.

But I hope I won't be thought ungrateful if I say that—even at the moment of greatest shock and astonishment—I had to ask myself if I really wanted to do this. I had already learned some hard lessons as I attempted to farm a relatively small acreage. Was I capable of assuming responsibility for a property this large, this historically significant? More importantly, did I *want* to?

There were problems, of course, and I could see them clearly—too clearly. The Casa Grande was undeniably grand, but Carol Stanley's twenty-year-old adobe restoration desperately needed attention. The roof leaked, the walls required repair, windows and plumbing had to be replaced, all of which would cost money. Would Mary be willing to fund repairs? She promised funding for the orchards and farm—but could I count on that?

As for living with Mary . . . well, I'd already had a taste of that. Could I manage it? What were her expectations of me during the four months or so she would spend in residence every year? What about those guests? And did she imagine me as an amiable, compliant Lucy Cabot, tending to her wishes and whims? If so, we were *both* likely to be infinitely frustrated.

And as my prudent father pointed out when I carried the news home, the project was imminently risky—less for Mary, more for *me*. I would be investing my most vigorous years in a tenuous enterprise (farming) that was quite likely to prove financially unprofitable. It was also quite likely that I would spend all my energy on the land, with nothing left for my writing.

Miss Wheelwright, on the other hand, would be gaining a full-time live-in ranch manager whom she already knew and trusted and who would have a strong personal stake in making the land more productive—a someone-always-nearby to whom she wouldn't be paying a salary. She would hold all the cards, my father reminded me quite sensibly. While her temper wasn't as volatile as O'Keeffe's, she was known to be whimsical, to act on impulse. If I disappointed or aggravated her, she could change her mind, and her will. To keep that from happening, I would have to stay in her good graces. Could I do that? Knowing me as he did, my father doubted it.

Those were the kinds of issues that made me hesitate, and quite naturally, I thought. But the only way to answer such questions is to go forward as bravely as you can, trusting that what you learn from the experience will be worth whatever it costs you. That answer, or something like it, was echoed by almost everyone I knew. Mr. Seth, Arthur Pack, my dear Dorothy and other Santa Fe friends, my mother, even Georgia. They counseled me to count my lucky stars, take what had fallen into my undeserving lap, and make the best of it.

And so I did. I accepted Mary's gift with all the fortitude I could muster while at the same time (to myself, and over and over again) questioning that acceptance and doubting that I had whatever it took to see it through. I reminded myself that I had no other options matching this one in sheer possibility and asked myself how I would feel in ten or twenty years if I *hadn't* seized this opportunity. As for the writing . . . Well, I hadn't exactly become Pearl Buck or William Faulkner in the four years I'd spent with O'Keeffe, had I? If I *really* wanted to write, I'd write, come hell or high water. Wouldn't I?

O'Keeffe, of course, had her own, evolving view of the situation. As soon as she got my letter telling her what had happened, she replied that she was pleased with what Mary had done. It couldn't be better, she wrote, "unless she just gave up the whole place to you now and that is too much to think of—It all seems so perfect I can scarcely think it can really be true."

That last, cryptic remark gave me pause, and I had to read it several times. Was Georgia simply expressing her astonishment at my good luck or was she questioning Mary's sincerity, or her intentions? She saw Mary frequently when they were both in New York. Did she know something I didn't? Had Mary said something to her that made her wonder whether she intended to keep her promise? Was this a *warning*?

That's what it was, and Georgia soon made it explicit. I would pay a steep price for Los Luceros, she cautioned. Mary was making "fine plans" for me, aiming to turn me into a lady, another Dear Lamb. "She believes that I have 'used you' during the four years we were together," Georgia said, and now she intended to turn the tables, so I had better watch out. She was saying, in essence, "Mary loves her beautiful garden with its lilacs and peonies, but she isn't so fond of the farmland. She says she'll support you if you try to make the orchards productive, but she won't. She once wanted to hire you as her museum director, remember? Now, she's giving you a place to live and time to write and enjoy the roses and peonies—with her, of course. And her perpetual yackety-yak will drive you crazy."

True, I supposed. A legitimate warning, yes. But I could read the rivalry hidden in O'Keeffe's letter, and it almost made me smile.

So I moved ahead. Over the winter, I read everything I could find on agricultural management, especially orchards. I planned to go to Santa Fe in late March, spend a few days with Dorothy, and then settle into Los Luceros. Georgia intended to come out in May, so I offered to open the ranch for her as usual.

And as usual, our letters that winter were full of the dailiness of our lives. I wrote that my father was growing more frail and feeble, and O'Keeffe sent me vitamins for him and my mother. She wrote that Stieglitz had another heart attack, that she had fired another slave, and that when it came to farming at Los Luceros, I should start with a single small field. I would learn from it things that would help me with the larger ones, she said—or I would learn that I was not interested. "Either will be worth learning," she said.

That was good advice, and I intended to take it. A small plot, fifteen or twenty acres, would allow me to test myself without making a huge investment of energy and effort, and without challenging Mary. What did I have to lose, I asked myself—and wasn't surprised when I couldn't think of an answer.

In one letter, Georgia told me a revealing story. She was hanging her usual February show at the Place, she said, when William Zorach, a well-known modernist sculptor, incautiously remarked to her that she wouldn't "exist as she did" if it were not for Stieglitz. I had met the mild-mannered Zorach and thought he might have meant simply that O'Keeffe's painting was built on some of the ideas that Stieglitz had worked with first, in photography. It might have been intended as a compliment. After all, Zorach and his wife Marguerite were recognized for *their* collaborative art.

But Georgia didn't take it that way. He meant, she thought, that she wouldn't have the reputation she had as a painter if Stieglitz hadn't promoted her work in the gallery. "I gave him a tongue lashing he will not soon forget," she wrote with undisguised relish. It was another reminder that Stieglitz's role in her artistic success was a continuing source of real pain—and of the sharp edge of her temper. I could imagine the red-hot scolding poor Zorach got, for I'd been the victim of several of those tongue lashings myself. And yes, they were truly quite unforgettable.

But I knew there was something else to be said, and I said it, straight out, in my reply. "I am beginning to wonder what you are coming to be," I wrote. "From time to time this winter I've had letters telling me of lashing this or that person with your tongue, of feeling like a whip. I would forgive you anything knowing that your anger comes of being out of touch with yourself. It was not Zorach that you whipped."

And it wasn't. It was Georgia, whipping herself for her dependence on Stieglitz and on the commercial art culture that bought her work and paid for the life she lived. Whipping herself because she feared that others would never see her as an independent artist. And if she failed to come to terms with that, *within* herself, she would continue to use her whip on others.

And I? My newfound independence might have freed me to say things to O'Keeffe that I had long kept to myself. But while I was no longer bound to her, I was bound to Mary, wasn't I? I might stand to gain more at Los Luceros than at Ghost Ranch, but hadn't I just traded one kind of dependency for another?

I would never quite answer these questions. They would live at the center of my life for the next fifteen years.

❖

The bleak Texas winter of 1944 and 1945 was lightened by my news about Los Luceros. But good news from the various war fronts was always darkened by the costs.

The US had a new long-range, high-altitude bomber, the B-29 Superfortress. Deployed from China and then from the Mariana Islands, the B-29s would turn Tokyo into a graveyard. The Red Army attacked in Poland and overran East Prussia, millions of civilians fleeing before them or dying under their boots—and the Russians were our *allies.* In the Philippines, American troops recaptured Manila at last, but the city itself was destroyed, along with its historic and cultural treasures. And at home, pale and wan, Franklin Roosevelt beat Thomas Dewey in an election that wasn't even close, but with a vice president—Harry Truman, a senator from Missouri—that nobody but a few politicos had ever heard of.

I went to Los Luceros in March, telling myself that I'd give it a year and see what happened. The winter snowfall had been heavy, there was deep moisture in the earth, and it looked like a promising season. I was starting small, so Armando and I put a fifteen-acre, fall-plowed field into alfalfa, applying extra fertilizer to make up for the years of neglect. Charlies, an Indian from the San Juan Pueblo who knew everything there was to know about orchards, showed me what we needed to do to rejuvenate some of the old peach and apple trees. I bought two hundred mail-order pear trees and Charlies and I planted them to replace those that were no longer fruitful.

That wasn't all of it. Joe Posey, the most experienced of Mary's workers, began teaching me what I needed to know about the rest of the farm: how to manage the cows, the chickens, the gardens, the prewar Fordson tractor, the even older Ford truck, the fences, the ditch system. All of this came with its own idiosyncrasies and challenges, each a career in itself.

For instance, who could have guessed that setting a pair of broody hens in orange-crate nests—fifteen eggs to a hen—would be such an intriguing adventure? Joe and I carried out our task on a chilly March midnight. Beneficent chicken thieves, we stealthily snatched the sleeping hens from their roosts, carrying them with their wings folded close to their bodies and placing them on the new nests gently, so they didn't panic and break the eggs. Joe had learned this from his grandmother, a good German hausfrau who always added a prayer for her broody hens' maternal success.

The *acequia*, too, was an adventure, but of a different kind—less intrigue, more brute force. Los Luceros was the largest and oldest estate of the dozens of smaller farms and orchards on the main irrigation ditch and had first rights to the water. But the ditch hadn't been entirely cleaned out during Mary's tenure and apparently not for years before that. Armando, Polito, Joe, and I, dressed in jeans, boots, and long-sleeved shirts, spent days cutting and burning the invasive black locust and cottonwood sprouts that crowded the waterway, chopping them out by hand and digging up the roots. The job required long hours of backbreaking physical work with hoe, mattock, and machete. But seeing a long stretch of clean, free-running ditch gave me a great deal of personal satisfaction, sort of like cleaning out your bad habits and getting right with the world.

I also enjoyed being with the guys, who were surprised—and appreciative—when I picked up a mattock, joined willingly in the work, and invited them to my cottage for a beer when the day's work was done. It felt right to me and it radically changed my relationship to the men. I was still their "boss lady," yes, responsible for directing and managing the work that had to be done. But I was also a working member of our four-man team, just one of the guys getting my hands dirty along with the rest. And more, which they couldn't know: I was no longer a hired man on O'Keeffe's corner of desert. I had a stake in this land. I'm proud to say that I held my own out there with a machete and a mattock, and the men respected me for it. It was a lesson I would put to good use in Abiquiu the next year.

And there was a gift in this for me. At Ghost Ranch, I had loved the great wildness of the empty desert and cared less for the more settled area east of the Rio Grande. But while I was out there working on the *acequia*, I found myself learning to love Los Luceros for what it was. To the west, the lush green *bosques* of cottonwood and willow along the slow-moving river. To the east, the badlands and wooded uplands and snow-peaked mountains. To the north and south, the broad ribbon of river—and all of it, river and land, land and river, open to the breathtakingly vast, open sky.

And unlike the spare, sparse desert of the Piedra Lumbre, Los Luceros was a land of abundance, of substance, of *sustenance*. I might see a pheasant or a dusky grouse darting out of the coyote willow, a great blue heron standing stilt-like and still in the margin of the river, a tumble of wild roses and wild raspberries spilling down a bank, the tips of wild asparagus, exuberant, poking up through last year's leaf litter. Los Luceros lacked the stern, severe splendor of the desert, the vivid colors of the cliffs, the solidity of Pedernal. Its beauty was mutable, softer, more generous, a blessing. This land wasn't mine, of course, any more than it was Mary's—any more than Pedernal was O'Keeffe's, no matter how many times she painted it. It belonged to itself and to the countless beings who, over the eons, had made homes here and found bounty and pleasure in the land along the river.

But I couldn't help feeling that I might have a custodian's claim, however tenuous, to this place, and I began to take that seriously. One evening I wrote to Georgia that I had been in Santa Fe all day in a dust storm with two men and the heavy truck, loading three thousand pounds of fence posts and a thousand pounds of native fir to build new irrigation boxes for our long section of ditch. The boxes themselves would prove to be an intricate task that required me to learn how to construct, how to caulk, how to waterproof, and where to put the finished boxes. And the fences? Who knew just how damned complicated it was to put in a row of proper fence posts and tension the barbwire so it wouldn't sag?

These challenges had another dimension. Finding help to build a fence or plant a field was nearly impossible. We had been at war for going on four years. Between the military draft and the allure of steady, better-paid work at Los Alamos, there was almost no help to be had. I spent one whole afternoon tramping through the rain in Española hunting a seed drill and a man to work it. I got soaked and chilled to the bone and came back to Los Luceros empty-handed. But I was able to find fence-makers, I wrote to Georgia a couple of weeks later, Pueblo men with fine braids and bright eyes, adept at stringing fence wire through mists of white-flowering wild plum. I wished the spring meant that to me, I told her, instead of broken irrigation locks and rusted wires and cajoling people to work.

I kept Mary informed about what I was doing, of course, but she wasn't eager to hear my reports, perhaps because they reminded her of the things she might have—or should have—been doing to improve Los Luceros over the past two decades. Joe Posey believed that she gave me the land because she didn't want to be bothered with it, but she didn't want me to bother with it, either. He was right. When I came in sunburned and muddy from a day in the field, Mildred (Joe's wife, our cook-housekeeper) said I smelled honest and good, like newly turned earth.

But Mary gave me lavender oil for my bath, to make me smell "like a lady," and a pink lotion to take the burn off my cheeks. She would have loved it if I'd put on my best dress (actually, my only dress—I spent my life in jeans) and joined her in the *sala* with a book of poems, or tended peonies with her in the garden, ladies of the manor, both—the "peony life," as I called it in one of my letters to Georgia. That I refused to become the woman Mary wanted me to be was a disappointment to her, just as it was to my mother.

And while I was engrossed in these personally satisfying matters of planting and clearing and irrigating, of herons and wild plum and lilacs and sweet, damp earth, the nation suffered a catastrophic loss. President Roosevelt died on April 12. The entire nation was suddenly plunged into the realization of just how much FDR had meant to all of us collectively, to each one of us, individually. Whether we had liked him or hated him, whether we had voted for him or for Hoover or Landon or Willkie or Dewey, we had known he was *there*, someone always nearby, with a determined hand on the helm and a sure eye on the horizon.

And who was there now who could bring an end to this wretched war? A Harry-Who, that's who. A nobody from Missouri whose chief claim to fame was having been elected to the Senate by the Kansas City Prendergast machine. A vice president who (we learned later) knew nothing about the Manhattan Project until after the president died. A lightweight who, when he went to the White House on the evening of FDR's death to ask Mrs. Roosevelt if there was anything he could do for her in her time of trouble, heard her reply: "Oh, no, President Truman. Is there anything *I* can do for you? You're the one who's in trouble now."

She was right—and wrong. Most Americans felt that *we* were the ones who were in trouble now, and that Harry-Who didn't have what it took to get us out of the mess we were in.

But there was light at the end of that very dark tunnel. Some eighteen days after Franklin Roosevelt died, Adolf Hitler killed himself. A week after that, the Germans surrendered. Japan was left to fight on alone, and President Truman was left to figure out how to stop them.

And while all this was happening on the international front, I was considering how I could help Georgia get settled at the ranch for the summer—without her experienced hired man. She wrote that she planned to hire Orlinda to do the cooking and housework. But Orlinda didn't have a driver's license, so I offered to drive over on weekends and bring groceries and drinking water, crank the water pump, and do whatever minor repair work she needed.

That's when Georgia surprised me. But no, I can't really say that it was a surprise, because she had already mentioned Maurice Grosser several times in her letters. Maurice had been to dinner frequently at the New York apartment, sometimes with others, sometimes alone. Maurice had brought her a buffalo steak from the Fulton Street Market. Maurice had taken her to the Museum of Modern Art, where one of his paintings had been exhibited the previous year.

Now, she wrote to tell me that Maurice would be spending the summer at the ranch and added that she knew it would annoy me, which would be "very foolish." Anyway, since he would be there to help with the chores, it wouldn't be necessary for me to make weekend trips. I could visit the ranch any afternoon, of course, she went on. After I had thrown one of my "little tantrums" and called her a few names, she added in an amused aside, she was sure that I would feel better.

O'Keeffe already knew how I felt about this, but I wanted to say it straight out in a letter: *I hate what you're doing with Maurice because it makes you look old and foolish. It is vampish. It diminishes you.* But she had often reminded me that our letters might end up in a library or archive somewhere and I didn't want to write something that might embarrass her. Anyway, I knew what she would say. *You can't own me, Maria. You're too possessive—you want to manage my life and my friends and I won't have it.*

And I understood and sympathized with her—with the way she felt, that is, not with the way she acted. What kind of physical affection had she and Stieglitz shared in the fifteen years since the advent of Mrs. Norman? What kind of reassurances did Georgia need, did she want, did she *crave*, to feel herself still an attractive woman? I understood this, and loved her for being real and human. It pulled her off her pedestal and revealed a woman with needs and desires and cravings like my own.

So I couldn't let it go without saying *something*. My first couple of attempts at a reply to her letter were too deferential. With the third draft I finally came up with something close to what I would say when I saw her:

> Well if you think you're right about Maurice you are right. Temporarily. In the long run it will be me, Georgia. Because I care—about you and about your way of life. And you know it. No I don't want to come to your house while he is there . . . I love that place too much.

But I was wrong, for in the long run, it wouldn't be me at all.

And this is important, not to her, of course, just to me. I would no longer idolize Georgia as I did in the beginning, although we would remain friends for the rest of our lives. But I would finally outgrow the need to take care of her and begin to learn how to take care of myself. Outgrowing that need opened me to the rest of my life.

She didn't outgrow the need to be cared for, however. And it wasn't Maurice, as she would learn that summer. It couldn't be Eliot Porter or Orville Cox, because both were definitively married and unavailable. Or Spud Johnson or Richard Pritzlaff, who were exclusively gay. Or even Henwar, who would insult her beyond measure by bringing another woman to the ranch. It wouldn't be anyone special—until Juan Hamilton, and then it would be just Juan until the end, an ultimately more amenable and satisfying version, I suppose, of Maurice. I wonder if she ever called him her hired man.

And in the short run, what about Stieglitz? How would he feel if he learned that his wife and Maurice were spending the summer together, alone? I wouldn't hurt him, or Georgia, by spilling the beans— although Mabel or even Ansel Adams (neither of them O'Keeffe fans) would love to do just that.

But in the longer run, I discovered that I didn't have time to obsess about Georgia's affair with Maurice (if that's what it was), for my life at Los Luceros was too demanding, too full. And on top of that, I was seeing Dorothy, who was recuperating from a serious surgery, whenever I could. I spent several weekends with her in Santa Fe or she came out to Los Luceros, where we could walk along the river and through the orchards. I was also trying to accommodate Mary's wishes and whims as much as I could, given the demands of spring alfalfa planting, ditch cleaning, and the arrangements I'd made with the coalition of Colorado planters who had offered to lease fifty acres of Los Luceros land for their cauliflower crop. And on top of all this, my mother fell and fractured her hip. Georgia gave me a check to help cover the cost of the plane fare, and I spent almost three weeks in San Antonio, managing nursing care and seeing my mother through the most difficult part of her recovery.

The short run turned out to be very short. Georgia had said that Maurice would be spending the whole summer, but when I got back from San Antonio, I learned that he had already gone—not on the most affectionate of terms, apparently. All she would say was that he "bothered" her so "he must go." He never came back.

And she never spoke of him, which was odd, because we had talked freely about our lovers. For her, before Stieglitz, there had been Arthur Macmahon and Ted Reid and Paul Strand, any of whom she might have married. After Stieglitz, briefly, a fling with a man she met in Hawaii during her weeks there and (more seriously) with Jean Toomer, whom she thought she might even have loved. She'd heard the rumors about her bisexual life and thought it was "funny" that people believed she'd had an affair with Beck James that first summer in New Mexico. And with both Mabel Dodge Luhan *and* Mabel's Indian husband Tony.

Of course none of that had ever happened, she told me with a half-smile, as if she and Beck and Tony and Mabel had planned their deceptions and it amused her. But even if it were true, I knew it wouldn't have mattered for longer than the time it took. Her life had always been about work, not about people. People got in her way.

But while I heard about all the others, she said nothing at all about Maurice. She was hurt when he left, but she didn't offer to tell me what happened between them, and I didn't press her. I guessed that he decided he wasn't her hired man and didn't like running errands or doing repairs. Or perhaps he told her that he was going back to Virgil Thomson. Or (the most hurtful) that he wasn't in the market for a lover who was almost old enough to be his mother. Whatever happened, I never heard her speak his name again.

And I didn't bring him up, either—until three decades later, after Hamilton came into her life. I asked her then if she remembered Maurice Grosser. "Maurice who?" she asked blankly. When I reminded her about the summer of 1945, she gave me that withering O'Keeffe look and snapped, "Don't be ridiculous, Maria. This business with Juan is nothing at all like *that*."

But it was, I thought. It was the very same thing: an aging woman's desire for a younger lover. Except that there was a difference. Maurice had a strong sense of direction, of what he wanted from life. He came for a visit and moved on. Hamilton had no sense of direction until Georgia gave him hers. He moved in and stayed.

I wasn't unkind enough about the Grosser affair to say "I told you so," although I might have. Instead, I said "Well, then, since he's gone, let's take a little trip." I came to the ranch, packed her car with the usual supplies and equipment, and we spent the weekend at the White Place, where she painted and I managed the meals and wrote in my journal. In September, we visited the Santa Fe market, where we bought a large *ristra* of dried chiles from the Zia Pueblo and another of garlic, enough to last a full year. In October, we drove to Santa Domingo for an Indian dance. In early November, we made a trip to the Black Place.

All this companionable travel might have seemed like the old days, but it wasn't. Changing Woman had worked her magic again. My new life at Los Luceros had already changed my relationship with Georgia. I cared for her and wanted to support her as much as I could, but she and the house at Ghost Ranch were no longer the lodestars of my life, nor my exclusive focus. Like Maurice, I had moved on, and I felt good about it.

I had other friends, too. There was Dorothy, of course. And Alice

Marriott, who often stopped for the night at Los Luceros on her travels for the Red Cross, and my county-nurse friend, Augustine Stoll, who kept me informed about the doings in the pueblos. All three of us were working on the Abiquiu clinic project, which looked like it was actually going to happen.

And there was Becky James (Georgia's friend, the former Beck Strand), who lived in Taos and whom I always saw when I went there. Becky had gotten into the habit of dropping in for a quick drink on her way back from Santa Fe, where some of her intriguing artwork—reverse painting on glass, as well as several pieces of her *colcha* embroidery—was on display at one of the local galleries.

"Of course it's not true about an affair," Becky said in her low, husky voice, over a second whiskey sour and a plate of the nachos I had learned to make on one of my trips to Mexico: refried beans, chorizo, cheese, and pickled jalapeños. We were sitting on the patio at Los Luceros, enjoying the afternoon sunshine, the summer roses and honeysuckle fragrant around us. "Georgia and I pretended to be lovers for the fun of it. She isn't interested in women. She has an eye for men, especially the young ones."

"I've noticed," I said drily.

With a smile, Becky tossed her head. "Pot calling the kettle black. My Bill is nine years younger than I am. Even Mabel makes eyes at him, although it doesn't do her a bit of good. Bill just pokes fun at her."

I knew that the transition from Beck Strand to Becky James had marked an enormous change in Becky's life. For ten years, Beck had been Georgia's closest friend and the wife of Paul Strand, a photographer, Stieglitz devotee, and one of Georgia's pre-Stieglitz lovers. Beck had been close to Stieglitz, too, exchanging letters and posing nude for him.

But a dozen years before, Becky had gotten a Mexican divorce from Paul and left the East Coast to settle permanently in Taos, where she pursued her painting. She adopted cowboy shirts, slim trousers, and boots and married Bill James, the owner of the Kit Carson Trading Post, where tourists taking Fred Harvey's Indian Detours always shopped for souvenirs. Now, Becky and Bill took an active part in the Taos social scene, especially when it came to dancing, playing poker, and drinking Taos Lightning with rowdy friends at Mike Cunico's saloon and dancehall—far removed from Mabel Dodge Luhan's elegant, upper-crusty art salon.

But there was something I wanted to know. And Becky was the right person to ask. "People say that Georgia and Mabel's husband slept together," I said. "Georgia told me it never happened. What do you think?"

"Oh, *that* happened, all right." Beck folded a match out of a paper matchbook and lit it with a flick of her thumbnail. "Mabel was out of town at the time, O'Keeffe spent several nights at the villa, and Tony had—still has, for that matter—enough personal charm to win over an ice maiden. Georgia was no ice maiden." She put the match to her cigarette. "But if you ask me, she was less interested in screwing Tony than in jerking Mabel's chain. And in holding it over Stieglitz—getting even with him for Dorothy Norman. At the time, you know, that affair was going hot and heavy. Georgia hated it." She blew out the match and dropped it in the pottery ashtray I'd put on the table for her. "Of course, even Norman couldn't change the way Georgia felt about Stieglitz. She loved him then, loves him now, so far as she's able to love anybody. And she owes him, of course. Owes him for everything."

I raised my eyebrows. "Owes him? O'Keeffe wouldn't like to hear you say *that*."

"You bet your boots she wouldn't." Becky picked up her whiskey.

"She might even slap my face. Which doesn't change the fact that it's true." Peering at me over the rim of her glass, she added, "You and I have something in common, you know, Maria. When it comes to O'Keeffe, that is."

"We do?" I was curious. "What?"

"I was her first slave. You were her second. For a while, anyway." She waved her hand. "Before you got smart and moved over here."

"Her slave?" I stared at her, startled. "*You?*"

"Well, *I* never thought so. But that's what she called me. Stieglitz told me what she'd said and it hurt—because I cared for her, you see. I admired her. I wanted to think we were *friends*. I would have done anything to make it easy for her to get on with her work, even though I knew, deep down, that it was a way of avoiding my own."

This all struck close to home, very close. I wasn't sure what to say. After a moment, I settled for "But just look at you now. Your own work, your own shows—"

"It certainly took long enough." She was intense. "This is something I've thought about a lot, Maria. O'Keeffe may look small and fragile, but she is a powerful woman. It's easy to let yourself get trapped in her orbit, to let her become the thing you circle around." Her pale eyes darkened. "I know this. It happened to me."

I turned my glass in my fingers. "It was cruel of Stieglitz to tell you," I said finally.

"Maybe." She shrugged. "*Slave* is certainly an ugly word. But it's *her* word. It's the way she thinks about people who are useful to her. They don't exist for themselves, they exist to take care of *her*. And I needed to hear it, don't you think? When Alfred told me, that's when I knew I had to get away from her. I had to grow up, be myself, stop being her *jeune fille* copycat. I wore my hair like hers—why, I even wore those ridiculous

163

all-black outfits, just like hers." She looked down at the red plaid blouse and flounced Mexican skirt she was wearing that day. "I loved her, you see. But I could never be myself, as long as I tried to be her."

I said nothing. She tapped the ash from her cigarette and leaned back in her chair, casting a glance at the Casa Grande and then at my cottage. The smell of rich, damp earth came from the nearby irrigation ditch. From the alfalfa field, the cheerful sound of Joe's tractor, mowing.

She said, "I'm glad to see you've declared your independence."

Was that what it was—my independence? Or had I simply moved into a different, less magnetic orbit? "That's not exactly what happened," I said slowly. "It's . . . complicated."

"Of course it is. Anything involving O'Keeffe is complicated. To tell the truth, I was surprised that she let you go." Becky tapped the ash off her cigarette, regarding me critically. "What I heard was that you told her she shouldn't get involved with Maurice Grosser. When she wouldn't listen, you checked out."

I stared at her, nonplussed. "Did *O'Keeffe* tell you that?"

"No. Maurice told me. We've known each other for years. I ran into him at Cunico's the night he left Georgia's ranch. He was in Taos, seeing people."

I should have thought of that. All the artists between Santa Fe and Taos were "old friends"—except for Georgia, who held herself aloof. It was no surprise that Becky knew him. That they had talked. What did surprise me was that O'Keeffe had told him what I had said. I had imagined it was just between the two of us.

"I . . . I hope Maurice doesn't blame me," I said slowly. "I like him, you know. He's a decent guy. I just hated to see her throw herself . . ." I stopped. "I mean, I didn't think it was a good idea for her to . . ." Frustrated, I rolled my eyes. "Oh, *hell.*"

"Exactly." Becky picked up her glass again. "And you're right, Maurice *is* a decent guy. He said he hated hurting her—although he thought she was more angry than hurt. He said she let him have it with both barrels. And didn't quit until she ran out of ammunition." She sipped her whiskey. "He said she expected him to be her slave. Number three, I suppose."

"She told *him* that?" I was startled.

"I doubt it. But that was the word he used. He said he didn't mind running a few errands, but there was never enough time for his own work. And there was the other thing," she added obliquely.

I sighed. "She let him know what she . . . wanted."

"That was the hard part. For him, I mean. He thought it was all on the up-and-up, no strings attached. A few weeks in the desert, time for him to relax and do some painting. He had no idea it was going to be just the two of them, à deux. He thought you would be there, and other people in and out, the way it was last year and the year before. But he was a gentleman. He blamed himself. He said he should have been able to see it coming." Another sip. "That's what Tony said, too."

For a moment, I was confused. "Tony? Mabel's husband? Back when he and Georgia—"

Becky nodded. "He told me he would never have dared if O'Keeffe hadn't made the offer, although I suspect he didn't hesitate to take her up on it. Anyway, Maurice has gone back to New York, to Virgil. His orbit." She glanced at her watch. "Hey, look at the time. Gotta head back north—Bill will be wondering where I am. Will you be in Taos again soon? If so, come and have supper with us, and we'll go dancing." She stood. "You can stay the night, you know. We always love to have you with us."

It was good to have a friend.

PART THREE

Going Away
1945–1981

CHAPTER EIGHT

The Faraway Nearby
Maria

If you get there next month I wish you would stop at Cook's and find out if my three bundles of Encyclopedia Britannica arrived & if Orville will put in the grease trap in the kitchen. . . . It must be fine up there [now] in a deep snow—only a rabbit or two hopping about.
—Georgia O'Keeffe to Maria Chabot
New York, February 3, 1945

I will see about your encyclopedia packages—and about the grease trap. I am happy that you will let me do such things for you. It is hard to cut out of my heart that house and that country.
—Maria Chabot to Georgia O'Keeffe
San Antonio, February 8, 1945

A couple of days after I saw Becky, the mail brought a brief note from O'Keeffe, inviting me to drive up to the ranch for the weekend and bring some fruit, if I had any. She also included a list of things she wanted from the market in Española. I thought of what Becky had said about slaves, then popped a reply in the mail, saying I would do her shopping. I knew I didn't have to go and I didn't have to shop for her. But something interesting had just come up, and I wanted to tell her.

It was July and the peaches and apricots were ripe in the Los Luceros orchards. So early Sunday morning, I put a bushel of each in the car, along with her groceries, and drove out to the ranch. That afternoon, Georgia and I peeled, sliced, and packed the peaches and apricots in quart Mason jars. The kitchen was hot, the air muggy with a summer rain shower and sweet with the rich, ripe scent of fruit. While we worked, I told her my news.

"I saw Katherine Ferrally when I was in Santa Fe last week. The realtor, remember? She's finally been able to talk to the new archbishop about the house at Abiquiu. She says she thinks he might be interested in doing something about it."

"Oh, really?" Georgia didn't seem surprised. "I thought it was completely out of the question."

"Apparently not. Sounds like there could be a possibility that the archbishop will sell, if the deal is right. Katherine says he can see that the place isn't doing the diocese any good, the way it is. They invested quite a bit of money in the new church ten years ago and there were hard feelings about it. They're not going to put another penny into that village if they can help it."

There was a story behind this. Isn't there always? The "new" church was designed by the well-known architect John Gaw Meem. In cruciform shape, it was sited so that the main doorway faced east. This was a marked change, since the old church (originally built in the 1750s, burned and rebuilt in the 1870s) faced south. The priest, the archbishop, and the architect preferred east, the sacred direction honored by Christians since the second century. The new stone foundation was laid out that way—until the villagers noticed. They loved their old church and wanted their new church to face in the same direction: south.

Did they also remember that south was the direction sacred to their ancestral Tewas, where the sun—the source of all light and life—

stood highest in the sky? Probably. But whether it was that or a matter of tradition, the Abiqueños were stubborn folk who knew what they wanted. They were providing the labor, gratis, so they simply stopped work until the matter was settled to their satisfaction.

Georgia and I had heard the story in various versions. Depending on the teller, it was either a drunken school bus driver with his bus, a tipsy Model-T driver with his Ford, or an organized effort by villagers with oxen, mules, and plows. However it happened, somebody demolished the unfinished foundation and somebody else stepped in to fix it. The next time the parish priest—Father Bickhaus—dropped by, he saw that the villagers had reoriented the foundation of their church, rebuilt it, and had begun laying up the adobe walls. The doorway now faced south. Abiqueños had already earned a reputation as unruly renegades. This was proof of their rebelliousness, and the priest and the archbishop went away with hard feelings.

"I don't plan to get my hopes up about the house," Georgia said in a practical tone. She poured boiling water into the last jar of sliced peaches—sugar was still rationed, so we weren't using syrup. "The idea still seems so far away." She put a rubber ring on the jar and flipped the wire bail to clamp down the glass lid. "Anyway, I'm not sure I should buy it, even if the new archbishop wants to sell."

The canning kettle with its rack of pint jars was sitting on the kitchen range. I added the last jar, poured in enough hot water to cover them, and turned on the burner. When the water boiled, we would let the kettle simmer for twenty minutes before taking the jars out to cool.

"Far away?" I turned to look at her. This was not what I expected. "You're saying you don't want the house after all?"

That seductive old wreck of a house had been the topic of untold hours of conversation between the two of us. O'Keeffe would buy it as a winter residence and a place to entertain friends. I would manage the restoration, using what I had learned when I watched Kate Chapman work on Dorothy's and Margretta's Santa Fe adobes. I had seen her bring mud-brick ruins back to beautiful life and knew that it was possible to construct a fine building on the foundations of an old, mostly melted adobe.

Of course, rebuilding a century-old ruined hacienda wasn't anybody's idea of an easy thing to do, given the problems of gathering and crafting local materials and working with the local craftspeople who understood adobe construction. But managing the Casa Grande repairs at Los Luceros and at Georgia's Ghost Ranch house had already provided me with a hands-on education in how and how not to build with the local mud, fir *vigas*, and cedar and aspen *latillas*. I knew people from the pueblos who could do the work. And I, too, had been seduced by that fine old Abiquiu ruin and was eager to jump into the project—although like O'Keeffe, I had considered it out of reach. Now, perhaps it wasn't.

Georgia was frowning at me. "Of course I want the house, Maria. I've wanted it for nearly a decade."

Well, then, what was it? "You don't have the money to buy it?"

Another frown. "I have the money, I suppose. But rebuilding seems . . . so difficult. And who would I get to do it? I know we talked about you managing the restoration, but that was before you took on Los Luceros. You have your hands full with Mary's work. She couldn't possibly spare you to rebuild a house for me and even if she could, she wouldn't. And you need to keep Mary happy," she added. "She might very well decide that she isn't going to leave that property to you, no matter how much work you've put into it. If she changes her will, where will you be?"

Much later, I would see the irony of this remark. Georgia left the Abiquiu house to me in a will she made in the late 1940s—at least, that's what she told me. She changed her mind later, and changed her will, leaving me out. But now, I didn't much like her suggestion that Mary Cabot Wheelwright's fickle wishes defined all the areas of my life.

Anyway, Mary had left it to me to decide what I did and didn't do at Los Luceros. I was supposed to be able to make time to write, wasn't I? If I chose to use that time to work on O'Keeffe's house instead, that should be my decision, shouldn't it? As for keeping Mary happy—well, that was something I would have to negotiate as time went on. I already knew it would be a challenge to balance her wishes against my own. How was this different?

But it was, as I should have known. Later, I would remember my conversation with Becky James and wonder whether I had allowed the Abiquiu house to indenture me, once again, to Georgia. But that thought didn't occur to me now.

"This has nothing to do with Mary or Los Luceros." I squared my shoulders. "If you buy the Abiquiu house, I will do my best to build it, and I will make you proud of it." I smiled, liking the sound of those words. "Shall I ask Katherine to set up a meeting with the archbishop?"

O'Keeffe was silent for a moment, as if she were debating with herself. When she spoke, she didn't sound celebratory. "If the archbishop is willing to talk, I suppose I ought to be willing to listen. And if I bought it, I wouldn't have to do anything with it right away."

"Exactly," I said with satisfaction. "That house has been melting away for decades. Another year or two of Joe Ferran's pigs won't make much difference."

"Well, then, I'll talk to him." She eyed me. "You'll go with me?"

I was surprised. I thought this was something she would want to do by herself. "Sure. If you want me."

"It would be a good idea. If I buy that place, you'll be the one doing the work." She gave me a direct look. "It's a massive job. I hope you know what you're asking for, Maria."

Did I? It was a memorable moment. But I only said, with the utmost sincerity, "Of course I do." Of course I didn't, but I wouldn't know that until this was over.

She hung up the dish towel. "It's going to be a gorgeous evening. You could stay overnight and we'll sleep on the roof." Georgia loved to sleep on the roof, but not by herself.

"Let's do it," I said. Polito and I were fixing the east orchard fence tomorrow. But here at the ranch, we were always awake at dawn. I would be back at Los Luceros before Polito finished his breakfast.

A thunderstorm had marched across the empty desert that afternoon and the evening air was fresh and clean, lightly scented with warm earth and wet sage. As it got dark, we climbed the wooden ladder that always stood beside the *portal*, equipped with bedrolls and pillows. I brought a flashlight and a bowl of popcorn and Georgia carried our latest book, *The Rubaiyat of Omar Khayyam*. When we had finished our popcorn and settled down, I read aloud, taking pleasure in the rhymes and rhythms of the Victorian-era translation and the brushing kiss of a light breeze. When it was done, we fell asleep under the infinite canopy of silent stars studding the black velvet canopy of sky. Both of us slept soundly.

Until 5:29 the next morning, when we were awakened by a dull shudder, felt rather than heard. We jerked upright and looked toward the south, where a new sun seemed to be rising low in the southern sky beyond Pedernal—a shimmering halo of yellow, then red, then an iridescent purple. A new sun, against the wrong horizon, and with it the world seemed to tilt. Wide-eyed and silent, we watched as it brightened, then faded, then disappeared. Thirty minutes later, the real sun, the *ordinary* sun, rose as it should, in the east.

The following day, on page six of the July sixteenth *Santa Fe New Mexican*, I read the press announcement from the commander of the Alamogordo Air Base. It was headlined, "Magazine Lets Go at Alamogordo." An ammunitions depot had exploded accidentally at the base's bombing range, the newspaper reported. The shockwave had shattered windows a hundred and twenty miles from the blast and was felt some two hundred miles away. "There was no loss of life or injury to persons," the commanding officer reassured the public.

It would be almost a month later—August 6, the day the atomic bomb was dropped on Hiroshima—and half a world away before Georgia and I knew what had awakened us that early July morning. It would be even later before I would learn that it was the successful July Trinity atomic test that prompted Harry-Who, Winston Churchill, and Chiang Kai-shek to issue the Potsdam Declaration, warning the Japanese of "prompt and utter destruction" and demanding Japan's unconditional surrender.

And still later, I would read that Trinity had prompted Robert Oppenheimer, the soft-spoken, mild-mannered man with whom I had played bridge at Ghost Ranch the summer before, to recall the somber line from the *Bhagavad-Gita*, "Now I am become death, the destroyer of worlds." To his fellow scientists, relieved, he would only say, "It worked."

However cruel, the bombs at Hiroshima and Nagasaki had their intended consequence. The Japanese surrendered and the long war was over at last. The men would come home and women would be released from factories and fields and sent back to their kitchens. Rationing would be over and you could buy a washing machine and an electric stove and a new car and all the gasoline you wanted. The Chile Line was gone, but you could find a seat on a train again or buy a ticket on an airplane, and a new hard-surfaced highway would soon replace the old gravel road to Abiquiu and beyond. A dam would be thrown across the Chama River. Electricity would light the night and telephone service would link Ghost Ranch to the rest of the world. And in Santa Fe, there would be meetings where people expressed their worry and fear of what had been done in secret on the Hill.

We had won the war, but it would be an altogether uneasy peace.

❖

My responsibilities at Los Luceros crowded the rest of that eventful 1945. I spent almost no time at my typewriter, but while my novel suffered, the orchards and fields prospered. The alfalfa I planted in spring was green and lush enough for cuttings in August and again in November, when we harvested 140 bales to the acre and I sold all of it except what I kept back for Mary's cows. In early summer, the Colorado growers who leased the fields hired Puebloans from San Juan to plant cauliflower for a late fall harvest—and signed the fifty-acre contract I offered them for 1946. By winter, I had plowed and disked the fields, turning their naked earthiness up to the cold sky. In the orchards, Polito and Armando and I pruned the salvageable old trees and Joe and I planted new ones. The four of us repaired miles of fences and burned off long stretches of ditch.

And I enjoyed almost every day of it. The neighbors might be surprised to see a woman on a tractor. But for me, farm work was really no different from needlework or housework—except that it was done outdoors, where I had the entertaining companionship of my fellow workers and meadowlarks and the old river's fine wild smells. Mary had gone back East, and in the evenings I built a fire in her *sala* and read William Blake and the Greek poets and listened to music on the radio—a peaceful end to a day of satisfying outdoor work. On several weekends, Dorothy visited or I drove to Santa Fe to see her.

In September, Georgia decided to roast a pig to celebrate the end of the war. She invited friends from Ghost Ranch and Taos—Dorothy Brett; D. H. Lawrence's widow Frieda and her husband, Angelo Ravagli; Becky and Bill James; and Mary Callery, a sculptor who had been staying at the ranch for several weeks.

The party was fun but a lot of work for me, since Georgia asked me to find a small roasting pig and round up the rest of the food, using the grocery list and the ration points she sent me. After several hours of trekking around, I located a piglet that weighed only about twenty-five pounds on the hoof, about right for a dozen people. I couldn't find a butcher who would bother with such a small animal, so I took it to my Puebloan friend Charlies. We got busy with our butcher knives and washtubs of boiling water, and the little fellow was clean as a whistle when we were finished with him. We hung him in the pueblo's cold house and Charlies' wife roasted him for Georgia's party. It was a memorable day—memorable, too, for the blowup the next day.

Afterward, I wrote to Georgia that it was too bad that every visit with her had to end as this one had, in another argument. Maybe the lesson for me was to keep my visits short, especially when there was company in the house—always a stressful time for her. I wondered if Georgia noticed that the old tearful, impassioned apologies were gone.

I had nothing to apologize for. Her tirade was not my fault. I had decided that my refusal to apologize was an indication of my increasing independence and maturity. I still think so. But I suppose that's open to interpretation.

There was another memorable day in mid-October: Archbishop Edwin Byrne met with O'Keeffe and me. The recalibrations of our relationship hadn't changed my enthusiasm about the Abiquiu house. I was intrigued by it, challenged by it, and (foolish or not) still eager to manage the restoration. I won't even try to pretend otherwise. And years later, Georgia would tell an interviewer that I had been "crazy to do this house."

She was right, of course. I was enthusiastic, even wildly enthusiastic—crazy, in other words. But I also had no idea what I was getting into, the years of my time and attention it would consume or what it would cost me, physically and emotionally. There's no two ways around it. I was crazy.

Part of my enthusiasm was due to the historical significance of the house. It had belonged to Abiquiu's leading family. A Spanish Colonial, it was the oldest extant dwelling in the village—and in all the neighboring pueblos, for that matter—and the largest and most architecturally important. Another part of it was my desire to do what Kate Chapman had done with Dorothy's and Margretta's Pueblo Revival adobes in Santa Fe—to carry on Kate's legacy.

Tragically, Kate had died just the year before, from complications following an emergency appendectomy. But Dorothy knew a great deal about adobe building and had helped Kate write and publish *Adobe Notes*. She would be able to answer my questions and offer advice, and I would be thrilled to belong to the honorable lineage of women adobe builders.

And yet another part was the opportunity to craft a unique home and a studio for O'Keeffe. When I first began working for her, I had helped make a home at Ghost Ranch, and it delighted me now to think I might have a hand in her Abiquiu house. I thought of it as a unique gift to her, something that no one else could give. Perhaps I should have guessed that my notion of making a gift of my work on the house might cause trouble between us, but I didn't. Not then. That would come later.

Archbishop Byrne appeared at our meeting dressed in the traditional black cassock and capelet with red-violet piping and a full row of red-violet buttons. In his early fifties, he was a tall, slender man topped with an elaborate wave of silver hair. His eyes were large behind round metal-rimmed spectacles and he had a curious habit of tilting his head to look over the shoulder of the person he was talking to, as if someone else might just be coming through the door. He was friendly enough, but remote and not easily persuaded that it was in the best interests of the people of Abiquiu to have a famous artist living in their village. Perhaps, I thought, he feared that she might give wild parties, like Mabel's soirees in Taos, of which he had certainly heard. But Georgia had worn a black dress, black stockings, and eminently sensible black shoes, and her hair was pulled back into its usual severe bun. She looked like one of the silent sisters who ministered piously to His Excellency. I was dressed circumspectly as well, and the sight of us might have allayed some of the archbishop's fears.

The conversation proceeded decorously. O'Keeffe told him of her long interest in the house and her intention to live there. She assured him that the restoration, to be managed by her assistant, Miss Chabot, would preserve its Spanish Colonial style. I pledged to use native materials—adobe, foundation stone, fir, cedar, aspen—and local craftsmen and women as far as possible, and to restore the old garden to something like its original beauty. We stressed all the possibilities for the derelict place. It was almost as if we had rehearsed our presentation, as indeed we had, if only to each other, in our many conversations over the years.

His Excellency seemed to feel uncomfortable with the idea of selling property that had been bequeathed to the church. I wondered if that was behind the long delay. But he finally agreed to transfer the deed to Georgia in return for a substantial gift to the church (making it a tax write-off for her). The possible amount of the gift—three thousand dollars—was mentioned once and then not again. Both agreed that the details could be ironed out between the church's attorney and O'Keeffe's attorney, J. O. Seth. Seth was also Mary Wheelwright's lawyer, with whom I often worked on Los Luceros matters. By the time we shook hands and left, the archbishop had agreed that the property was O'Keeffe's, if she wanted it.

The second week of November, I took Georgia to Albuquerque to catch a plane to New York. A few days later, Stieglitz wrote ebulliently, exclaiming that she had arrived home safely after an absence of "six months & 11 days!!" He closed with an odd sentence: "Never forget that I am ever fully aware that I am eternally in your debt."

It was an intriguing expression. Was he thanking me for doing what I could to make life in New Mexico easier for his beloved Georgia? Did he know about Maurice Grosser and believe (mistakenly) that I had a hand in the man's banishment from his wife's life? Did he imagine that he owed me for something else?

I never knew. I replied as obliquely as he: "I hope someday we will meet again. For a talk. And yet the most important things never get said—as they never quite get painted . . ." It was quite true. There were so many things I longed to say to him, questions I yearned to ask. But the time for that had passed and would never come again. This exchange was our last.

For nearly two months, O'Keeffe couldn't make up her mind whether to buy the house. But finally, on Christmas Eve, she sent a check to her lawyer. "I have a fine time thinking about it here," she wrote to me. She added, with her customary pragmatism, "The reality will undoubtedly never be as good as the thinking but it will be good."

And a couple of months later, she let me know that she hadn't told Alfred what she was doing. "He is the sort of person who will probably think me crazy to have another house. . . . Anyway I don't care."

I suppose she meant that she didn't care what he thought—Stieglitz wasn't going to stop her. I also suspected that she hadn't told him because she didn't want him to know that she had sold several paintings and was using the money to pay for the house. But perhaps also because she wanted to hold the knowledge to herself for at least a little while longer, her own precious secret. And perhaps because it was another house, like Ghost Ranch, that would be completely hers. She would never share it with him.

The Abiquiu ruin, the faraway that she had dreamed of for over a decade, was at long last nearby. But before it was fit to live in—before *she* could live in it—it was mine to rebuild. And we would learn that our house would be something like Oppenheimer's bomb. In ways that neither Georgia nor I could appreciate or foresee, it would change that dusty little village forever.

ABIQUIU

———

The Pueblo of Abiquiu—and Abiquiu was, in every sense of the word, a Native American pueblo centuries before it was a Spanish village—is unlike any community in the Southwest: it is an Indian community whose ancestral trails reached hundreds of miles to the Anasazi, Tewa, Hopi, and nomadic Native American tribes of the Great Plains and West; it is also a Hispanic community whose residents proudly trace the branches of their family trees directly to the first Spanish New World colonists.

—Lesley Poling-Kempes
Valley of Shining Stone

Abiquiu put itself on the map long before Georgia O'Keeffe bought the old Chávez house and Maria Chabot began its restoration.

Archaeologists think that the mesa, sixty feet above the valley of the Rio Chama and with its own unfailing source of spring water, has been home to humans for nearly five thousand years. It first served as a defensible site for nomadic camps, then as a series of waxing and waning agricultural pueblos, built by Tewa migrants from farther west who tended gardens and fields on the fertile green banks of the river below. That's prehistory, recorded in the bones and potshards interpreted by those who dig beneath the surface of the village's ancient *plazuela*.

Abiquiu is a Spanish variation of two Tewa words: *abechin*, meaning "hoot of an owl" and *pay sha boo-oo*, "timber-end town" or "town where the trees stop" (and the desert begins). Its recorded history began with the Spanish, who arrived to settle the region in 1598 and struggled against indigenous invaders for nearly a century until they were evicted by the Puebloans in 1680. When the Spanish returned to their frontier a dozen years later under the command of Don Diego de Vargas, they knew they had to do a better job of defending their northern border. Since Abiquiu was strategically located along an established trail that led out of Santa Fe and north along the Rio Grande and then northwest along the Rio Chama, it seemed a logical site. In 1742 the governor of the territory of Santa Fe de Nuevo México dispatched a Franciscan friar and a small flock of twenty-three Tewa families to build defensive works, resettle the ancient pueblo, and replant the fields. This first effort lasted all of three years, until a Comanche band swooped in, killed several men, and snatched up two dozen women and children to be sold or bartered for guns and horses. Prudently, the survivors fled.

Still trying to cobble together a frontier defense, the governor tried again. This time, carrot in hand, he turned to a hardier group, including members of the Spanish militia. In 1754, he offered a grant of sixteen thousand acres to thirty-four Genízaro families in return for their skills and experience as soldiers and their willingness to settle in Abiquiu. Genízaros were Indians from various tribes who had been enslaved by the colonists, learned Spanish, adopted Spanish customs, and intermarried. Because they had few rights under the Spanish *casta* laws, military service was their likeliest ladder to land ownership and higher social status. To capture this coveted prize, these entrepreneurial folk were willing to risk armed encounters with hostile Ute, Comanche, Kiowa, and Apache bands. Which explains how, one historian says, Abiquiu became such a unique place: a "pueblo for non-Pueblo people." And might also explain how it got its reputation as an often unruly community of people who didn't quite fit elsewhere.

One thing that everyone notices about Abiquiu is its horizon-wide view of the faraway. You can look south toward the Jemez Mesa and the Jemez Mountains, west to Pedernal and the Piedra Lumbre, north across the green Chama Valley to the ivory limestone cliffs of Plaza Blanca and the Tusas Mountains, and east to the rugged peaks of the Sangre de Cristo Mountains—all of it domed by the brilliant sky.

This remarkable panorama was also enjoyed by the Montoyas, the colonial family who built the first small adobe dwelling on the northern rim of the Abiquiu mesa—although *enjoyed* probably isn't the right word. Nervous residents of this little house likely spent most of the day on lookout duty, keeping a wary eye peeled for Indian attackers. The village grew on the ruins of previous residences, the small, single-story adobe-brick dwellings huddled together around a plaza, unlike the multistoried pueblos at San Juan and Taos. The villagers held all sixteen thousand acres of the Abiquiu grant in common: families grew vegetables in the community garden, raised grains and maize and cotton in the community's irrigated fields along the river, and tended their flocks and herds in the community's meadows above the village.

They lived the rest of their lives as a community, as well. They set up looms and pottery and basket workshops in the plaza, where trade fairs and meetings were also held. They baked their bread in communal beehive ovens called *hornos*, gathered for Mass on Sundays in their small adobe-brick Church of St. Thomas the Apostle, and attended the friar's catechism as required. They celebrated their neighbors' weddings, midwifed their neighbors' babies, and buried their neighbors' dead.

But even though Abiqueños might be baptized and observe Christian ritual, many refused to relinquish the tribal beliefs and traditional practices that grew out of their ancient understanding of the seasons, the stars, and the plants and animals upon whose lives their own lives depended. The friars were frightened by these spiritual practices and called them witchcraft, the work of the devil, giving Abiquiu its enduring reputation as a village where black magic flourished. Illness, accident, unexplained death, loss of property—every scrap of bad luck was another evidence of sorcery.

The church, of course, employed all its considerable muscle to root out the guilty parties. *Curanderos* were persecuted for prescribing native herbs for healing and managing women's reproduction—more evidence of magical work. In the 1750s and 1760s, accused *brujos* and *brujas* were arrested, tried, flogged, and tortured for witchcraft. Indian "idols" and ancestral shrines were destroyed and their evil spirits exorcised. Ancient petroglyphs, condemned as satanic symbols, were obliterated or defaced.

The persecutions ran their ugly course after a decade or so, but many Abiqueños continued to cling to their traditional practices. Children were warned to be wary of attractive strangers with bewitching eyes. *Brujas*, they were told, are notorious shape-shifters. That *tecolote* might be a real owl—or it might be the old grandmother who lives in the *bosque* at La Cuchilla. That slinking coyote, an ill-intentioned neighbor. And Ghost Ranch? There is a reason for that name, isn't there? Better stay out of those canyons—and if you go there, keep an eye peeled for Vivaron, the mythical giant rattlesnake that slithers out of the red-walled canyons to eat babies.

It wasn't long before the Abiqueños got in trouble with the church for a different reason. Following Mexican independence from Spain in 1821, the Spanish recalled the Franciscan, Dominican, and Jesuit missionaries and dispatched a handful of deacons instead. As a result, many remote settlements like Abiquiu found themselves without a priest for most of the year. The men in these communities undertook the task of providing community aid and celebrating weddings, funerals, and holy days. Called Los Penitentes and the Brothers of Light, they became known for their severely ascetic practices, including flogging themselves, carrying heavy wooden crosses, and enduring a form of crucifixion. Abiquiu quickly became the center of Penitente observance in northern New Mexico, a fact that did not endear the community to the Catholic Church.

But the church wasn't the only force shaping this remote village. By the early decades of the eighteenth century, Abiquiu had become a commercial center that boasted nearly fourteen hundred citizens, the third largest settlement in Nuevo México. The fur trade was in full swing and Indian, Anglo, and French hunters and trappers converged on the village to trade their buffalo, antelope, deer, elk, bear, and beaver skins, as well as enslaved Indian captives, illegal after Mexico won its independence from Spain in 1821 but still trafficked.

More Anglo and Mexican settlers and adventurers arrived after Spanish Nuevo México became the Mexican province of New Mexico. Still more poured into the village after the American Civil War ended and word of gold and silver discoveries in Sierra and Socorro counties hit the newspapers back East. Throughout the 1800s, annual weeks-long Abiquiu trade fairs created a brisk exchange of local commodities: horses, mules, and guns, as well as woven blankets and serapes, pottery, tools, hides and furs, turquoise, maize, and chiles. Abiquiu was a bustling trading hub, the place to be if you had something to sell.

And more. In the 1800s, the narrow dirt track that led northwest out of Abiquiu along the Rio Chama became the Old Spanish Trail, the famous (or infamous) twelve-hundred-mile three-month mule-train route over terrain so difficult that carts and wagons couldn't manage it. The pack trains assembled at Abiquiu and followed the tortuous trail northwest into Colorado and Utah, then angled sharply southwest across the toe of Nevada and the Mojave Desert to the San Gabriel Mission south of Los Angeles, then a village of about sixteen hundred souls. They usually left Abiquiu in early November, when the winter rains filled the watering holes. With luck and the blessings of the trail gods, they got where they were going in early February. California was short on wool and weavers, so the pack mules were loaded with New Mexican woolen blankets and serapes to be traded for horses and mules, of which there were plenty. The usual barter was two blankets for one horse, three for a mule. Mules were stronger and had better endurance. Returning, the trains left in early April, aiming to reach Abiquiu before the snowmelt flooded the rivers. Throughout those years, Abiquiu saw a brisk trade business.

And sometime during the early part of the nineteenth century, the Montoya house, there on the cliff overlooking the Chama Valley, became the property of Francisco Antonio Chávez, whose Spanish great-great-grandfather was a captain in the company that reconquered New Mexico in 1692. Chávez moved his young family, including his four-year-old son, José María C. Chávez, to Abiquiu. The boy would grow up to be an important citizen, recognized for his bravery and strong military and civic leadership under three governments: Spanish, Mexican, and American. He served seven terms as a member of the Territorial Legislature, as a judge, and even as a school commissioner. He would live in the Abiquiu house for nearly all of his century-long life, welcoming such notable visitors as Kit Carson (in his Indian agent days) and General Stephen Kearny (who took New Mexico for the United States).

The one-story adobe-brick house would undergo many architectural changes throughout its Montoya and Chávez ownership, The original

1730s dwelling appears to have been a single file of three rooms, each with an outside door but without connecting doors. Sometime around 1840, the Chávez family added a wing, enclosing a courtyard known as a *plazuela*. This courtyard was entered by a double-wide *zaguan* (entry hall) that was fitted with a massive double wooden gate, wide enough to admit a horse and buggy, with a smaller, inset door for foot traffic—the doorway that so entranced Georgia O'Keeffe in the 1930s. A walled garden was added, with irrigation ditches to water the plants and trees.

After Chávez's death in 1904, the house stood deserted. Without regular maintenance, adobe buildings deteriorate quickly, and within a decade or two, the roofs had collapsed, the mud walls were melting away, and villagers stole the foundation rocks. The garden was rented to the Ferrans, who used some of the rooms to corral their pigs.

Abiquiu changed too, during and after the general's long life. The Spanish and Mexican governments were replaced by the Americans. The trappers ran out of furs by the 1830s. The gold and silver in the Jemez Mountains petered out quickly. The raiding Indians were moved to reservations, and the railroad replaced the pack trains. Land agents and lawyers pilfered the land grants throughout the area, doing their best to separate the Native communities from their lands.

Abiquiu had become the dusty little back-of-beyond it was when O'Keeffe finally bought what was left of the Chávez house.

And, when, enthusiastically, Maria Chabot set to work on the renovation.

CHAPTER NINE

The House at Abiquiu
Maria

Draw me a picture of how you want the garden to look. And right away, Miss O'Keeffe! Spring doesn't wait—
—Maria Chabot to Georgia O'Keeffe
San Antonio, February 5, 1946

The garden came first.

O'Keeffe wanted to plant vegetables that summer. That meant that the tumbledown adobe wall surrounding the old garden had to be rebuilt, which would also be good practice, a trial run for the rest of the project.

The ruined wall—two hundred fifteen feet on its long side, the village side; one hundred thirty-five feet on the shorter side—needed to be close to six feet high to provide protection for the acre-and-a-half rectangle and the trees and plants within it. I aimed to make the wall look natural, not like a fortress built to keep the woman within safe from the villagers without.

"I don't want you to look like a walled-in *millonaria*," I told O'Keeffe. "It should look like you and your house belong in the village." Belonging was likely to be a challenge for her, though. I had seen how difficult it was for O'Keeffe to tolerate her Anglo neighbors at the ranch. How would she fare in the village, where she didn't even speak the language?

But that was not my problem. I had to get the place built first. I rented two trucks and hired eight men from Los Luceros, Española, and the pueblo to haul rocks for the wall's foundation. It was something like building the pyramids, I wrote to O'Keeffe on the day we trucked in fifteen loads of rock, telling her that we had already changed the ancient face of Abiquiu—and we hadn't even begun.

But as I would learn, building a house in Abiquiu required extended negotiations with the people to whom this little village and its surrounding lands really did belong, in ways it would take me a while to understand and appreciate. The land—some sixteen thousand acres—had been given to them in 1764 by the New Mexico governor Tomás Vélez Cachupín, and it was still theirs. The rocks were free, but to take them from the quarry, I had to file a formal appeal to the owner of the village cantina, Alfredo Maestas, who administered the Abiquiu Land Grant. When I needed dirt from the cemetery for the bricks and *vigas* and *latillas* from the mountain, I would have to ask for those, too. While it was true that O'Keeffe had bought the house, everything else in that grant belonged to the people of Abiquiu—not just all of the land, but the rock, trees, the dirt, and even the water that came from the spring.

I doubted if O'Keeffe understood the implications of this. Why should she? She had a canceled check and a deed (from the archbishop, no less!) to the property. She had purchased the right to think of it as hers. But these encounters and many others like them required me to see the house and its renovation in a different way. In the villagers' mind, the place was still part of the communal land that had been legally theirs for over two centuries. That might change as the generations passed, and

Georgia might even believe it was hers. But in truth, it was still *theirs*. I was shaken by the thought of what I had gotten myself into—and how little I actually understood it. Not about the construction—that, I would learn from the Puebloan adobe builders I had met and from Dorothy and the other women adobe builders in Santa Fe. But about the way this historic house fit into the past and present life of the ancient village, and what that might mean to anyone who lived in it.

Less confident now but not wanting to share my trepidations with O'Keeffe, I began to work. We couldn't build the wall until we had made the mud bricks and we couldn't do that until the weather was warmer. But I got the men started rebuilding the wall's foundations and began to think about the garden itself. I had included Georgia's fruit trees—apricots, plums, apples—in my January order of new trees for the Los Luceros orchard; they would be shipped in April.

But now Flora told me that the garden was a "made" garden. Decades before, old General Chávez had brought in wagonloads of soil from the mountain to cover the *tierra blanca* (as the villagers call the native hardpan) and create a soil bed deep enough for planting. So I asked a soil conservation agent to take a soils test and tell me what had to be done before I could plant Georgia's trees. He reported that the hardpan was an impermeable bentonite clay and lime. For each tree, we would have to blast a ten- or twelve-foot-deep planting hole and fill it with a mix of soil, manure, and gypsum. Given the work involved, I reduced the number of trees, putting in a peach (Alton, an older variety), three apples, a Russian apricot, two pears, and the weeping willow Georgia had requested.

In the plan I sent to Georgia, the garden consisted of three terraces separated by raised walkways. The upper terrace to the south would be filled with fruit trees, while the lower two terraces would be dedicated to vegetables, herbs, and flowers. While the men continued their work on the wall, I rented Balta Maestas' four-wheel-drive truck for an unreasonable twelve dollars a day—my only option. I hitched a chain to the dead trees in the garden and dragged them off. Then I borrowed a tractor, a scraper, and a disk from a Los Luceros neighbor and spent a weekend leveling and disking the garden. I would open the irrigation ditch so the whole area could be watered, then allow it to settle so it could be leveled again. That project underway, I turned my attention to getting the old well cleaned out and the debris hauled out of the house so we could start work on the foundations.

All this cost money, of course. At this point, I wasn't buying much in the way of supplies, but there was the rent on the vehicles as well as the men's pay. To Georgia I wrote that the workmen were costing $25 a day and since Saturday was payday, she needed to send me a check. The discussion of money became complicated and unwieldy, though, so I asked her to open an account at the Santa Fe bank. She did, but cautioned me against tackling too many tasks at once: "You have a habit of thinking that you can manage what it takes four or five people to handle," she reminded me. She had said this before, and of course she was right. I had a great deal of energy and I tended to focus it on whatever I was interested in. Right now, I was obsessed with that house. I woke up in the morning thinking about it, worked on it all day, and went to bed with it on my mind.

Unfortunately, our discussion of money for supplies and labor did not include a discussion of how I was to be paid—my fault, of course, since it's not a discussion O'Keeffe herself would have initiated. I mentioned it occasionally, lightheartedly, in my letters. "I keep a record of the time I have worked for you—so you can pay me off and be done with all obligation. Not even a handshake, Miss O'Keeffe." But I was as ambivalent about this as I was about everything I did for her.

The next January, however, she insisted on paying me for what I had done in 1946: $600 for six months of work on the house. I tried to return the check (yes, my ambivalence) but she was sternly insistent and that was the winter my father was dying. I took the money (again, a compromise with my intentions) because my family needed it. In her letter, she added, "I know I cannot pay you for the spirit you spend on this thing you do—If I live I pay you in one way—if I die I have made adequate provision to repay you in my will." She had left the Abiquiu house to me, she said. She would change her mind later, of course.

What I know now: I wanted her house to be my freely offered gift of friendship, given with no expectation of reward. I suppose I thought this would finally require her to acknowledge me as her friend. But I know now that she would never be able to do that. To her, I would always be just another of the never-ending procession of slaves who did things for her. Knowing that, I know now—sadly—that I should have made sure that we both agreed on how much she was to pay for my work on her house and insisted on regular payments.

But that was in the future. Right now, I needed to understand the old well and what we could expect from it. In Española, I found a local expert named Clarence Bell. He came to Abiquiu and we spent two hours looking closely at the well. Located for defensive purposes inside what had once been a walled courtyard, it was likely dug when the Montoyas built the first dwelling here, perhaps on the site of a natural spring. Cleaned out, it proved to be about fifty feet deep, with ten feet of cold, crystal-clear water. It looked like a very good well, Mr. Bell said, but we couldn't know how much water it would produce until O'Keeffe actually started to use it. Which wouldn't happen until we could put a pump on it. Which depended on when we got electrical power to the house.

And when would that happen? A year? Maybe more? In the meantime, I would have to bargain with Mr. Bode, who managed what there was of a village utility. He owned the generator that powered his store and his residence and sold electricity to four or five nearby neighbors. The constant *thrum* of Bode's generator was one of the background noises in the village, and on crisp early mornings, the stink of his diesel mingled with the sweet piñon smoke that flavored the air.

The next job: getting the trash out of what remained of the house so I could take a good look at the foundations of the exterior and interior walls and get measured dimensions of each existing room. But before I could do that, Joe Ferran's pigs had to go. Joe had a bushel of excuses for not moving them, and I got tired of arguing with him. So one March morning, at Georgia's recommendation, I accidentally opened the gate and the pigs made for freedom, leaving Joe no choice. He was afraid that one of them might wander into someone's house and come out as hams and bacon. He rounded them up, pronto, and built a proper pigsty elsewhere.

Georgia was living her New York life, so we carried out our discussion by letters, figuring out the changes in floor plans that had to be made, possible uses for the rooms, where to put interior doors and how to locate skylights and new windows, which would be much larger than the old, smaller windows typical of adobe construction. The discussion was often frustrating, because our letters overlapped and some confusions were never quite corrected. O'Keeffe was very busy that spring, too, and even my urgent questions often went unanswered for so long that I began to wonder if she was still interested in her new house.

The most pressing thing on my mind was an idea I suggested in early March. The studio and bedroom ought to be on the edge of the mesa, I told O'Keeffe. That would be the northeast side of the house, where you could still see the remains of the old garage and corral—the *tepeste*. This would give her plenty of north light and a fabulous view. Georgia didn't like my plan and for weeks, either put off replying or actively resisted the idea. Later, when the house was being nominated as a National Historic Landmark, she told an interviewer, "I hadn't intended to use that part of the place at all, but Maria made such a fuss about it, I said well go ahead and fix it. I thought the studio would be where the garage is."

I *did* make a fuss about it, and I'm glad I did, for the studio complex is clearly the most dramatic part of the house. Separated from the house by the courtyard, it is sixty-four feet long, twenty-four feet wide, and offers a spectacular view of the Chama's green valley, the white cliffs, and the blue mountains beyond. I laid out a suite of three rooms, including a studio/office with an immense, open interior space, a small bedroom with an unusual corner window, and a bathroom. This would give Georgia a whole new way of placing herself in the landscape, I told her. It would be "something new and big and fresh, opening out to the world instead of turning into the house."

Which was true: the studio was outward looking, open and expansive. But there was something else behind my insistence, based on years of day-to-day living with this difficult woman. The studio/bedroom complex would divide O'Keeffe and her work—her painting—from the people who did her cooking, cleaning, laundering, and gardening. This separation would not only give her more privacy but would reduce (I thought) some of the inevitable friction between her and the people who worked for her. The old house could be her kitchen, her laundry, her tool room, her storerooms and garage, I told her—even a place to meet people and lodge guests. But I wanted her to live and work where she could see the dawn and feel the wheel of the seasons. It was a good idea. I stuck to my guns.

While I was building her house, Georgia was busy with New York things. As usual, she hung a show of her previous year's work at Stieglitz's gallery. She began collaborating with a young woman at the Whitney Museum of American Art to catalog her canvases. With Anita Pollitzer, she went to Washington to be feted by the Women's National Press Club. She worked on a piece of sculpture at Mary Callery's studio and went to dinner with Callery and her famous architect friend Mies Van der Rohe (who had designed Mary's studio on Long Island, she told me). Henwar took her to see *Othello* again, but there was still no mention of Maurice. On weekends, she retreated to the Johnson farm in New Jersey.

Most importantly, she was involved with her show at the Museum of Modern Art and couldn't get to New Mexico until after the mid-May opening—and probably not until June. It was the museum's first retrospective devoted to a woman artist. Stieglitz was always contemptuous of MOMA and she spoke slightingly of it in her letters. But I knew the show was a landmark event in her career. Organized chronologically, it included some of her early abstractions on paper as well as the giant flowers for which she was famous and her more recent New Mexico work.

The show was positively reviewed, of course, although Georgia was annoyed at Henry McBride for writing (in the *New York Sun*) that, as an artist, she had been "very lucky" at the beginning of her career, when Stieglitz exhibited his portraits of her. (McBride didn't mention that most of the portraits were nudes.) He also placed her "securely in the top position among women artists." That remark annoyed her even more, for she disliked being categorized as a female artist—even though that was the premise of the exhibit.

I knew the house was on Georgia's mind, but she was so busy that spring that she lacked the energy to pay attention to the project. I understood, of course, but I was regretful. I wrote her that I was sorry she couldn't be here to watch the house grow and change from the village pigpen and garbage dump to a splendid dwelling. It was beginning to look loved.

Well, I loved it, anyway—sometimes (I thought) in spite of O'Keeffe. I loved it because I was creating something, at last, worth creating. Not for Georgia, not for the artist, and not even for my compatriot adobe builders in Santa Fe. But in some strange, unfathomable way, for the house itself, a being that had long deserved a renewed life. And for the village and the villagers, who were taking an increased interest in what was happening at the edge of their mesa.

And for myself, too, for building the house gave me a new self-confidence and a renewed appreciation of some improbable things. Like the banner day I was able to lay my hands on four tons of straw for Georgia's mud bricks by making a nine-dollar gift to the San Juan kiva. Or the day I contracted with Alfredo Maestas to make twenty thousand of those bricks at thirty dollars per thousand, using the nine-dollar San Juan straw and free dirt from the Abiquiu cemetery—the very same earthy place where, over two centuries before, the original bricks had been made of the very same gummy *tierra blanca* clay. Straw and clay, small things, insignificant, beneath our notice. But large and immeasurably significant in the long and important story of this house, and something I wanted Georgia to appreciate. Would she, ever? Really? I couldn't be sure.

I also took pleasure in working within a tight budget. Most of the rooms had split cedar in the ceilings or old boards that I salvaged, aiming to reuse them. One day a man quoted me a hundred and eight dollars per ceiling for aspen *latilla* and I could say no, because I knew I could get a permit from the Forest Service and cut my own aspen in the Sierra—for free.

But it wasn't just the money. It would be a fine thing to spend a day, I told O'Keeffe, cutting the ceiling off the living side of a mountain. And I took an enormous satisfaction in the idea that we were making the house from the land, out of the native soils and rocks and trees—in the same way that the Puebloans made their houses from the land and their baskets from the river reeds and pots from the native clays and knives from Pedernal's flint.

I had my frustrations, of course. The sawmill in Copper Canyon broke down, and after it was repaired, the boss fell in love with a lady in Albuquerque and could never be found when I needed lumber. During Lent, I had more helpers than I needed and had to make work to keep them. But come summer, when I needed them to make bricks and lay up the walls, the best workmen had gone to their sheep camps in the mountains. The war had been over for months but tires were still hard to get and when one of the trucks lost both front tires, our rock hauling was interrupted. And the day Orville and I got the gas company to install the new propane tank at O'Keeffe's ranch, a storm came up over Navajo Canyon, the waterfalls roared, the arroyos ran over their banks, and Canjilon Creek was a raging river, unfordable for six hours. There we sat, three cars, five men, and the enormous gas truck—none of us going anywhere until the water went down. I woke up the next morning not having heard from O'Keeffe in nearly three weeks. I hope I can be forgiven for thinking that she would never live in the Abiquiu house and wondering why in the hell I bothered.

Then I, too, was pulled away from the house by the obligations of my double life. In May, Mary Wheelwright arrived on the Super Chief, the wartime blackout shield removed at last from its headlight. I picked her up at Lamy and went back to work at Los Luceros. I had planned a relatively easy year there. Joe, Polito, and Armando managed the spring work without much supervision from me. The fields I had leased to the Colorado growers were plowed, disked, and ready for their cauliflower crop. I would only have to manage one cutting of alfalfa, and we had already taken care of the worst of the fence repair. But there were new trees to be planted, the *acequia* had to be cleaned, and Mary claimed me for a ten-day trip to Navajoland.

"Oh Georgia," I wrote in a kind of comic despair, "I don't know which is worse. Your servitude to the museum show or my slavery to Mary's land. Both seem pretty senseless in the long view of things— which isn't long at all, but too damn short."

Too damn short. Yes, that's the truth of it.

I saw Mary off for China at the end of May. On June 6, I met Georgia's plane at Santa Fe's small airfield and drove her to Ghost Ranch. For the next month, we spent three or four days a week at the Abiquiu house, discussing options and making the decisions I had held for her consideration: where to put interior doors, what flooring to use in this room and that, what to do about windows and skylights. Georgia even began a painting, one of a series of *Patio* oils she would do at the Abiquiu house. We worked through those first weeks of summer productively and even pleasantly, with only a few uncomfortable sessions.

Until Changing Woman intervened yet again. On July 6, Stieglitz suffered a major angina attack—his seventh in the last eight years, most of them when Georgia was away. His doctor ordered him to bed in the apartment and telephoned O'Keeffe to urge her to return to New York.

But years of her husband's emotional coercions had made Georgia wary. Instead of returning, she telephoned Stieglitz's nephew, who agreed to stay nights with his uncle until he recovered. The housekeeper would be there all day, and of course, Mrs. Norman was on hand, as she always was.

He didn't recover. Four days later, he suffered a stroke and was taken to Doctors Hospital. Georgia and I were shopping in Española that morning. The boy from Western Union caught up with us at Cook's General Store, where we were looking for nails, still hard to get, even though the war was over. I drove her—wearing her comfortable old red ranch dress and shoes—to Albuquerque, where she caught the next flight to New York.

CHAPTER TEN

Always There, Always Going Away
Georgia

August 11, 1946. I may get out for September and October but I do not know yet—It would probably be the best thing to do but I have little desire to move—Henwar took me to the Bronx Zoo this morning—it was a fine cool clear morning.

August 23, 1946. I hope to get away by the 7th or 9th of September—but I also may not get away at all.

September 11, 1946. At present I hope as usual to get away next Tuesday or Wednesday . . . will wire you if I can get off.

September 23, 1946. I seem to have spent all this time—some 10 weeks or so—always thinking I will get away next week—I am still thinking that—I hope to really . . . I will wire if l am coming.
> —Georgia O'Keeffe to Maria Chabot, from New York

Georgia is there three days later, when it is over, when he is gone. Three days of watching, of waiting, while he lies unknowing, unconscious. A great pity, she thinks. He would enjoy the attention.

He dies in the early dawn of July 13, a Saturday, chilly for a summer weekend. Georgia has sat beside his hospital bed hour after long, vacant hour, watching him die, waiting for him to die, trying to grasp what his death means to her. Trying to imagine herself a free woman, no longer obligated to shape herself around his needs when they are together or write to him daily when they are apart. She has anticipated this freedom so often.

Anticipated. Is that the right word? Has she looked forward to it? Yearned for it, feared it, dreaded it? She doesn't know. She only knows that she's mostly numb—except for the leaden guilt that weighs on her shoulders. Guilt for things done and undone, for words said and unsaid, for leaving when she knew he was ill and for refusing to return when the doctor telephoned, for not being with him when it happened.

And except for the anger, so much of it, for so many years that it cannot be easily dismissed. Anger at him for the humiliation and anguish of his philandering. At his family for being who they are and how they are. At herself for not leaving him a decade ago. And for leaving him this year, when he was failing. For not coming back when she was called.

Oh, and yes, the fear. The fear of his absence, of being alone— separate, untethered, unconnected—for the first time in nearly thirty years. The terror of too many choices. The dread of decisions, right and wrong. The apprehension of silence, which has always been filled with his words, spoken or written or echoing in her head. But before she can deal with any of that, which she must, there must be *this*. This . . . ending.

No funeral, he has insisted. "No music or flowers or eulogies. Just a small gathering, all personally invited. A plain pine coffin. That's all." He said much more than that, of course. He *always* had more to say. But that's the gist of it.

She forces herself into a semblance of control and spends the day trying to locate a coffin. Alfred's brother Lee has insisted on an elegant

Jewish funeral home—the Frank Campbell Mortuary on Madison at Eightieth—and Georgia has no will to fight him.

But she does battle Lee over the coffin ("Plain pine, it's what he *wanted*") and finds it, finally, in the Hasidic Jewish neighborhood of Williamsburg in Brooklyn. She will tell friends that she spent the night ripping out the lining of pleated pink satin and replacing it with plain white linen. Later, she will amend this dramatic little fiction, telling a Yale librarian that she merely gave the funeral home a white cotton sheet and instructed them to use it to cover the pink lining.

The Sunday morning obituary in the *Times* has announced that no funeral is planned, so only twenty or so mourners—the family and closest friends—meet at the funeral home. Stoic, aloof, without tears, Georgia retreats within herself, acknowledging no one. The family is tight-lipped, resentful. Dorothy Norman (of course) weeps loudly, half-hysterical, and one of Stieglitz's nieces comforts her with a stage whisper loud enough for everyone to hear. "We never worried about Alfred because we knew you were always there, caring."

The unkindest cut, Georgia thinks, and bites her lip until she tastes blood. No one comforts her. No one dares. When the ordeal is over, she climbs into the hearse and takes Stieglitz in his coffin to the Fresh Pond Crematory in Maspeth, Queens. In a few weeks, she and his niece Elizabeth will bury his ashes under a tree near Lake George. "He loved the water," she says. "I put him where he could hear it."

Georgia maintains a distant dignity at the funeral home, but that is only a façade. Beneath it, anger seethes. The next day, she telephones Dorothy Norman and explodes, her rage fueled by the public humiliations of the long, embarrassing affair. "Your relationship with my husband was absolutely disgusting," she says through gritted teeth, and inflicts a long, slashing tirade, demanding complete control of An

American Place. "I'm taking over the gallery," she says. "Remove your belongings and return your keys. And stay away. I don't want to see you there ever again."

Naïve and almost guilelessly romantic, Dorothy Norman has always considered her affair with Stieglitz to be fatefully preordained, a spiritual joining of two soulmates with nothing of the tawdry about it. Now, she dissolves in tears, so deeply wounded by Georgia's violent hatred that she cannot speak.

Having disposed of Dorothy, Georgia closes herself into the apartment, refusing to see the Stieglitz family or friends. Or Maria, who has followed her to New York on the train, arriving too late on Sunday to come to the funeral home. At Georgia's request, she has brought personal things from the New Mexico ranch: the checkbook, important papers, clothes and shoes, as well as her leather paint box. She is met at the station by Henwar, whom she knows from his visits to the ranch.

Henwar takes Maria to Georgia's apartment, where she waits in the lobby while he carries the things upstairs. Georgia dispatches him back downstairs to tell Maria that she isn't seeing anybody. Apologetic, visibly uncomfortable with the message, Henwar invites Maria to stay at his apartment. He can stay with the Normans—he and Dorothy are friends.

Grateful but reluctant to impose, Maria checks into a hotel and spends the next several days visiting Georgia's exhibit at the Museum of Modern Art, seeing one or two Broadway shows, talking with some of the people she knows from their ranch visits, and making repeated efforts to see Georgia.

But when Georgia finally consents, the meeting only creates another rupture in their increasingly fragile relationship. Maria brings a basket of food, a book, and a Beethoven recording, hoping to recreate one of their evenings at the ranch. Georgia, gaunt and hollow-eyed, still tightly wound and barely under control, accuses her of trying to manage her, to possess her, to *smother* her. She subjects her to a tongue lashing for a sadly trivial thing: a canvas stretching tool is missing from the leather paint box she asked Maria to bring to New York. (It later appears that the tool was taken from the box when it was stowed in the train's baggage car.) With a casual cruelty, Georgia introduces Maria to her current housekeeper as one of her "New Mexico slaves."

Has Maria presumed too much, hoped for too much? Has she thought that with Stieglitz's death, Georgia might turn to her for comfort? Has she imagined that some sort of new bridge might be built between them? That they might become, finally, friends? If so, she must be disheartened—and even more so when Henwar tells her about the cruel treatment of Dorothy, who (Henwar says) does not deserve O'Keeffe's fury. Rebuffed, Maria takes the train back to Santa Fe. A few weeks later, she will write, "Listen, O'Keeffe, you made me feel as though I suffocated you in New York—and I haven't gotten over it yet—the damned things I learned and the hurt of it."

Georgia will wonder, briefly, what those "damned things" are. Maria can't be still thinking about that business with the housekeeper, can she? Really, it is very foolish to be upset by something so silly. She *is* a slave, isn't she? Anyway, whatever the problem, Maria will get over it and apologize. She always does. Georgia dismisses the whole affair, for it is such an inconsequential thing.

But not for Maria. A month after her return to New Mexico, Maria will write, with a caustic humor, "I have always felt that I ought to save you from something. And I don't know quite what nor quite why." Perhaps, she thinks, she is trying to save Georgia from herself.

On reflection, she adds with a bitter resignation, "I think I would so much rather write to you than ever see you again."

Maria isn't the only one who is about to give up on Georgia. Those of Stieglitz's friends and family who watched his health fail and saw her leaving him every year now view her behavior as unforgivable. Members of the family go to court to contest Stieglitz's will (in which he left everything to his wife) on the grounds that she was not dutiful, that she left him alone for a full half year, every year, and that she kept her own name.

Beaumont and Nancy Newhall, devoted friends who were with Stieglitz a day or two before his death, are deeply troubled by what they see as her irrational behavior. In a letter to Stieglitz's friend and photographer Ansel Adams, Nancy writes that Georgia gave Dorothy Norman a "malignant whipping" over the telephone, and that in May, Georgia arrived at a party at the Newhalls', glimpsed Dorothy, screamed, and rushed back to the elevator. Nancy is afraid that the tirade Georgia inflicted on Dorothy may be a prelude to another complete nervous breakdown, like the prostration Georgia suffered a decade before. And Adams, who has traveled with Georgia and who took the photo of her coyly seductive glance at Orville Cox, replies sadly, "I am convinced that Georgia is psychopathic."

She might well be, especially in the days immediately after Stieglitz's death. The guilt she feels is agonizing, ferocious, a tiger gnawing at her insides, keeping her from sleeping or eating proper meals. She knows she should have returned to New York when the doctor telephoned with the urgent news of the angina attack. She will spend the next three years doing penance in a vain attempt to expiate that guilt.

And even that won't be enough. Her burden of culpability will trouble her for the rest of her life—until someone knocks at her door, a lean, dark, handsome young man come to be her hired man, then becoming something else altogether. Juan Hamilton was born in the year Stieglitz died and looks so much like her husband that she will believe he might be a reincarnation. The young man will believe it, too, and will out-Stieglitz Stieglitz in as many ways as possible.

But until that happens, Georgia must live with the loss. She admired and loved Stieglitz, although she would say later that he was "much more wonderful in his work than as a human being" and that living with him required her to put up with a "great deal of contradictory nonsense." But as much as she grieves his loss as a part of her daily life (all those letters!), she cannot share that grief, can only keep it entirely to herself. She knows that others see her as cold and uncaring, but she is accustomed to their disapproval. She simply does now what she has always done when she felt besieged.

Late in the year, she leaves New York and returns to New Mexico, lost in relief that it is over at last and grief that he is gone—and guilt, of course, always that guilt. She paints, the best one a memory of Stieglitz, "Old Crow Feather," a name he sometimes called himself. The painting is called "A Black Bird with Snow-Covered Red Hills" and depicts a stylized crow, soaring across a blue sky between two white mounds. Years later, in her autobiography, she would write, "One morning the world was covered in snow. It became another painting . . . a black bird flying, always there, always going away."

But even if she felt urgent about painting, there wouldn't be time. Her guilt and sense of obligation drive her to manage the massive legacy that Stieglitz left behind. It will be no easy task.

For starters, there is his 1937 last will and testament, naming her as his primary heir and executor. There is some $148,000 in stocks and bonds, part of it in a Stieglitz family trust valued at $130,000. When some members of the family contest the bequest, she will hold out for three years, then prevail, with an agreement to accept only the income for her lifetime—and is much amused, years later, when she realizes that she has outlived the last Stieglitz challenger.

There are other more consequential matters to be settled. An inveterate collector of modern art, Stieglitz owned (and often exhibited) paintings and drawings by Picasso, Kandinsky, and Rodin; Toulouse-Lautrec posters and prints; bronzes by Matisse and Brancusi—and more. Altogether, his estate contains some 850 paintings, watercolors, drawings, and sculptures. In addition, there are hundreds of photographs, over fifty thousand letters and documents, and shelves and boxes and stacks of books. What to do, what to do, *what to do*?

Stieglitz never pursued exhibits of his collections outside his galleries. But Georgia conceives the idea of honoring him with a show—no, two shows. Calling on her friends James Sweeny and Daniel Rich, both museum curators, she arranges for a double exhibit: Stieglitz's own work, together with the works in his collection. Art critic Henry McBride remarks off-handedly in one of his *Sun* pieces that of course her reputation will also be burnished by shows of Stieglitz's work, but she simply wants the exhibits done well. She puts a great deal of effort into the selection and the hanging. Both open together in 1947 at the Museum of Modern Art in New York and later travel to the Art Institute of Chicago.

But the larger and even more daunting task is disposing of Stieglitz's collections, to which Georgia dedicates herself for the next three years. Most of that time she spends in that dark, cramped little apartment on Fifty-Fourth, eating meals cooked for her by her cook-housekeeper (one after the other), and walking a daily block to the Place, where the art is stored and where she works with her new assistant, Doris Bry.

She chooses only a very few things to keep for her own. To Maria, she writes, "Going over Alfred's photographs adds much to my life—Rodin adds—Toulouse-Lautrec says something—Picasso a little—Mostly I came to some conclusions that summed up mean that I don't want or need any of those things."

So, determined to be rid of it, Georgia gives it away, almost all of it, eight-hundred-and-some pieces. Stieglitz resented museums, accusing them of serving as stodgy arbiters of the art world's status quo who habitually neglected the avant-garde, where new ideas and concepts are born. But Georgia wants people to see his collections and since he left no instructions, it is up to her to decide where each piece should go. After a great deal of thought and extended discussion with possible recipients, she divides the lot among seven museums, on the condition that they will keep the work accessible. The largest groups go to the National Gallery of Art in Washington, the Metropolitan Museum in New York, and the Art Institute of Chicago. Smaller groups go to the Boston Museum of Fine Arts, the Philadelphia Museum of Art, the San Francisco Museum of Modern Art, and Fisk University. She doesn't think Stieglitz would be especially pleased. In fact, she imagines him peering over the tops of his spectacles at her list and growling, gruff and surly, over each of her decisions. But by the time she is finished, she simply doesn't care what he would have thought. She is just glad to find respectable homes for the massive collection, homes that reflect well on him. And on her.

Stieglitz's photographs must go, too. But these are his artistic legacy in a way that his collections are not, and the task is even more difficult. She copies each of Stieglitz's prints and gives a master set—at least one print of every mounted photograph in his possession at the time of his death, 1,317 altogether—to the National Gallery. Prudently, she keeps the negatives.

And those nude portraits? What to do with them? Stieglitz had told Nancy Newhall that he expected Georgia to destroy them. Instead, she includes one print of each of her nudes in the master set. Out of the more than 150 photos he took of his mistress, she includes just nineteen.

But the most mammoth task of all is the disposal of Stieglitz's fifty thousand letters and papers. Georgia settles on the Beinecke Library at Yale University. She very much likes Donald Gallup, the erudite, charming thirty-something curator there. Unlike the art and the photographs, though, she decides that the documents are not to be immediately accessible. For example, the twenty-five thousand letters she and Stieglitz exchanged between 1915 and 1946, some of them running to fifty or more pages, will be sealed for twenty years. Later, she will decide that they should be sealed for twenty years after her death. She bundles them into boxes. She doesn't read any of them.

While Georgia knows that her work represents penance for sins of omission and commission, she is fully aware that she could not have managed it without the excellent, experienced help of Doris Bry. Doris is a slender, dark-haired, young woman in her late twenties. She wears neatly tailored suits and flat heels and is quite familiar with Stieglitz's photography. In fact, when Georgia meets her, she is working for Dorothy Norman. Georgia takes a distinct pleasure in luring her away. Her offer of $65 a week is higher than the $35 Mrs. Norman was paying. And indisputably higher than the $17 a week she pays Maria for nine months of construction work on the Abiquiu house.

Doris is undoubtedly worth the money. The daughter of a Jewish woolen manufacturer and a classical violinist, she is the cultured product of a cultured family, prestigious private schools, and Wellesley College. She will be an enormous resource for O'Keeffe for the next thirty years, working at first as her assistant, then as her curator, agent, and exclusive dealer, a post that Georgia encourages her to believe she will hold for the rest of her life.

But Doris is wrong. She will hold that post until the tall, dark, handsome young man knocks at Georgia's door, the young man who might be a reincarnation of Stieglitz. He comes to be her hired man, but soon becomes her intimate friend, her companion, her caretaker, her heir. Within a few years, replacing Doris, her curator, her agent, and her dealer—a second Stieglitz.

The replacement is painful for everyone. The ensuing lawsuits, countersuits, and arbitration will damage reputations, cost huge amounts of money, and take eight years to settle. "There's no way anything can pay for eight years wasted like that," a bitter Doris will tell the *Washington Post*. "It was a Kafkaesque game, and I'm sure my life has been shortened by it."

But until then, the competent Doris does her job. "When O'Keeffe hired me," she tells a later biographer, "she wanted to teach me everything so she could be free to paint. After a while, I did most of the work while she was in New Mexico." Thoughtfully, she adds, "I'm always a little irritated to read how she spent years settling the Stieglitz estate. She did the thinking, but if a letter went to a museum, chances are that I drafted and wrote it. There is a certain amount of drudgery in taking care of eight hundred paintings." Maria Chabot could undoubtedly sympathize with Doris's irritation after hearing Georgia tell countless people how she had rebuilt the Abiquiu house without ever mentioning Maria's name. Bry adds that O'Keeffe was a "very strong person" while she herself was young at the time, easily influenced and "easily consumed." Maria might sympathize with this, too.

In these early years after Stieglitz's death, Georgia has engaged another helper, as well—this one entirely unpaid. She uses Dorothy Norman to do the massive work of putting Stieglitz's piles of disorganized papers into order—perhaps, in Georgia's mind, a kind of consolation prize. Or a punishment. Or both. If Dorothy resents Georgia, she keeps it well hidden. She was always eager to serve Alfred during his life and his death hasn't changed a thing. She agrees to this labor of love, writes to Stieglitz's many correspondents requesting copies of letters they may have exchanged, and begins assembling and sorting. In the end, her editorial contribution to the archive will amount to hundreds of hours and something like fifty thousand pages. O'Keeffe doesn't acknowledge it.

About Dorothy, Georgia tells Maria, "I have let her put all his papers in order—it had to be done—I didn't intend to do it . . . she likes doing it so why not do it—I've just never thought she was creative and I never change my mind about it." O'Keeffe knows her women. Doris, Dorothy, and Maria free her of work she wants done but doesn't want to—or can't—do herself.

There is one more person Georgia will find essential to her future, but only for the next decade or so. Edith Halpert is a powerful, squarely built, forty-something woman with gray-streaked dark hair, emphatically dark eyebrows, a fondness for vivid scarlet lipstick, and an assertively confident style. Halpert opened the Downtown Gallery in 1926. A Russian Jew, she is among the few art dealers Stieglitz tolerated, so he sometimes loaned works by his artists to her shows.

Georgia knows that Halpert will be glad to exhibit and sell her work, but she wants to try *her* hand at that first. She has renewed the lease on the Place and, with the help of artist and friend Charles Marin, tries to keep it open. But she doesn't take readily to bargaining. When a collector asks if he might purchase her *White Canadian Barn*, she replies brusquely, "If I sell it the price will not be low and I am not at all sure that you would be interested." And anyway, the small Stieglitz circle has become even smaller. Dorothy Norman is no longer around to pay the gallery rent and handle the dreary business of keeping it open. And Georgia is simply not as congenial a gallery owner as Stieglitz, who thrived on extended conversations with strangers whom Georgia can barely tolerate. Everyone agrees that without him, it's just not the same.

But she perseveres at the Place until October 1950, when she hangs thirty-one canvases, almost everything she's completed after Stieglitz's death: eight of the Abiquiu patio (there's that *door*), nine cottonwood trees, several landscapes, flowers, and antlers. Confident of the critics' reception, she writes to Alfred's nephew (now her financial advisor), "I have always been willing to bet on myself you know—and been willing to stand on what I am and can do even when the world isn't much with me . . . I don't even mind if I don't win—but for some unaccountable reason I expect to win . . ."

But the critics see little worth praising, attendance is sparse, and sales are sparser. The *New York Times* slights the show with a single brief paragraph. Georgia takes the canvases down, closes the Place, and moves her work to Halpert's Downtown Gallery, now located on East Fifty-First Street, uptown. She may be philosophical about it, but the critical failure of the show leads to a retreat from the easel that will last for several years. Still, her arrangement with Edith Halpert allows her work to be shown in New York, in a well-regarded gallery by a woman she knows and whose judgment she trusts, at least for the next decade.

And at last, she can begin to give her full attention to her new life in the New Mexican desert, in the house Maria has built for her.

Chapter Eleven

Choices
Maria

This is Good Friday . . . In a few minutes I will go up to Bruce Hayter's to dig up chrysanthemums—and from there to Abiquiu. I have poplars I dug up yesterday in the car. We've planted many cottonwoods and locusts—very good big trees rooted up [by] the SCS [Soil Conservation Service] bulldozer I've had working at Mary's. Saturday I hope to have help at Abiquiu—to plant. Then Sunday in the Piedra Lumbre. Anselmo [the cat] will go with me . . . It will be fine fun when you come. I look forward to it very much.

Or maybe you're dead? I've not heard in so long—

—Maria Chabot to Georgia O'Keeffe
Los Luceros, April 15, 1949

While O'Keeffe was paying her penance in New York, I was occupied with her house in Abiquiu and with other, more personal challenges. It would be three full years before I finished the work and came up for air—work tedious to describe at length but tough to telescope without blunting the significance of what I was doing and what it meant to me.

The house was more difficult than it might have been because I was balancing O'Keeffe's construction project with my obligations to Mary Wheelwright and the orchards and fields (and the ditch!) at Los Luceros, and to my parents in San Antonio. My mother had never fully recovered from her hip fracture, and now my father was dying—not with a generous suddenness, like my brother and Stieglitz, here one moment, gone the next—but with agonizing slowness, a wasting-away that stretched like a ghostly diminishment over a long six months.

I was my father's last child, born when he was in his late forties and his first two children were already adults. He was now in his eighties, and whatever we had once been to one another was submerged in the painful present of his illness. Day after silent day, I watched him lie in his bed, sometimes awake, more often asleep, his world narrowing to the business of each breath and bowel movement, to the swallowing of a few spoonsful of biscuits softened in milk. Life—if that's what it can be called—continued through the autumn of 1946 into March of 1947. We could not afford nurses, so Mother and I did that job as faithfully as we could. He died on March 5, undoubtedly glad to be done with it and with us.

I wrote often to O'Keeffe in those months, mostly with questions about the house. It was a snowy winter in New Mexico and no work could be done there—and anyway, I was in Texas. But choices had to be made, many choices, about many things. About the electrical system, the water supply, the plumbing, the windows and doors and floors. Does it matter whether we have willows or aspen for the *latillas*? Does Georgia want a skylight in the studio? If so, at which end? Is there to be a fireplace in her bedroom? A corner door in the kitchen for better access to adjoining rooms? Would it be cork or rubber or tile for the floors? Metal cabinets in the kitchen, or wood?

The issue of my payment came up again, too. She sent me a check for $600, which I chose to return. "What I am doing for you at Abiquiu," I wrote huffily, "is a thing that is well paid or not paid at all. I don't think $600 for nine months of work is good pay. Any laborer we hire gets more than that and he doesn't use his head in the matter or his heart . . . I smile just a little bit, Miss O'Keeffe, at the shortness of the string you hold me on."

Georgia returned the check with a reply that was both curt and oblique, informing me that while she didn't consider the money an "adequate" final payment, she thought it "protected the finality of payment" (whatever that gobbledygook meant) and that she had made "adequate provision" for me in her will (which of course could be changed, as my father liked to point out). But I finally accepted her money. It went toward my father's doctor bills.

On and on it went, a litany of choices, almost without end. O'Keeffe might be living her New York life, but if she didn't tell me what she wanted, construction on her house would stall. Or I would be forced into making the choices myself, based on what I imagined to be her preferences—which is what usually happened. In May, she wrote that she had so many decisions to make and things to tend to in New York that she simply could not put her mind to the Abiquiu house.

"You decide," she wrote.

And so I did. But there were still a great many decisions to be made when Georgia finally arrived in New Mexico in late June of that year—1947, the first full year after Stieglitz's death—and I was usually able to prevail on her to spend two or three days a week with me in Abiquiu. My mother was with me that summer, too, and I saw Dorothy when I could. Which meant that there were plenty of ways to divide my attention.

But we muddled through, and by the time O'Keeffe went back to New York that December, I was satisfied. The adobe walls were up. The *vigas* were placed and the *latillas* laid and the roof was on. Most of the floors were in, although the floor coverings—linoleum, tile, cork—were not yet chosen. Altogether, the project was coming along better than I had any right to expect. I enjoyed working alongside the local builders and subcontractors. I was learning what I needed to know about house-building and also about myself as a manager, especially when it came to dealing with a large and disparate group of men who had never worked for a woman. I was learning about managing money, too. At the end of the year, I sent Georgia a detailed accounting of expenses.

While all this was going on, I was also learning about farming in New Mexico—and about myself as a farmer. At Los Luceros, the corn was in by the first of May, the wheat was up, and the alfalfa field was a lovely leaf-green carpet. Estelle, the Los Luceros sow, had produced a litter of eight squirmy piglets and I was mothering twenty-five just-hatched turkey poults. I slept with them the first couple of weeks because somebody had to keep an eye on the tricky kerosene stove that warmed the coop.

I had persuaded Mary to buy a 1941 ton-and-a-half Ford flatbed and a new plow for the tractor, so we were entirely mechanized now. She couldn't help but see that her ranch—after two seasons in my care—was the neatest and best run in the valley. As for me, the more I did, the more I knew I could do and that gave me the confidence to try even more. To choose *new* things, like the dozen grapevines I planted in the Los Luceros garden: four Black Monukkas and eight white, nearly seedless French grapes called Seibel 9110, both good for eating and for wine. I bought enough for the Abiquiu garden, too.

Something worth mentioning happened in the early autumn—worth mentioning because it fits into the pattern that included O'Keeffe's young men: Maurice, Henwar, Eliot, Cady, Johnny. Georgia had agreed to take part in a film that Henwar was making for the US State

Department's state-by-state series on artists and their environments. It was to be a short documentary called *The Land of Enchantment.*

Henwar had told me about the film when I was in New York after Stieglitz's death and asked for my suggestions about Navajo or Puebloan artists to include. "The people at State want an Indian," he said. "You've got connections out there—who do you suggest?"

I recommended Maria Martinez at San Ildefonso Pueblo, on the Rio Grande not far from Los Luceros. She made blackware pottery, elegant glazed pots with matte black decorations on polished black surfaces, fired in a beehive kiln at the pueblo. I had met her a decade earlier, when I was working with the Santa Fe Indian Market. Now, I saw her whenever I dropped in at the pueblo, which was quite often, since some of the men were working with me on the Abiquiu house and we had become friends. With Maria's help, I also arranged with the pueblo's leaders to do a costumed rain dance for the film.

I was at the ranch when Henwar and his camera crew arrived to film O'Keeffe's segment. Ill-advisedly, he brought the attractive young woman he was seeing. All smiles, Georgia came out of the house to greet him, but when she saw that he wasn't alone, she exploded. "Nobody comes to work with a woman!" she yelled, and stormed back into the house. When I finally persuaded her to participate in the shooting, she wore a scowl during every single frame. And poor Henwar was banished for life, cut off for having offended her.

When Georgia flew back to New York in December, I wrapped up the year's work at Abiquiu and took the bus to San Antonio to be with my mother in a house that was much too large and expensive for her and would be sold as soon as she could bring herself to do that. I had finally wrapped up my novel, although I didn't have much confidence in it. Neither did the publishers I submitted it to. One of them thought it needed a stronger story line. Another remarked that there wasn't much of a market for a novel about Mexico in these postwar days. Still another said I had promise as a writer and suggested I try my hand at a novel about an Indian princess. He thought that would sell.

But since I didn't know any Indian princesses, I wasn't inclined to take that advice. I had to conclude, sadly, that I didn't have much of a future in fiction. Maybe I should consider nonfiction—writing about northern New Mexico, for instance. I knew I could do that: witness my published magazine articles about Navajo and Puebloan arts and crafts. When I first met O'Keeffe, I had thought I would write about her and her life at the ranch. I still had some ideas about that, although she had made it even more clear that I wasn't to write about her. I also thought about a collection of our letters. A publisher might be interested in that.

But the way the new year—1948—was shaping up, there wouldn't be much time to write. In January, O'Keeffe sent me a thousand of the three thousand dollars I needed to start work on her house that year and promised the other two thousand when the project got underway again. I added, casually, that she could pay me whenever it was convenient for her. "I'm not building the house for compensation," I wrote to her. This was true. And so was this ungraceful addendum: "If I had I would have quit long ago. So do not feel indebted."

I might think better of those words at the end of another year, but at the time, they felt right. I said what I meant. Foolish as it might seem, I was building the house because of the house itself, which was a personal challenge. And because I admired O'Keeffe. And because I'm loyal to my friends—although by this time it should have been clear that my claim to O'Keeffe's friendship was not matched by hers to me.

At Los Luceros that year, the Colorado Growers Association was doubling their hotbed output to eighteen million cauliflower plants and I was planting a ton (literally—two thousand pounds) of field pea seed. I had agreed to feed the Colorado team when they came to work, and one week, there were eight of them. I put a turkey in the oven—the second twenty-five-pound turkey I had executed, plucked, dressed, roasted, and served that week. To Georgia, I wrote that putting a turkey in the oven was beginning to seem as easy as frying a skillet of bacon. Oh, and by the middle of April, Joe Posey and I had planted six hundred new peaches, apricots, and pears in Mary's orchards. We had started a small vineyard down by the river and were planting vines. Dawn to dark, we were busy.

But there were beautiful moments. One April day as the Fordson and I were plowing the lettuce field, a young hawk flew along with me, staying within three or four feet of the tractor. He was intent on catching whatever might be stirred up: snakes, field mice, a frightened rabbit, grasshoppers. He had beautifully translucent wings and a rosy tail that he spread wide. He seemed entirely unaware of my presence, content to view me and the tractor as another hybrid creature in his springtime universe of creatures. I was never so close to the daily affairs of birds as I was that spring on the tractor.

My life got even busier and more complicated when I agreed to take on the Lucero *acequia.* Joe and Polito and I had spent the early spring months cutting the willows and chamisa out of miles of secondary irrigation ditches, all of which ran off the Acequia Madre, the mother ditch that supplies water to large tracts of land on the east side of the river. It left the Rio Grande some three miles upstream of Los Luceros and returned to the river two miles south. Along that five miles, smaller ditches—laterals—branched off, taking water to each of the farms along the river. These laterals were controlled by headgates that were opened to let the water flow in and closed to stop it from flowing, all on a prearranged schedule. The mother ditch was closed for the winter in November and opened again in late March, but before the season's irrigation could begin, it had to be cleaned. This was a community effort in which all the *parciantes* (the individual irrigators who owned rights to that water) removed the invasive weeds, willows, cottonwood sprouts, dead skunks, and tin cans from their sections.

There were about 125 *parciantes* on the mother ditch. When it came time to elect the ditch *mayordomo* for 1948, they chose me. Some people thought it was strange that the *parciantes* would elect a *gringa*, much less unanimously, as they did. Half the men were glad to have me do the dirty, hands-on, time-killing job that nobody else wanted. The other half were afraid of me. But since Los Luceros was the largest farm on the ditch and entitled to the most water, I felt obligated to accept their choice. Like it or not, I was the new *mayordoma*, with a lot to learn.

The cleaning had always been done by hand, with shovels, axes, machetes—whatever the job required. The work usually took two weekends plus a couple of extra days plus a chorus of bellyaching. But when the appointed day arrived, I brought in an excavator with a hydraulic shovel. I had walked the ditch often enough to know where the three-foot-wide channel needed to be widened—*más ancho*, wider here, wider—or where the bank was overgrown with willows and wild rose canes that needed to be dug out. So I was able to direct the excavator where it could do the most good. With plenty of additional shovel work, we were done in half the usual time, ready for the frothy, churning roil of muddy water that would fill the ditch and its laterals when the main headgate was opened to let the river in.

The ditch ran better than ever that year, and I became something of a local celebrity. When I met one of the *parciantes* at the market in Española, he would take off his hat respectfully. I was entitled by law, you see, to go wherever the mother ditch went, and I usually spent several hours a week, checking headgates and making sure nobody took more water than they had a right to. This meant many more hours on the telephone, refereeing the distribution I had organized. It was my job to deliver bad-with-the-good messages: "You'll be happy to know, Emiliano, that you can have water for four hours every Thursday." (Brief pause for thanks.) "But please don't be too unhappy when I tell you that your hours are between midnight and four a.m." (Longer pause for Emiliano's muttered curses.) It is a nerve-wracking business, this responsibility of water.

The work was eminently satisfying, but between the orchards and the alfalfa, the grapes and cauliflower and lettuce and the ditch, I had my hands full. There was O'Keeffe's house, of course, which required me to spend at least three days a week in Abiquiu. We were installing the kitchen and the bathrooms and the heating system that summer, and it all had to be done right—and done over again when it was (inevitably) done wrong. I had made a deal with Mr. Bode to buy power from his generator at twelve dollars a month. Fair, I thought, since that was what he charged the church. In May, I was able to tell Georgia that the fir *vigas* for her ceilings had bleached out beautifully, naked and white and dry. The aspen poles, though, would have to come from the Sangre de Cristos. I would drive up to Truchas to see what I could find there.

And since the outside perimeter wall was now completed, I could get started on Georgia's garden. She was one of the *parciantes* on the Abiquiu ditch, so that cleaning had to be done, as well as restoring the laterals in the garden itself. In late March, I planted another bed of strawberries there, more grapes, and more fruit trees: a Peking persimmon and a black American persimmon to fertilize it. And apricots, filberts, and almonds, as well as tamarisks and white roses. Now that the weather was warming, the garden would quickly transform itself into a lovely green oasis, a lush, protected *refugio* on that dry and dusty mesa where the wind never seemed to stop blowing.

But we were facing an interesting—and frustrating—problem, quite small by definition but large in its implications. For a hundred-dollar contribution to the health clinic fund, I had persuaded the village to give O'Keeffe a quit-claim to the eastern side of the Arroyo de Los Muertos, which lay along the west of the house. When the deal was done, I planned to install the large butane tank there, out of sight. The problem: a neighbor named Finiano had erected a tiny hut about the size of a packing crate on the edge of the arroyo, where he kept two old Barred Rock hens and a Rhode Island red. He adamantly refused to move his three chickens, who had called this coop home all their lives.

Of course, it wasn't just his chickens that Finiano was defending. Everyone in town (including me) understood that he felt it his bounden duty as a courageous Abiqueño to raise his fist in the face of the Anglo invader—symbolized in this case by three old hens pitted against a butane tank the size of a pickup truck. Some were grateful that he took his obligation and the principle upon which it was based with such seriousness, while others brushed it off as a futile and quixotic gesture. For them, the house was just the latest manifestation of the Anglo annexation of Nuevo México that had begun nearly a century before. It was time to capitulate, they advised, especially since the health clinic (another Anglo invasion, this one benign, unless you were Father Bickhaus) had recently opened and nurses were available most days. The wisdom of this advice was demonstrated when Martina

López sprained her ankle bringing a bucket of water from the spring and had only to hobble across the plaza to be treated.

Still, Finiano's chickens turned into a matter for the entire village to resolve, and everyone had a point of view. Their discussions took a month or more. But the chickens were finally accommodated elsewhere, Finiano was appeased, and the butane tank was installed. The rest of the village would be burning piñon in their fireplaces and cookstoves, but O'Keeffe would be warm in her butane-fueled winter home.

The story stayed in my mind. It reminded me of something I'd once heard in Taos, where Mabel Dodge Luhan's adobe mansion comprised three stories, seventeen rooms, central heating, and bathtubs and indoor toilets, along with five guesthouses, a gatehouse, barns, and stables—while Mabel praised the local Puebloans for their inherent "lack of materialism." They were spiritually pure, she thought, caring nothing for the trappings of modern life. One local Taos Indian took offense and wrote to the *Taos Star*, offering to trade places with her. She could come to the pueblo and drink the muddy water that flowed down from the mountain, while he and his wife and five children would drink clean water from her many faucets.

The tale of Finiano's hens versus the butane tank fueled my own increasingly uneasy ambivalence about this project. Watching the house come to life and begin to resume something of its former importance in the village, I was on the one hand deeply satisfied and the Abiqueños—most of them, anyway—were pleased, as well. Whatever the poverty of their small dwellings and the difficulty of life on that mesa, they took it as a personal achievement that this important house in their little village was being restored to its former glory and would be occupied by America's most prominent *gringa* artist, with modern plumbing, gas, and electrical systems, as well as radiant-heat wall panels to warm the cold rooms in winter. And all for one single woman, while some of them lived with ten family members in three rooms. But I was uncomfortable, for O'Keeffe's was the only house in Abiquiu that had so many modern conveniences. It stood out, in the same way that a castle must have stood out in a medieval village.

And that wasn't where we'd started. Back when O'Keeffe and I had first talked about the house, both of us had imagined something much closer to the traditional Native houses. In it, Georgia said, she hoped to live what we called the "hogan life"—a modest Native structure, few possessions, the aesthetic of simplicity. She often said that she could live with nothing but a bed to sleep in, a tree stump for a table, and an orange crate to sit on.

But as we began to confront questions about how she might actually *live* in the Abiquiu house, the compromises began. Big windows and skylights, easy-to-care-for floors, warm rooms, plugs in the wall—all this was quite natural and necessary for a mid-twentieth-century householder. But when you start adding large modern windows, plumbing, and electricity to a traditional dwelling in an ancient village, you necessarily create a hybrid structure. Years later, when the house would be nominated as a National Historic Landmark, the supporting document would point out that among the many compromises, the "most assertively modernist" was the addition of those large picture windows.

"That is the painful truth," I said to Georgia. "Your house may look like a traditional adobe, but it is a mish-mash, a compromise. It obviously belongs to an Anglo *millonaria* who lives behind a wall."

Georgia didn't respond. I didn't expect her to. She had more than enough on her plate and an ambiguous house that was or wasn't a hogan was not something she wanted to think about. But I had to think about it because I was *building* it. And beside the traditional adobes of Abiquiu, this one didn't feel much different from the generic postwar ranch-style houses with big picture windows that were going up in the new suburbs around San Antonio—except that the walls were built of adobe, with a hand-hewn wooden door that opened to an enclosed patio. And it had a fabulous view.

But it was what it was. I had mostly given up writing and O'Keeffe's house was now my art. What Georgia had seen, she liked, and over the three and a half decades she would live at the edge of the mesa, it would become her own powerful work of art and an image of her mythic personage.

And if I wasn't entirely pleased with it . . . well, I wasn't going to live there. And I didn't have much room to talk, did I? I was living the peony life at Los Luceros.

❖

The year brought another, different, and (for me) more troublesome complication. Her name was Doris Bry, a snobbish Easterner a few years younger than I and with a vastly superior education. At least, she thought so, although I daresay I had read more widely and traveled more extensively than she had, for all her expensive years at Wellesley. She also thought my Texas accent was "amusing" and wondered aloud whether I spent a lot of time at rodeos and roundups when I went back to San Antonio for the winter. O'Keeffe told me with satisfaction that she had hired her away from Dorothy Norman and that she was an excellent slave, especially when it came to typing, filing, and sending letters to museums.

But Doris hadn't yet learned that she was a slave, or that her responsibilities were supposed to be confined to typing, filing, and letter-writing. The two of us had rubbed each other the wrong way the previous fall, but this year . . . well, it was much more explosive. She had a habit of telling me what I should be doing when it came to the Abiquiu house—and the Ghost Ranch house, too, although I no longer had any responsibilities there.

Still, I probably wouldn't have minded if Doris hadn't insisted on jumping in and making silly changes in the Abiquiu garden, where I had been working for three summers and was just beginning to see results. And if she hadn't had the temerity one day to command Chopo to leave the work he was doing on the subflooring (which had to be finished before we could lay Georgia's cork flooring) and plant some flowers she had ordered for the garden—tender flowers that might thrive in her part of the country but could not survive our desert heat or our bitter winter cold.

Not only that, she had him pull out some of the native herbs I had transplanted into the garden from the wild places where O'Keeffe and I had foraged for them in the canyons behind Ghost Ranch. I thought Georgia would like to have them here, where she could harvest them more easily, and they might remind her of the wild things we had found together. There was *chimaja*, always the first green thing to appear in the spring, best when it lent its assertive wild-parsley flavor to a pot of beans or stew or to meat or roasted vegetables. There was wild spinach, *quelites*, and *cebolla*, wild onion, perfect for *cebolla en escabeche*, or pickled onions. And for tea, of course *yerba buena* (spearmint) and *poleó* (peppermint). Chopo protested that these were important plants and should not be destroyed, but to Doris' Eastern eyes, they were weeds and nothing would do but to have them out, now, today, before they went to seed. Is it any wonder that I blew up when I saw the carnage?

And it wasn't the first time Doris had tried to make her mark on the garden. The previous fall, she had ordered two hundred raspberry plants (when a dozen would have been more than sufficient), to be delivered in October, precisely the wrong time of year. We plant berries in late March and early April here, so I'd had the serious bother of keeping the damned things alive all winter. To make matters worse, they were sent without identification, so I had no idea what varieties they were, or whether summer fruiting or ever-bearing, or how tall or how wide they might be when they matured, which you need to know at planting time.

So yes, it's true. I blew up at Doris and I'm sure I behaved rudely—not because I was jealous but because Doris was one of those know-it-alls who don't know much of anything—except typing and filing, of course. To Georgia, later, I wrote, tongue-in-cheek, "Naturally I want to know if you are bringing Doris out. Better let me hear about that ahead of time! Keep her in New York. There isn't room enough out here, and I haven't time—this year—to fight—nor strength—with all there is to do."

Tongue-in-cheek? Well, that's probably what I wanted Georgia to think. But I was being honest. She would call it jealousy when she berated me about my rudeness to Doris, but that's because she enjoyed it when people around her (her friends, but especially her slaves) were jealous of their positions with her, when they began to compete with one another. She cultivated that. I think it made her feel special, superior, in charge.

And you may call it jealousy if you choose. But I was working hard, long hours to build a house for a woman who didn't seem sure she would actually live there. I was deeply annoyed when Doris (who would *never* live there) marched in and began ordering the hired help to do things in the garden that—

Enough. There's never any point in getting stuck in somebody else's problems. But when O'Keeffe came to the Abiquiu house when Chopo and I were laying new gravel in the patio and began scolding me for being rude to Doris, I blew up again. I accused her of not caring about the Abiquiu house and of extending her time in New York because she was enjoying her friends and the art scene there, where people made a great deal of her as a famous artist. There would be none of that here, and she'd just have to get used to it.

O'Keeffe wasn't prepared to hear this any more than she had been prepared to hear the things I had said to her about Maurice several years before. As far as she was concerned, I was not only jealous, but psychologically immature and behaving like an ill-tempered child. And once again, she managed to convince me that I was all those things. Accused with such steely authority, I fell back into my old, self-destructive habit. I took all the blame. I apologized.

Now, looking back on this exchange with the objectivity born of time and distance, I can see that I was obsessed with building the house—partly for the sake of the house itself and partly for Georgia—and wanted nothing more than her validation of my work. I think now that it was the last act of my childhood, carrying the hope of achieving a blessing from one of my parents.

Georgia, on the other hand, was obsessed with absolving herself of her decades-long debt to Stieglitz so she could leave New York with something like a clear conscience. At the same time she must have been terrified of stepping out of her life at the center of the art world, where she had gained so much public recognition and admiration. She knew she could continue painting when she moved permanently to New Mexico, but without Stieglitz's gallery to exhibit her work, how would it be seen? Had she come to the end of her career?

But those questions were not my concern now. I had served my purposes, first as her hired man, then as her contractor. The house was finished. The windows were washed, the floors were swept, the rooms were empty except for the few pieces of furniture O'Keeffe had shipped and the many boxes of books that were stacked away in what we called the "book room."

Georgia left New York for the last time in June, 1949. She stayed at the ranch but spent several days a week getting settled in the Abiquiu house. I was busy that year with the usual demands of the Los Luceros growing season, the mother ditch, and my own mother, who came to stay through October, out of the heat and humidity of a San Antonio summer.

After I had handed the keys to O'Keeffe, the two of us saw less of one another. But that didn't mean we lost touch. Both electricity and the telephone had finally come to Abiquiu, and a phone booth had been installed outside of Bode's General Store. The booth had electricity, although when you wanted to make a late-evening call, you brought your own light bulb, screwed it in, and unscrewed it and took it home with you when you were finished. (If you forgot, it wouldn't be there when you went back for it.) It was now very easy for Georgia to telephone me at Los Luceros when something didn't work the way she expected at the Abiquiu house—or at the ranch, too, for that matter. There were quite a number of calls and several letters about an ill-fitting garage door before we finally declared that the house was finished.

We didn't actually settle accounts, though, at least, not to my way of thinking. I had managed the construction bookkeeping scrupulously, documenting the payments for labor, supplies, equipment, and so on. She was sometimes slow with money for the project, but it was never really an issue. But I had left it to her to pay me what she thought my work was worth, and in the end, she did just that. For three years, she paid me roughly a hundred dollars a month for six months' work—reminding me several times that she had made additional provisions in her will. If she did, they were gone by the time of her death. I'm glad I didn't count on them.

❖

Our relationship—O'Keeffe's and mine—didn't end when I handed over the keys to the Abiquiu house, but it changed. It changed because I changed and Georgia changed and we no longer needed one another as we had during the war and the years immediately after.

Illness and loss marked the 1950s. Georgia suffered from shingles in 1950 and lost a breast in 1955. William Schubart, her trusted financial advisor and Stieglitz's nephew, died in 1950. Her sister Anita's husband killed himself in 1958. And she lost friends—or rather, she separated herself from them. Henwar was gone in that argument over the woman he brought to the ranch. Ansel Adams no longer visited. She was estranged from the Porters. And she said about her New York friends that she had left them behind, "all shut up in an odd pen" that they couldn't escape.

And worse for me lay ahead in the middle of that decade, when Dorothy, always so dear, died in a hospital in Mexico City, at Christmas, 1955. We had changed too, not separating but drifting softly from passion into a sweet and profound affection that was deepened and enriched by all we had been and wanted to be to each other. She had undergone breast surgery in the 1940s and brain surgery some eighteen months before this. We both knew she was very ill.

I wanted to stay with Dorothy in Santa Fe but reluctantly agreed to Mary Wheelwright's insistence that I take her to Oaxaca for the Fiesta de la Virgen de la Soledad in early December. I had just checked the two of us into the Hotel Monte Alban, next to the cathedral, when there was a flurry of telegrams. And then Dorothy, at my door.

"If I have to be sick," she announced cheerfully, "I'd rather be sick where I can hear Mexican street music."

She was sick, very sick, for the next week and the next. Just before the end, I left Mary in Oaxaca and took Dorothy to a hospital in Mexico City. We were there, together, when she died—in the place where she had loved to live, where we had met one another a long and eventful two decades before.

At the San Juan flower market the next morning, I found a vendor of violets, Dorothy's favorite flower. I took a fragrant little bouquet and the tattered New Testament I'd found in her suitcase and made my way to the Agencia Funeraria Gayosso where her body lay. Feeling somehow that she couldn't go on this journey without something fresh and true in her hands, I left both to be placed with her when she was cremated. Then I walked through the rain-wet streets until I found a cafe where I could celebrate her life by eating a tamale, as we had often done, together.

My time at Los Luceros changed me in more ways than I could count. I won't say it wasn't a continual challenge, for it was, especially in the mid-1950s, when Mary's exorbitant travel expenses and the upkeep on her properties in the United States and abroad began to eat into her financial resources. There were months when there was no money for salaries or the necessary maintenance. I cut expenses, took out bank loans, sold cattle, and leased the alfalfa pastures. But in spite of my efforts, it was clear that farming Los Luceros was a losing proposition.

It had been difficult to approach the subject with Mary. In response to one of my pleas, she wrote that she hated talking about money, that she was a coward about it, which I understood, for I'd had my own share of cowardice on the subject. But things got to the point where I knew I would have to take a job off the ranch and asked Mary for a deed to the land I had been managing—just the land, not the big house and its gardens. She agreed, and I had what I needed.

But when Mary unexpectedly died the next year—in July, 1958, at the family estate in Maine—I was surprised to discover that she had left the house and almost five acres to her museum in Santa Fe. Mr. Seth, the lawyer, told me that she had made the change in her will only six weeks before she died. "I tried to talk her out of it," he told me, "but you know Mary. She was a Cabot. She listened only to God."

It was a jolt, yes. But on reflection, not an enormous loss. The adobe hacienda that had been rather hastily built in the 1920s was now a white elephant desperately in need of a great deal of work. I couldn't have afforded it without selling a big part of the land. And by now, I had realized that while I loved living and working at Los Luceros I could not support myself or the place. I put the fields and orchards up for sale. About the same time, the museum sold the Casa Grande to Charles Collier, an old friend of O'Keeffe's. After a good deal of back-and-forthing, Collier bought my land, too, for $70,000—less than it was worth, I thought, and less than I had asked.

But it was what it was. Dorothy had left me her Galleria on Canyon Road, where she had hosted so many marvelous parties, and thirty-five acres on Atalaya Road. I lived at the Galleria for a time, while I thought about what I wanted to do. I hadn't given up the possibility of writing, especially now that I had free time. I could stay in Santa Fe. I could build an adobe for myself on a distant piece of desert land I'd acquired. Or I could—

But Changing Woman had another idea.

Chapter Twelve

Changing Women
Maria

Dear Dana—

I found your cooking pot. It accidentally got packed with my roaster of the same genre. I will send it by post . . . I wonder if you have found my earring? If so, wrap it in a Kleenex and mail it in an envelope, please.

Today I saw O'Keeffe off at the airport. She is off for two months to the Aswan Dam. She asked about you and wished to be remembered to you. The whole country is abuzz about my divorce—even Abiquiu!

—Maria Chabot to Dana Bailey
Albuquerque, February 18, 1962

The marriage was a surprise to me, too.

Dana and I had met at Oxford during one of the golden summers before the war. A Rhodes Scholar studying astrophysics, he was a friend of my cousin, Cresson, who introduced us. We enjoyed one another—both of us young, bright, energetic, optimistic—but our lives took us in different directions. I came back to the States with Dorothy. He went off to Antarctica on a scientific expedition, then on to a career in astrophysics research at what was then the National Bureau of Standards in Boulder, Colorado. I heard from him intermittently until early 1959, when he came to Los Alamos to work on a project. We reconnected as I was selling Los Luceros and considering new directions.

And there we were. Unmarried, in his mid-forties, and at the peak of a brilliant research career, Dana considered himself in want of a wife. I was once again without a plan for myself, as I had been in Mexico in 1933, when I met Dorothy and she took me to Santa Fe with her. And in 1941, when I was twenty-seven and O'Keeffe made me her hired man at Ghost Ranch. And again in 1944, when I was thirty-one and Mary dropped Los Luceros into my unsuspecting lap—or (to use her metaphor) hung it like a millstone around my neck.

Now forty-six, I was substantially older and presumably wiser, although not, as it proved, by much. Was I in want of a husband? Did I love this man? I suppose I thought so at the time, although now, I think not. I resisted for a time, like Georgia resisting Stieglitz's continued nagging to marry. I suggested we live together. But Dana had a reputation to maintain. For him, that just wouldn't do.

And so we married (to the astonishment of everyone who knew me) in Santa Fe on Valentine's Day in 1961. In June, I moved to his home in Boulder and we set up housekeeping. In the fall, we took a honeymoon trip to the Far East; he went on to Australia for a research project and I came home via Hong Kong, Cambodia, South Vietnam, and the Philippines. By November, we had agreed, mutually and more or less amicably, to divorce, for reasons both of us understood very well and thought it best to keep to ourselves.

To my therapist, Dr. Ross, I wrote that we were sexually incompatible—sex without affection was both mechanical and miserable—and that I simply couldn't understand why, after five years of therapy, I had gotten myself into such a fix. To my mother and Dana's (Mother Bailey and I exchanged frequent letters), I offered another version, claiming a large share of the blame for being an independent woman, so long accustomed to living on her own terms that she found it difficult to conform to her husband's expectations. To everyone else, Dana and I simply said we had discovered that we were better friends than spouses and left them to speculate as they liked. For my part, I learned that it is easier to marry than to divorce, even when there are relatively few financial entanglements. I don't know what Dana learned—he didn't share that with me. But he never married again, and neither did I.

That experiment ended, I moved to a small house on Sixteenth Street in Albuquerque and found my mother a duplex to rent not far away. The sale of Los Luceros and Dorothy's Santa Fe properties made me financially comfortable. Two years after moving to Albuquerque, I was able to buy a snug adobe-style house from Erna Fergusson (a writer whom I had known from the early days in Santa Fe), on Veranda Road, just a couple of blocks from the Rio Grande River. It was large enough for two, and my mother joined me there. Our decade together would be reasonably pleasant, complicated only by the increasing frailties of her old age. I missed her when she was gone.

And O'Keeffe? Once she was living in the Abiquiu house, there were often questions about this or that, which we usually were able to resolve by telephone. We saw one another on holidays and I enjoyed the postcards she sent from her travels to exotic places. She asked me to help with several renovations at the ranch and at the Abiquiu house, and I was always glad to lend a hand—a friendly hand. The writer Calvin Tomkins was bemused by Georgia's demand that he fly to New Mexico to review notes she was making about a possible autobiography. "Typical O'Keeffe," he said. "She had no hesitation to make demands on people." She continued to make demands on me, and I complied because I enjoyed her company, at least for a half-day or so. But I only had to drive over from Albuquerque, not fly from New York.

Georgia might be settled, but she didn't go back to the old routine of daily painting outdoors or in the studio. She had a yen for world travel and began, as one of her biographers put it, to plunge into the "diversions of a wealthy widow, the most lavish being a travel schedule that would have daunted a teenager." She went to Mexico and the Yucatan, to Europe, North Africa, and Peru. After that, an around-the-world tour with a group of art fanciers to Southeast Asia, the Far East, India, the Middle East, Italy. Then another Asian trip: Cambodia, Japan, Taiwan, Hong Kong, Saigon, Bangkok, Fiji, Tahiti, Korea, the Philippines. Then Egypt, Greece, the Near East. She invited me to go with her, but I had the good sense to decline. As her companions would report, traveling with O'Keeffe was not a collaborative adventure, and it wasn't much fun. Like Mary's Dear Lamb, you went along and managed the luggage.

When she was at home at the ranch or Abiquiu, the place was filled with people. Becky James—Beck Strand, from the early days—visited often until she became ill in the mid-1960s and died in 1968. There were others; O'Keeffe's sisters and their families; Doris Bry, now functioning as her curator and agent; the hired girls who kept her house and did the cooking and shopping; and the hired men who planted and tended her garden and did the maintenance work on the house. And there were the writers and photographers who came to document her solitude, for she continued to insist that she lived alone in the desert. She was known as a remarkable hostess.

But she also became famous for her rejections. She wouldn't answer a knock, or she would stand behind the closed door and shout, "Go away. I don't want to see you." When somebody told me about that, I was reminded of what Ghost Ranch owner Phoebe Pack once said, remembering her in the 1930s and 1940s. "I had to stay right there and see that she didn't kill someone. She hated strangers." In the 1970s, when a group of art students appeared at the Abiquiu gate asking to see her, she faced them. "Front side," she said, and turned around. "Backside. Goodbye." And when Laurie Lisle, a writer from *Newsweek*, attempted to interview her for a planned biography, O'Keeffe refused permission to quote her letters or reproduce images of her work and threatened legal action if Lisle went ahead with the project.

She did, successfully. Lisle's *Portrait of an Artist* was hailed by critics as an inspiring portrait of a truly original, courageous woman. I enjoyed the book, although I jealously resented it, too, knowing that *my* book about O'Keeffe would have told a truer story about her life in the desert.

And that was always a great frustration to me. I continued to write about our lives together, but she had made it clear that she would never allow it to be published. Even if I hadn't wanted to accommodate her wishes, I knew I was an unknown author and that a frown from O'Keeffe would kill any publisher's interest. Then I suggested that we assemble our many letters into a volume and asked her for copies of those I had written. At first she just put me off, saying that she didn't know where the letters were (they were in boxes on the floor in her book room), or that she was too busy to look for them. Then the excuses became *no*, the last one so angry that I stopped trying.

I wasn't the only one who heard "I said *no*—and don't ask me again." The art historian Barbara Rose, whom Georgia knew quite well, had been offered access to the Stieglitz correspondence and then told to go away and not come back. Anita Pollitzer, her oldest friend, had believed for many years that she had Georgia's agreement (and even her encouragement) to write her biography. But when Georgia saw Anita's manuscript, she rejected it as too personal, too intimate, too revealing. Anita was completely devastated when she received an icily formal letter offering to buy the manuscript for a "reasonable compensation." I understood why this gentle soul whom I had liked very much might feel like a hired girl being offered a position in the kitchen. And when the book finally came out after both women were gone, I was glad to read a glowing review in the *Los Angeles Times*. The reviewer described it as "a book that makes you long for a friend as loyal as Anita Pollitzer," It was a damned shame, I thought, that Georgia O'Keeffe hadn't been as loyal a friend as Anita.

Between her many trips, O'Keeffe occasionally painted, her work becoming more abstract and minimalist, more geometric and angular, like her *Patio* series of the 1950s. Flat, too, with less of the subtle depth of shading and the dimensioned contrasts you can see in her paintings of the 1930s and 1940s. Art critics sometimes describe this as a return to her earlier abstract watercolors, or as a maturation of her work. I'm no expert, but what I saw in her painting was a demonstration of her encroaching blindness. It was the epic tragedy of her later life that she could no longer see the vivid colors and strong shapes she loved and lived for, or manage the challenges of oil paints.

I've seen it reported that her eyesight began to fail in the 1970s, but Peggy Kiskadden puts it much earlier, in the spring of 1964, when Georgia was seventy-seven. She was driving her Buick convertible from the ranch on a brilliant New Mexico day, when she rounded a curve and felt as if she had just driven into a fog across the road. That evening, her panic escalating, she telephoned Peggy in Los Angeles. "My world is *blurred*!" she cried. Peggy, who had been close to Georgia since the 1940s, said it was a cry of unendurable agony.

Peggy was right. In the fall of 1964, when I saw Georgia off on a trip to New York, she told me that she had an appointment to see her doctor, Constance Fries, about her eyes. Dr. Fries sent her to Frank Constantine, at the Manhattan Eye, Ear & Throat Hospital. Constantine diagnosed macular degeneration and told her that it would progressively erode her central vision, leaving her sightless. There was no cure. She would soon have only peripheral sight, and eventually that, too, would be lost. I wondered whether it might be due to her decades-long devotion to the Bates eye exercises—staring at the sun while fluttering her eyelids—and to her refusal to wear sunglasses in the desert's glare. I'd tried to tell her that both were dangerous, but the O'Keeffe way of doing things was always the right way. I doubt she even heard me.

Georgia kept her failing eyesight to herself for as long as she could. She didn't want the art world to know, of course. She continued traveling as long as she could, always with people she trusted to keep her secret—her sister Anita, her old friend Richard Pritzlaff, with whom she went to Vienna to see the world-famous Lipizzaner horses. (Richard arranged for front-row seats so she wouldn't miss anything. She peered at the show ring through her opera glasses.) And later, with Juan Hamilton, the young man whose strong arm and commanding presence made her feel safe.

But there was no stopping or even slowing the loss of vision. When I visited Georgia at Ghost Ranch not long after she and Richard came back from Austria, she said sadly, "The sun must be shining but it looks so gray." We went out into the patio where we had shared so many good meals and lively conversations. I put my hands on her shoulders and turned her toward Pedernal.

"Can you see that?" I asked. "Changing Woman, on the horizon."

"No," she said quietly, "but I know she's there. And that she will always be *mine.*"

Losing her sight was a tragedy of indescribable dimensions. She coped with an almost ferocious intensity, but she was increasingly dependent on the sighted people who worked for her. Worse, the loss robbed her of painting, the necessary thread—as she said—that ran through all the other things in her life. But she didn't give up. There were several failed paintings, then, in desperation, she began enlisting helpers, like the Renaissance masters who kept entire workshops full of assistants.

One of these was John Poling, a twenty-three-year-old hired man who started out painting window trim at the ranch and ended in front of a canvas with one of the artist's brushes in his hand, following her directions as she coached him. Later, he told a journalist how they worked. "O'Keeffe would sometimes sit close to the canvas but at other times would stand at the back of the room and study the canvas through a pair of binoculars," he said. "Her vision was sort of blurring all over, but there were little holes in it where she could see through."

The first painting they did together (one of the patio door series) took five days to complete. When they were finished, she said, "I should give you something for this." She wrote her name on a postcard and handed it to him—her autograph. Soon, though, he was promoted to studio assistant and was earning five dollars an hour.

John Poling's assistance at Georgia's easel might never have been discovered. But when he saw a photograph of a painting he'd worked on in the magazine *ARTnews* and found no mention of his involvement, he was troubled. "It wasn't ethical," he said. The episode made him feel that he had been an unwitting partner in a deception. "I wasn't asking for credit," he insisted. "I just thought people should know that it wasn't entirely her work." But when he went to talk with O'Keeffe, she accused him of asking for "something" for himself—recognition or money. Hamilton, now serving as her manager and agent, sent him away.

So Poling went to the *Santa Fe Reporter*, which sent a journalist to get Georgia's side of the story. She was still reluctant to acknowledge her loss of vision, and it must have been incredibly painful to admit that she could no longer put paint on her own canvases. But the reporter had several insistent questions for her. How would the use of an assistant impact the value of O'Keeffe's art? How long had she been producing paintings in this way—without acknowledgment? How many assisted paintings had she done? And most troubling: might questions be raised about the authenticity of paintings in museums or on the walls of private collectors?

O'Keeffe was offended at the reporter's impertinence and angrily refused to answer her questions. How she painted was nobody's business but her own. As for John Poling's assistance, she said, it was simply insignificant. He was, she said, a mechanical tool, "the equivalent of a palette knife."

I shook my head at the utter cruelty of the remark, reflecting that if he had been a palette knife, I had been a hammer and a handful of nails. But I also cringed for Georgia: how humiliating, for that proud woman, so assured of her artistic power and her reigning place in the art world, to be revealed as a blind old lady who could no longer do what she most loved. And worse, an ungrateful, vindictive old lady who insulted those who wanted to help her.

And I was sorry for John Poling, whom I hadn't met but whose ethical sense I had to respect. For years, I had watched Georgia fail to credit people for the work they had done. For my work on the Abiquiu house. For Doris Bry's work with the Stieglitz art collection. For the work of the many gardeners who produced the vegetables and fruit she claimed to grow in her garden. John Poling, the palette knife, was just another in a long line of those of us who had once been of use to her and were useful no longer. "Slaves," she had called us. As for myself, I had long ago grown accustomed to this habit of hers and was no longer hurt by it.

But Doris Bry was desperately hurt and when Georgia found that she was no longer useful, Doris would take her distress to court, filing a "malicious interference" suit against Juan Hamilton for getting between her and O'Keeffe. The eight-year scandal created a great deal of national interest. But that part of the story involves Georgia and Hamilton, the last—and most lasting—of her young men. It's not my story to tell, so I won't attempt it. I'll only say that, while I resented Hamilton's control over Georgia, I also felt deeply sorry for him. He was a talented young man, surrendering his most creative and productive years to the service of an old woman. I had been enriched by her company in those early days. I hoped he would gain something in return for being someone always nearby.

My last visit with Georgia was in September 1981 at the ranch, on a day when Hamilton was absent. She could no longer see and her hearing was failing too. But she was alert and lively and we had a pleasant afternoon, remembering the best of the times we had spent together in those early desert days when the cliffs shone like polished gemstone behind us, Pedernal held blessings before us, and the sky— and our futures—arched beyond us, infinite.

We shared an embrace as I was leaving and I asked if I might come back and read to her from Basho's recently translated collection of haiku, *Narrow Road to the Deep North*. She agreed eagerly and we made plans for the next week. But a few days later, I received a typed letter, signed with a scrawl that was nothing like the stylized script I knew so well. *Dear Maria: It was good to see you again, but I do not think I can have you at the ranch. I feel it is best if we leave things as they are.*

Had Hamilton written this? I thought so then and I think so now. I doubted, in fact, whether Georgia even knew that he had sent that letter—and if to me, then perhaps also to others who wanted to visit but weren't welcome. She wouldn't be isolated, because his friends were her friends now, and there were plenty to care for her. We were the ones who were isolated from her.

My conclusion was bolstered by my conversations with Carol, a young woman who had been working as O'Keeffe's caregiver. She was keeping a detailed journal of her weekends at the ranch and at Abiquiu: records of the meals she and Georgia shared, the music they listened to, the books they read—the kind of story I wanted to write and was still in a manuscript draft, stowed away in my bottom desk drawer. Carol and I met in a tai chi class in Albuquerque and saw one another occasionally after that. Eager to share her story, she told me that, in the beginning, she had been drawn to O'Keeffe for the same reasons I had. She admired her artistic achievements, was inspired by her indomitable strength, and was captivated by the orderly elegance of O'Keeffe's life, which she saw as an art itself. But after seven years of organizing her time around O'Keeffe's unpredictable needs, Carol was told she was no longer needed. She never knew why. Their last meeting ended abruptly.

"Let's get this over with," was all O'Keeffe said as they stood together at the studio door that last day. "Goodbye." Not "thank you." Not "I've appreciated your help." Not "I wish you the very best." Just "Let's get this over with."

Carol grieved for the loss of O'Keeffe's company. But she came to understand what I had understood, nearly four decades earlier, what Becky James had understood before me, and what Doris Bry would understand after me. "I was losing my life to her," Carol told me one brilliant spring day, when we were walking in the park near my house. "I needed to find a future for myself, to become whoever I was meant to be." She was meant to be a poet and a teacher, and that's who she became.

I wasn't the only one who was excluded from Georgia's company, of course. Other friends told me that they were kept away. Georgia's relationship with her sister Claudia was threatened when Claudia jokingly called Juan a gigolo. Peggy Kiskadden, who told me about the episode, was also there and reported that she and Claudia sang a few bars of "Just a Gigolo," while O'Keeffe and Hamilton glowered. Later, when Hamilton was "spectacularly rude," Peggy told Georgia that she couldn't come back if he was allowed to insult guests. Georgia's silence ended what had been an enduring forty-year friendship. When Peggy wrote saying that Georgia (alone) would always be welcome at her home in Beverly Springs, O'Keeffe replied that she was astonished to learn that Peggy imagined that she might wish to visit or even speak to her. "So there we are," she concluded, with a note of triumph. "Finished!"

So, too, Frances O'Brien, a friend of five decades. When O'Brien supported Doris Bry in her lawsuit against Hamilton, Georgia ended the friendship and demanded the return of paintings she had given Frances years before—as she had demanded the return of the paintings she gave me and Anita Pollitzer. We complied, of course. We loved her, or we thought we did. We didn't know what else to do.

"Stieglitz says that art is wicked," O'Keeffe had told me years before. "But it is who we are."

They were right, of course. Art is wicked.

❖

I made several more efforts to visit Georgia after Hamilton moved her to Sol y Sombra, the sprawling ten-acre estate he bought in her name in Santa Fe. But I was barred and even relatives were turned away. Georgia's niece June was sent packing and Raymond Krueger, a favorite grandnephew, was told that his visit was "inappropriate."

And there was Christine Taylor Patten, an artist who was O'Keeffe's sympathetic nurse for nearly a year and who wrote about their months together in a tender little memoir called *Miss O'Keeffe*. Her story is important because Christine was a vigilant, attentive witness who had a deep affection for O'Keeffe and admired her bravery in the darkness of her last years. She left after an escalating series of disagreements with Hamilton. Christine was surprised when she didn't miss Georgia, with whom she felt she had shared a real friendship.

The reason? "She was still with me," Christine writes in the last chapter of her memoir. "I didn't feel separated from her. It had nothing to do with my being there physically. I knew she had been present in the process of what I gave her and what she gave me. She knew it and that was all that mattered."

Yes, I thought when I read that. Yes. And when I heard the news that O'Keeffe had died, I felt the earth tilt in the same way it had tilted on that July morning, the morning of Trinity. I opened my copy of *Georgia O'Keeffe* and reread her inscription: "For Maria Chabot, who made the Abiquiu House a place to live and has dreamed other dreams with me here near the cliffs and the red hills."

She knew and I knew, and the cliffs and the red hills and Changing Woman know.

And in the end, that is all that matters.

AFTER

–

If human life is about loss—the procession of growth, acquisition, and accumulation, then the relinquishment of childhood, of naïve faith, of youthful health, of perfect love, of perfect children—then for selfish purposes I demystify Georgia O'Keeffe. I will not place her out of reach, will crank down the pedestal, touch the statue, and find it is a woman who could behave noxiously, act arrogantly and outrageously at close mortal range.

—Melissa Pritchard
"A Graven Space"
From the Faraway Nearby: Georgia O'Keeffe as Icon

Making your unknown known is the thing.
—Georgia O'Keeffe to Sherwood Anderson, 1926

From the Author

As I worked on this book, I thought often of a pair of sentences in Rebecca Solnit's memoir, *The Faraway Nearby*:

> To love someone is to put yourself in their place, we say, which is to put yourself in their story, or figure out how to tell yourself their story. Which means that a place is a story, and stories are geography, and empathy is first of all an act of imagination, a storyteller's art, and then a way of traveling from here to there.

As one of her biographers puts it, Georgia O'Keeffe was "a woman who lived the newspaper editor's adage that, if the myth is more stirring than the truth, print the myth." And there are plenty of myths to choose from, especially the one that the artist herself created: that of a monastic woman who led an ascetic, solitary Zen life, practicing her art in a starkly simple home in a remote desert. But perhaps the most intriguing are the myths framing her relationship with the hired man fifty-eight years her junior who became her companion, caregiver, curator, manager, agent, legal guardian, rumored lover and even husband in the last thirteen years of her life.

When John Bruce Hamilton appeared at O'Keeffe's ranch in the fall of 1973, he was twenty-seven, recently divorced, pony-tailed, and a conscientious objector to the Vietnam War, still underway at the time. Like Maria, he had no money and no clear focus for his future. For the previous few months, he had been working on the Ghost Ranch maintenance crew (a job arranged by his Presbyterian-official father) and telling friends that he had come to the desert to meet O'Keeffe. He got his chance when there was a problem with her plumbing and she called Ray McCall at Ghost Ranch to come over and fix it—a courtesy that the generous Presbyterians extended *gratis* to their unneighborly neighbor. McCall took Hamilton with him.

O'Keeffe was displeased. Hamilton recalled that the eighty-four-year-old artist looked past him as if he were transparent. In a more recent retelling (the details of the story have varied) he reports that she scolded McCall. "Don't you ever bring anybody else here again without asking me first," she said. "Well, so much for getting to know her," Hamilton thought to himself.

But this was a young man on a mission. He kept knocking at her door and eventually O'Keeffe asked him to pack some paintings for shipment. She had recently lost another in a long string of come-and-go secretaries, and when she learned that this one had not only four years of college but two years of graduate school and knew how a typewriter worked, she asked him to type some letters. She quickly discovered that Hamilton (like Maria) could communicate with the hired girls in fluent Spanish, could make himself useful in many of the ways that Maria had been useful, had a cynical, teasing manner, and refused to defer to her. What's more, he had studied art and art history and had trained as a potter. Out of that background, he was able to respond to her artistic needs and priorities, and she found herself relying on him.

And there was more. By this time, O'Keeffe had lost most of her eyesight but she could see well enough to notice that the tall, dark-haired, good-looking Hamilton bore a remarkable resemblance to photographs of Alfred Stieglitz as a young man. In fact, Hamilton would tell friends that he had been driving along the shore of Lake George when a premonition that Georgia needed care came to him out of the mist above the water—the spirit of Stieglitz, he thought, beckoning him to care for O'Keeffe. For her part, Georgia had never lost the profoundly mystical sense that informed so much of her art and had drawn her to Pedernal, the mountain that looked out for her. She believed in the supernatural and in omens. "Juan was sent to me," she would tell friends, who noticed that Georgia's face lit up when Hamilton came into the room. Others observed that the two seemed to share a common sense of belonging.

The young man and the older woman quickly developed a comfortable pattern of working together. Hamilton lived with O'Keeffe for some months until he found a house in nearby Barranco. She loaned him the money to buy and remodel it. (All loans to him were forgiven in her 1979 will.) Early each morning, he would drive to her home—either the ranch or the Abiquiu house—to be her guide on her morning walk. During the day, he supervised the household help, drove her where she wanted to go, managed her appointments, and answered her mail.

"I was an employee who became a friend," he told another biographer, confident words that resolved in a few months the paradox that bedeviled Maria for a full decade. Now in her eighties, her eyesight almost gone, O'Keeffe must have felt the need for someone always nearby much more than she did in her fifties and sixties.

The friendship developed rapidly when O'Keeffe invited Hamilton to go with her on a seven-week trip to Morocco in the spring of 1974. Many years later, Hamilton would tell *Harper's Bazaar* about the trip. "We went everywhere together, and we got along. I could help her feel independent. She would tell people, 'He is my eyes and my ears.'" She wasn't always a congenial traveling companion, of course. "She was pretty demanding. She was no flower. And when she was in a bad mood, boy, she was tough! But over time she developed an affection for me that I wasn't expecting or looking for."

Maybe not, but he reciprocated. The open affection the two displayed prompted the speculations of a December–May marriage, speculations that O'Keeffe seemed to enjoy and that neither she nor Hamilton bothered to deny. Long before, she had learned to invite notoriety and find it both amusing and profitable, and the idea of being cared for and loved by (or *seen* as being loved by) a handsome and much younger man must have been hugely appealing. It was Maria who said to Georgia in 1941: "I have told you before that someone should make a career of caring for you." Thirty-two years later, someone did.

From travel companions, the pair became a business partnership. In the late 1970s, they made a film together, produced several pots together, and worked together on the book that became the artist's autobiography, illustrated by photographs of carefully chosen paintings.

O'Keeffe could not see well enough to select the works, so Hamilton was her eyes on the project—and ears, since she was increasingly deaf. He was her legs, too. When the book went into production, he flew to New York and worked with the senior editor at Viking Press to review and approve the color plates. He was, by all reports, as discerning, demanding, and difficult as O'Keeffe. Since he did not have O'Keeffe's credentials or credibility, his demands did not always endear him to those who had to work with him.

The person who found it most difficult to work with O'Keeffe's new partner was Doris Bry, the young woman who had provided the secretarial support O'Keeffe needed during the three years she spent settling Stieglitz's estate. In 1963, O'Keeffe fired Downtown Gallery owner Edith Halpert in an apparent disagreement about the prices on her paintings. Not long after, she made Bry her exclusive dealer. Since Bry had no gallery, O'Keeffe's paintings were stacked in the dim recesses of the Manhattan Storage Company warehouse at Third Avenue and Eightieth Street. When potential clients appeared, Bry screened them, then personally escorted them to the warehouse for a private viewing of the paintings, which O'Keeffe priced at the high end of the market.

All this was, as biographer Roxana Robinson observes, "another element in the growing O'Keeffe mystique," an image constructed on "her isolated life in the distant desert, her lack of a commercial gallery, her general rejection of the New York art world, and the elitism attending the purchase of one of her paintings." *Buzz* may be a contemporary word, but the concept itself isn't new. When O'Keeffe first came to New York, she had felt "invaded" by what the critics wrote and said about her. But after five years with Stieglitz, she was able to tell a friend: "One must be written about and talked about or the people who buy through their ears think your work is no good—and won't buy and one must sell to live—so one must be written about and talked about whether one likes it or not."

The unusual arrangement with Bry encouraged people to talk about the absent O'Keeffe. It went on for ten or eleven years. But Doris, in her turn (and as Maria Chabot or Anita Pollitzer or Frances O'Brien might have predicted), fell out of favor with O'Keeffe. In 1976, Hamilton began working as the artist's agent, selling her work without Bry's knowledge. When Bry discovered this and objected, O'Keeffe fired her and demanded the return of the hundreds of paintings squirreled away in the Third Avenue warehouse. Bry was slow in complying. O'Keeffe sued. Bry returned the paintings but countersued O'Keeffe for breach of contract. For good measure, she also sued Hamilton—for some three million dollars, charging him with "malicious interference" in her relationship with O'Keeffe.

The Hamilton suit was finally settled in 1982, O'Keeffe's suit in 1985. The terms were sealed, but Bry told the *Washington Post* that most of the money she received went to pay her lawyers. Grimly, she remarked, "There's no way anything can pay for eight years wasted like that. It was a Kafkaesque game, and I'm sure my life has been shortened by it." The lawsuits clearly gave Hamilton the authority he needed. Roxana Robinson remarks, "Hamilton, who had long ago established power over O'Keeffe's private life, now reigned supreme over her professional life." The East Coast art community, which had never seen anything like this, was scandalized. Quite naturally, its sympathies lay almost entirely with Bry.

Hamilton was well aware that O'Keeffe's reputation as a painter had been enhanced through her association with Stieglitz and saw a similar opportunity for himself. His aggressive approach, however, created a certain uneasiness in the art world. In order to hang O'Keeffe's paintings, galleries were also required to exhibit Hamilton's pots. A museum to which O'Keeffe gave a major gift was obliged to use part of that gift to buy Hamilton's work. And while well-known collectors were named as purchasers of his pots and sculptures, their purchases were rumored to have come at Georgia's insistence. In general, art critics considered pottery a decorative (not a fine) art, and critical opinions of Hamilton's work were not uniformly high. People noticed that his pots and O'Keeffe's name and influence seemed "inextricably linked" and made the usual assumptions about the relationship. If O'Keeffe was trying to boost Hamilton's career in the same way Stieglitz boosted hers, the efforts did not have the same effect.

Given all these stressful circumstances, the hired help at the ranch and at Abiquiu were dealing with a challenging situation. Carol Merrill, who for six years served as O'Keeffe's weekend librarian, companion, cook, nurse, and reader, describes the household as a "medieval court of intrigue" and tells a carefully guarded story about staffers who tiptoed around a pair of combative people or jealously pursued the approval of one or the other. They must try to negotiate what Merrill candidly but compassionately describes as O'Keeffe's poisonous moods, her tantrums, and her negative energy. Her rages frightened everyone in the household (as they had frightened Maria decades before). When Merrill asked Hamilton how to deal with the tantrums, he advised her "to stand aside when the shit flies."

But Hamilton was part of the problem. He was rumored to use drugs, to be a heavy drinker, and to be abusive to the help. Staff members were required to sign nondisclosure agreements and warned not to talk about what went on in the house. In this toxic atmosphere, people worked for a time, found O'Keeffe too difficult or too demanding, and left or were fired. Others came for a time, found Hamilton too unpredictable, too temperamental, or too demanding, and left or were fired.

Merrill has given us a bittersweet poem about her six-year experience—which ended, as most did, in an abrupt dismissal.

> I can say how I felt today
> Washing Georgia O'Keeffe's white stockings
> In the basin . . .
> I can talk about hatred between
> Her friends and employees
> I can talk of history
> Of the Taos art scene
> Of New York in the 1920s
> I can talk about her clothes
> Ranging like Mandarins
> Conspiring in the closet.
> I can talk a lot
> But I cannot speak of
> Cloud shadow slowing crossing cliffs
> Or the look on her face when
> She turns her unseeing eye to sky
> And remembers blue.

The situation became even more troubling when Hamilton began breaking appointments, leaving without letting anyone know where he was going, and failing to meet his obligations. In the insular world of Santa Fe, he had developed a reputation as a big spender, buying three Mercedes-Benzes in O'Keeffe's name (she was no longer licensed to drive), and a BMW, Toyota Land Cruiser, and a Ford pickup for himself—all of them white. He was noticeably absent for stretches of time, and O'Keeffe, who by now was nearly completely sightless, began to wonder if she should send him away. She became so concerned that she arranged an extraordinary midwinter meeting with Phoebe Pack, who flew from Tucson to see her but was stranded in Española by a blizzard. O'Keeffe (who rarely ventured out in the winter) went to meet her. Pack listened to her complaints about Hamilton's rudeness, his inattentiveness, his unexplained absences—and then counseled her to maintain the relationship.

"That young man has made a different person of you," she said. "For heaven's sake, Georgia, don't let him get away. Keep him."

Phoebe Pack was right on that score. With Hamilton's help, O'Keeffe was able to travel, to publish several books, make a movie, produce some pottery, arrange for exhibits, and sell more of her paintings for more and more money. And his absences were explained when a young Arizona artist named Anna Marie Erskine moved into his house. O'Keeffe seems not to have been pleased (she fell into the habit of referring to Anna Marie as "that poor thing") but if she wanted to keep his professional services, she could hardly object to what he did in his private life.

Hamilton and Anna Marie were married in the spring of 1980. The ceremony was not public, the marriage was not announced in the area newspapers, and some felt that O'Keeffe was not fully aware of it. She was soon required to accommodate herself to Hamilton's children, however. The first child, a boy, was born in fall 1980, followed by another. O'Keeffe was reported to enjoy the babies—she told a visitor that she was a grandmother—and the marriage seemed to have a stabilizing effect on Hamilton.

But Georgia was in her nineties now, slowing down, submitting more quietly to directions, failing to recognize friends, experiencing the paranoias of old age, and often appearing confused about where she was and why she was there. It was increasingly difficult to find help who would come to the ranch, so Hamilton moved Georgia to her Abiquiu house, where girls from the village were available to serve as caregivers and kitchen help. He was frequently gone on business, and employees reported O'Keeffe's querulous complaints about his absences. There were repeated episodes involving Hamilton's questionable decisions about the artist's care, including a "grand drama of foolhardiness" (as one biographer calls it) when he put her on a jet plane with oxygen and nurses and took her to Florida, where he installed her in her sister Anita's Palm Beach mansion. The trip was an unmitigated disaster.

Finally, in O'Keeffe's name, Hamilton purchased (for nearly three million dollars—some nine million in 2022) a sprawling, twenty-acre estate called Sol y Sombra, known as the "storied jewel of Santa Fe." O'Keeffe occupied the ground-floor library suite. That was where, in 1984, she signed a codicil to her 1979 will, leaving "to my friend, John Bruce Hamilton," the bulk of her estate, which was estimated at the time as between sixty-five and eighty million dollars—one of the largest artist's estates on record. If Hamilton died before her, the estate would go to his heirs, not to her family. Christine Taylor Patten, O'Keeffe's nurse-companion, was concerned about whether O'Keeffe knew what she was doing when she signed the 1984 codicil. Patten believed that Georgia thought that she and Hamilton were to be married and that she was about to sign a marriage certificate. Her highly credible testimony would play an important role in the litigation to come.

Hamilton and his family were vacationing in Mexico when the housekeeper telephoned him to say that an ambulance had taken

O'Keeffe to St. Vincent's Hospital. He caught the next plane, but he was too late. She died at noon on March 6, 1986, at the age of ninety-eight. As she had directed, Hamilton took her ashes to the top of Pedernal and tossed them into the wind.

God may have told Georgia O'Keeffe that Changing Woman belonged to her, if she painted it often enough. Now, she belonged to Changing Woman.

❖

The story continued to unspool, of course. The family—Georgia's sister Catherine Klenert and a niece—filed suit, challenging both the 1983 and 1984 codicils and accusing Hamilton of exerting "undue influence" over an aging woman who was not fully aware of what she was doing. (Klenert called him "nothing but a tramp" in her deposition.) They did not challenge the 1979 will, however, which left the greater part of the artwork to various museums and made no provision for the family.

The sides lined up. The state of New Mexico had been left a bequest of artwork in the 1979 will and decided to join the suit. Hired by the state to investigate, an attorney discovered Christine Patten's record of her August 1984 conversation with O'Keeffe (when Georgia confided that she and Hamilton were to be married), and therapists subpoenaed by the family would make some damaging statements about Hamilton's drug use and alcoholism. Doris Bry would be called to testify, as would a number of former O'Keeffe employees. One of Hamilton's lawyers felt compelled to insist that his client was not "some Svengali or Rasputin in handyman's clothes." Articles about the astonishing market value of the artwork, the circumstances surrounding the codicils, and Juan Hamilton's expected inheritance popped up in dozens of newspapers and magazines around the country. According to National Gallery of Art curator Jack Cowart, the litigation was shaping up to be "trench warfare." Others thought it was more like a three-ring circus and were waiting for the clowns.

While the situation dragged on and Hamilton's legal and living expenses mounted, public opinion swung heavily—and perhaps inevitably—against him. It must have been a harrowing experience. He could not be sure what other accusations might come out or how the final judgment might go against him. To the *Washington Post* reporter, he sighed, "In a trial, lots of things go on public display, and have to get reexamined. And the whole time I was there in Abiquiu, there was a misconception about our relationship."

The end came sooner and with fewer fireworks than many expected. In January 1987, confronted by the likelihood that he could lose everything Georgia had given him, Hamilton agreed to settle. He accepted the terms of the 1979 will and the 1983 codicil. Forty-two paintings (valued at twenty million dollars) went to eight museums, the Beinecke Library at Yale got O'Keeffe's papers, and a charitable foundation—formed to "perpetuate the artistic legacy of Georgia O'Keeffe"—would be established to distribute the rest of the art and manage the house and studio at Abiquiu, the house that Maria built. The family members received paintings and cash to the tune of about a million dollars each, and the state of New Mexico received paintings worth $1.5 million (at the time) in lieu of estate taxes. Hamilton settled for the Ghost Ranch property, Sol y Sombra, and some twenty-four paintings as well as photographs by Stieglitz, O'Keeffe's letters, copyrights, and works of other artists. The bottom line: fifteen million plus change. Nothing to sneeze at, of course, but nothing like the sixty-some million he stood to inherit under the 1984 codicil—which O'Keeffe may have thought was a marriage certificate.

"It wasn't a compromise," one of the lawyers said. "It was a capitulation."

The hullaballoo was finally over. Juan Hamilton—who for thirteen years had been someone always nearby—was a very wealthy man.

❖

And what of Maria Chabot, the woman who enabled O'Keeffe to live comfortably and work productively at the ranch through the difficult days of the war and who transformed a ruined hacienda into an artist's living work of art?

After her divorce from Dana Bailey, Maria moved to Albuquerque. Never a woman to sit in the corner and watch while others worked, she became active in community affairs, especially in the establishment of the Rio Grande Nature Center, created to protect the river's bosque and its ecosystem. She also remained active as an advocate for Native Americans and for healthcare for women and girls.

In her later years, people began finally to recognize her work on O'Keeffe's now-famous Abiquiu house. In 1994, Richard Brettell, director of the Georgia O'Keeffe Foundation, credited her in a planned book on the house as its "architect, contractor and garden designer." Now a part of the Georgia O'Keeffe Museum, the house was designated a National Historic Landmark in 1998. Maria spoke at the ceremony. She must have been delighted at this recognition, however tardy, of her contributions to O'Keeffe's life.

The new O'Keeffe Foundation and Maria were also interested in something else: those hundreds of letters that Georgia and Maria had exchanged during the 1940s. Maria had apparently resigned herself to her inability to publish a memoir of her years with O'Keeffe, whether because Georgia discouraged or forbade it or because she couldn't pull the material together. In the late 1970s, she became seriously committed to compiling and publishing their letters. She had kept the originals of Georgia's (to which the artist held the copyright) and asked O'Keeffe for copies of *hers* (to which *she* owned the copyright). She wanted to incorporate them into a single collection, with extended notes that would tell the story of those years. Georgia refused, whether because she wanted to keep the correspondence private or because she preferred that all of her papers be managed through the Beinecke Library. Without Georgia's agreement, the project couldn't go forward, so Maria dropped it.

But in 1991, five years after Georgia's death, Maria renewed her request—this time, bringing it to the newly-established O'Keeffe Foundation, which now had physical possession of Maria's letters to Georgia. That was when it was discovered that they had been stored on the dirt floor of the Abiquiu house "book room," where they had been invaded by paper-hungry insects. They were heavily damaged.

Nevertheless, the Foundation agreed that the letters could make an important contribution to an understanding of a decade of major change in O'Keeffe's life. They provided Maria copies of the undamaged letters before they were sent with Georgia's other papers to the Beinecke. The following year, after the Beinecke conservators had stabilized the letters, Maria received copies of all of them and got to work assembling them (and drafts she had kept) with O'Keeffe's letters to her. Her own eyesight was failing, so she hired people to digitize the letters so she could print them in a large font. She also engaged editor Ann Paden to help with the compilation.

Maria died in 2001 at the age of eighty-seven, before she could finish compiling the nearly seven hundred letters. The project was continued by Paden and Barbara Buhler Lynes, a noted O'Keeffe scholar, the director of the Museum's Research Center, and the author of the O'Keeffe catalog raisonné. The Lynes-Paden book—six hundred and seventy-eight letters, with the editors' narrative comments and explanatory notes—was published in 2003. *Maria Chabot—Georgia O'Keeffe, Correspondence, 1941–1949.* It is the book on which *Someone Always Nearby* is based.

Maria's friendship with Georgia was complicated and went through many phases, like all long friendships. But it was deeply felt and genuine. In their letters we have an enduring record of their voices, their passions, their angers, their own stories and the stories they made up about each other—and about themselves.

And there is their love of the land, always the land, which lies like a peace treaty between them, a bridge linking two separate and distant islands, as in this letter that Maria in San Antonio wrote to Georgia in New York, on a cold, blustery December night in 1943:

> The moon is out. Do you know that? I wonder if in New York you know. I went down to close the big hall door tonight and I felt the moon outside. Texas is full of rain and fog and people and things far from the moon. I had forgotten the moon . . . the fulling and the waning . . . It is like losing one's balance. I shut the door—and finished off the moon like that—with a feeling that I did not know where I was standing. I had a sense of something being lost, and after that: of guilt. And then . . . I

knew what was wrong. And what I love, and what I longed for. Is it odd—to care for anything so much? . . . To want suddenly, so terribly, the big cold and the wide stars and the stillness? Yes, I think I am very odd. You do not even have to tell me that—for no matter how you say it you cannot say it wholly. Not for me.

ACKNOWLEDGMENTS

A book is never a single writer's effort. This one, especially, is a village. It could not have been written if it were not for the scholarship of numerous biographers and historians who did the exhausting work of collecting, sifting, documenting, and presenting the facts on which my fiction is based. In addition, important thanks are due to the archivists and staff at the Georgia O'Keeffe Museum in Santa Fe, who were helpful as I worked through the resources there; Paula Yost, who conducted onsite archive research and gave generously of her time and attention as coauthor of the *Reader's Guide*; Molly Mullins, who shared her memories of Maria Chabot; Kerry Sparks, literary agent par excellence; my skilled editorial team of Sandra Spicher and Sarah Masterson Hally; and the helpful folk at Greenleaf Book Group. As always, I am grateful to the caring and inspiring women of the Story Circle Network. And to Bill Albert, my someone-always-nearby. I can never thank him enough for his unfailing support and constant encouragement.

CREDITS

—

Quotations at the beginning of Chapters 1, 4, 5, 6, 7, 8, 9, 10, 11 and occasionally throughout are from *Maria Chabot—Georgia O'Keeffe: Correspondence, 1941-1949* by Ann Paden and Barbara Buhler Lynes. Copyright © 2003 University of New Mexico Press and are used with permission. In the narrative, I have indicated when a quotation comes from this letter collection, usually with an indicative phrase like "she wrote" or "her note said." The letters are reproduced here as they were written, without correction.

Quotations at the beginning of Chapters 2, 3, and 12 are from documents in the archives of the Georgia O'Keeffe Library and Museum and are used with permission.

Extending Your Reading Experience

An historical novel provides a fictional glimpse into a time and place where real things really happened to real people. Many readers want to extend and expand the reading experience by looking deeper into the past. If you're that kind of reader, here are fifteen books you may find of interest.

A Reader's Guide to Someone Always Nearby. Susan Wittig Albert and Paula Stallings Yost. Persevero Press, 2023.

> After an overview of the novel, each chapter of the *Guide* includes historical and geographical settings, plot summaries, and suggestions of issues to consider. "For Further Study" features an author commentary keyed to individual passages in the novel, explaining and expanding on the extensive research behind the fiction. Also included: questions for group discussion, an annotated list of characters, photographs, a map, a timeline of events in the lives of Georgia O'Keeffe and Maria Chabot, links to research articles and websites, and a full list of works cited.

Equal Under the Sky: Georgia O'Keeffe and Twentieth-Century Feminism. Linda M. Grasso. University of New Mexico Press, 2017.

> An important historical study of O'Keeffe's place in American feminist movements, 1910–1970.

Full Bloom: The Art and Life of Georgia O'Keeffe. Hunter Drohojowska-Philp. W. W. Norton, 2004.

> A deeply researched biography of the artist, her work and her often difficult personal relationships, called "the definitive life of O'Keeffe."

Georgia O'Keeffe, Art and Letters. Jack Cowart, Juan Hamilton, and Sarah Greenough. National Gallery of Art, 1987.

> Photographs of important paintings, quotations from the artist's letters, catalogs, and other writings.

Georgia O'Keeffe. Georgia O'Keeffe. Penguin Books, 1974.

> O'Keeffe's autobiography, with 108 color photographs of paintings she se-

lected, as well as her own commentary about her life and her development as an artist—because "no one else can know how my paintings happen."

Georgia O'Keeffe and Her Houses: Ghost Ranch and Abiquiu. Barbara Buhler Lynes. Harry N. Abrams, 2012.

Color photographs and extensive, detailed descriptions of O'Keeffe's famous New Mexico homes, as well as her paintings of the houses and the surrounding landscapes.

Georgia O'Keeffe: A Life. Roxana Robinson. Brandeis University Press, 2020.

An authoritative biography of O'Keeffe, written with the family's cooperation. A *New York Times* Notable Book of the Year.

Ghost Ranch. Lesley Poling-Kempes. University of Arizona Press, 2005.

The story of the transformation of el Rancho de los Brujos, a hideout for legendary outlaws, to the home of one of America's most famous artists and a premier educational and conference center.

Los Luceros: New Mexico's Morning Star. Michael Wallis. Museum of New Mexico Press, 2018.

The fascinating history of Los Luceros: from its earliest human inhabitants to its many occupiers, visitors, and owners—including Mary Cabot Wheelwright and Maria Chabot. Now one of New Mexico Historic Sites and a living museum. Add this to your list of magical places to visit.

Maria Chabot—Georgia O'Keeffe Correspondence, 1941–1949. Barbara Buhler Lynes and Ann Paden, eds. University of New Mexico Press, 2003.

A collection of nearly seven hundred letters written during the 1940s by Maria Chabot and Georgia O'Keeffe, the basis for the novel *Someone Always Nearby.*

Miss O'Keeffe. Christine Taylor Patten and Alvaro Cardona-Hine. University of New Mexico Press, 1992.

An intimate, insightful, and often troubling story of the artist's final few years, written by a compassionate caregiver, friend, and witness to the difficulties of later life.

O'Keeffe: The Life of an American Legend. Jeffrey Hogrefe. Bantam Books, 1992.

A behind-the-myth biography of the artist, with an emphasis on her years in New Mexico. The author's access to Juan Hamilton, Maria Chabot, Phoebe Pack, and others who knew O'Keeffe well provides a deeper look into her relationships.

Painting with O'Keeffe. John David Poling. Texas Tech University Press, 1999.

The memoir of a young man's instructive, rewarding, but painful collaboration with an artist who needed his help at the easel—and what happened after that.

Portrait of an Artist: A Biography of Georgia O'Keeffe. Laurie Lisle. New York: Washington Square Press, 1980.

The first O'Keeffe biography, written during the artist's lifetime after extensive interviews with her friends and colleagues. Important for its candor.

Valley of Shining Stone, Lesley Poling-Kempes. University of Arizona Press, 1997.

A comprehensive, highly readable human and natural history of one of the Southwest's most beautiful but endangered landscapes—the place that bewitched Georgia O'Keeffe.

Weekends with O'Keeffe. C. S. Merrill. University of New Mexico Press, 2010.

An engaging account of the author's years (1973–1979) as a weekend-assistant to O'Keeffe. Many insights into the elderly artist's personal life at the ranch and at Abiquiu during active but declining years, based on contemporaneous notes.

ABOUT THE AUTHOR

Growing up on a farm on the Illinois prairie, Susan Wittig Albert learned that books could take her anywhere in the world. She earned an undergraduate degree in English from the University of Illinois at Urbana and a PhD in medieval studies from the University of California at Berkeley. After fifteen years of faculty and administrative appointments at the University of Texas, Tulane University, and Texas State University, she left her academic career to write full time. She is the founder of the Story Circle Network, a nonprofit organization for women writers, and a member of Sisters in Crime, Women Writing the West, Mystery Writers of America, and the Texas Institute of Letters. She and her husband Bill live on thirty-one acres in the Texas Hill Country. For more: www.susanalbert.com

BOOKS BY SUSAN WITTIG ALBERT

For a detailed list, including the latest additions,
visit www.susanalbert.com

MYSTERY SERIES
The Crystal Cave Novella Trilogy (China Bayles Mysteries)
The *Pecan Springs Enterprise* Novella Trilogy (China Bayles Mysteries)
The Darling Dahlias Mysteries
The Cottage Tales of Beatrix Potter
The Robin Paige Victorian-Edwardian Mysteries
(with Bill Albert, writing as Robin Paige)

THE HIDDEN WOMEN SERIES: HISTORICAL/BIOGRAPHICAL FICTION
Loving Eleanor
A Wilder Rose
The General's Women
Someone Always Nearby

MEMOIR
An Extraordinary Year
of Ordinary Days
Together, Alone: A Memoir of
Marriage and Place

NONFICTION
Writing from Life:
Telling the Soul's Story
Work of Her Own

EDITED VOLUMES
What Wildness Is This: Women Write about the Southwest